MURDER IMPERIAL

MURDER IMPERIAL

Paul Doherty

headline

First published in Great Britain in 2003 by
HEADLINE BOOK PUBLISHING

10 9 8 7 6 5 4 3 2 1

Cataloguing in Publication Data is available from the British Library

ISBN 0 7472 2242 8 (hardback)
ISBN 0 7472 7263 8 (trade paperback)

Typeset in Trump Mediaeval by Palimpsest Book Production Limited,
Polmont, Stirlingshire
Printed and bound in Great Britain by
Clays Ltd, St Ives plc
HEADLINE BOOK PUBLISHING
A division of Hodder Headline
338 Euston Road
London NW1 3BH

www.headline.co.uk
www.hodderheadline.com

*In memory of Michael Akos of the United States Air Force,
tragically killed in August 2002*

PRINCIPAL CHARACTERS

THE EMPERORS

Diocletian:	the old Emperor, now in retirement
Maxentius:	formerly Emperor of the West, defeated and killed by Constantine at the Milvian Bridge
Constantine:	new Emperor of the West
Helena:	Constantine's mother, Empress and Augusta
Licinius:	Emperor in the East

IMPERIAL OFFICIALS

Anastasius:	Christian priest and scribe, secretary to Helena
Bessus:	Imperial Chamberlain
Burrus:	Helena's bodyguard
Chrysis:	head of Constantine's agents
Severus:	Maxentius' First Minister
Rufinus:	merchant banker, friend of Constantine

THE CHRISTIAN CHURCH

Militiades:	Pope, Bishop of Rome
Sylvester:	Militiades' assistant, principal priest in the Christian community in Rome

THE COURTESANS
Domatilla
Sabina

THE ACTORS
Zosinas
Paris
Iolus

AT THE SHE-ASSES

Polybius:	the owner
Poppaoe:	his common-law wife
Oceanus	
Granius	
Januaria	
Faustina	
Claudia:	Polybius' niece
Murranus:	a gladiator

Introduction

During the trial of Christ, Pilate, according to the gospels, wanted to free the prisoner. He was stopped by a cry that, if he did so, 'he would be no friend of Caesar's'. According to commentators, Pilate recognised the threat. Every Roman governor and official was closely scrutinised by secret agents of the Emperor, 'the Agentes in Rebus', literally 'the Doers of Things'! The Roman Empire had a police force, both military and civil, though these differed from region to region, but it would be inaccurate to claim the Empire had anything akin to detectives or our own CID. Instead, the Emperor and his leading politicians paid vast sums to informers and spies. These were often difficult to control; as Walsingham, Elizabeth I's master spy, once wryly remarked, 'He wasn't too sure who his own men were working for, himself or the opposition.'

The Agentes in Rebus were a class apart amongst this horde of gossip-collectors, tale-bearers and, sometimes, very dangerous informers. The Emperors used them, and their testimony could mean the end of a promising career. This certainly applied to the bloody and byzantine period at the beginning of the fourth century AD.

The Emperor Diocletian had divided the Empire into East and West. Each division had its own Emperor, and a lieutenant, who took the title of Caesar. The Empire was facing economic problems, barbarian incursions. Its state religion was threatened by the thriving Christian Church, which was making its presence felt in all provinces at every level of society.

In AD 312 a young general, Constantine, supported by his mother Helena, a British-born woman who was already flirting with the Christian Church, decided to make his bid for the Empire of the West. He marched down Italy and met his rival Maxentius at the Milvian Bridge. According to Eusebius, Constantine's biographer, the would-be Emperor saw a vision of the cross, underneath the words 'In hoc signo vinces' ('In this sign you will conquer'). Constantine, the story goes, told his troops to adopt the Christian symbol and won an outstanding victory. He defeated and killed Maxentius and marched into Rome. Constantine was now Emperor of the West, his only rival Licinius, who ruled the Eastern Empire. Constantine, heavily influenced by his mother, grasped the reins of government and began to negotiate with the Christian Church to end centuries of persecution. Nevertheless, intrigue and murder were still masters of the day. There was unfinished business in Rome and the Agentes in Rebus had their hands full . . .

Prologue

'From one crime we learn the nature of them all.'
Virgil, *Aeneid*, II.65

Rome: Autumn, AD 311

The Tiber slithered sluggishly like a serpent along its banks, twisting and turning past the temples, the high-rise slums, the thronging quaysides and the gardens of the patricians. Night was falling yet the Tiber flowed and ebbed as it always had, peaceful now, no longer choked with the corpses which had floated and bobbed for days after the crushing of the last conspiracy. The Tiber was accustomed to such horrors: the blood-letting, the usual sequence following a mass proscription, gruesome murders and bone-chilling death. Along its banks Christians had been lashed to crosses, covered in oil, then used as human torches for wayfarers on the river. Now that was all in the past. Nero's statue on the Palatine Hill had disappeared. His great golden house, his palace with the revolving roof which displayed the constellations of the

1

sky, all gone. Tyrant after tyrant had followed Nero, only to be swept away in the sea of blood they themselves had caused.

The criers now proclaimed a new Rome. In the catacombs beneath the city, the Christians no longer skulked, paying reverence to the bones of those who died before them in the amphitheatre of the Colosseum. All Rome was rejoicing. Constantine was preparing to march south and the usurper Maxentius was arming to meet him. What did it really matter? The Tiber flowed on. Thousands used it as a source of life: fishermen, merchants, traders and travellers. When the river ebbed, exposing the rich mud and silt, the poor of Rome, or the curious, would come out to search its banks for half-concealed treasures. The young woman and her witless brother were two of these. They came from a respectable home, or at least they used to. Now they stayed with their uncle, Polybius, self-styled entrepreneur, owner and manager of the She-Asses tavern. The young woman, Claudia, pulled the cloak her 'dear uncle' had filched off a guest from Ostia closer about her. She walked quietly, her sandalled feet squelching in the mud.

'Come on, Felix!' she called, then smiled.

Felix was wandering, hands dangling by his sides. He was not looking for treasure, but shells, the relics of life from the river. She ran back and shook him. His head came up, slack lips and empty eyes. He recognised his sister's face and, in the dim light, made out the signs her fingers made.

'You must keep up,' the message went. 'You should stay close to me. I've brought you here because you wanted to come.'

She stopped and half-listened to the noise from the city. Tomorrow she was to entertain her uncle's guests with a public recitation of Aesop's fables. Claudia turned away, Felix trotting behind her like a dog. They were so engrossed in their task that the man who stepped out of the shadows of the deserted quayside made them both start. Claudia couldn't make out his face, though his toga and sandals were costly. She glimpsed the chalice tattooed on his left wrist.

'Well, well, well!' he slurred. 'What have we here?'

He grasped her by the shoulders. Claudia fought back. She was used to such drunken attention, but now she panicked. The man was stronger than she thought. Felix came running up. He grasped the man's hand. The stranger threw him away. Claudia screamed. Her cry went unanswered. This part of the Tiber was near the Maxima Cloaca, where the sewers of the city debouched their waste from the latrines and cesspits. Felix closed again, his mouth open in a dumb scream. Claudia tried to prevent him. Her assailant moved like a viper. The knife he drew glittered in the moonlight, and with one quick slash he cut the young man's throat. Felix dropped like a stone. Claudia knelt down beside him, screaming, the tears flowing down her face. She heard a movement in the squelching mud. Felix's death had proved no obstacle: her assailant was above her, the knife coming down.

Rome: Spring, AD 313

She was beautiful enough. Her golden hair was decorated with a diadem. Pearls for earrings, a jewelled collar round her slim throat, its pendant hanging between swelling breasts. The circlet round her ankle was shimmering silver whilst the silk gown was cunningly dyed with purple. Her corpse lay sprawled beneath the black poplars in the Gardens of Sallust. Her pretty eyes were closed, the voluptuous mouth smudged with blood. The marks round her throat were still fresh. The angry red weals showed how her life had been throttled out.

3

The assailant knelt down and checked the pulse in the young woman's throat and then, beneath the silk, the beat of her heart. All silent. The flesh was turning cold. The courtesan's head was turned, the golden hair pushed gently back. The dark-garbed attacker, balancing the knife carefully, etched the bloody cross, first on the forehead and then on each cheek.

Chapter 1

'A snake lurks in the grass.'
Virgil, *Eclogues*, III. 64

Rome: Spring, AD 313

In the slaughterhouse of the Domus Julia on the Palatine Hill, the spy Claudia sat on an uncomfortable stool and looked impassively at the man in a red-trimmed white tunic perched on another stool carefully studying her. Claudia hid all emotion; fear or pity would achieve nothing. The slaughter-house was cold; an icy stillness reigned. She looked down to avoid the man's gaze. The floor was still covered in blood-soaked sawdust. She wondered whether this was from the beef hanging from the iron rail or the corpse of the young woman whose throat had been cut and a piece of rope tied round her neck before being hoisted on to one of the hooks.

Claudia rubbed her arms. Outside she heard the murmur of the palace, the distant cries of the guards on the late-night breeze. She had considered running, but where could she flee to? It was only a matter of time before Caesar's dogs hunted her down. Anyway, she wanted to stay. She was both intrigued and frightened. She had been busy in the kitchen, washing the fleshing boards in barrels of hot water, when the Augusta's secretary, Anastasius, had come to collect her. He'd smiled but gripped her by the elbow. Once they were outside, he'd made those signs with his fingers that she should accompany him. She had been brought here and made to sit. Anastasius had lit oil lamps and placed them carefully on the floor around her as if she was some statue or Lares, a household god to be honoured and reverenced rather than frightened.

Claudia glanced at the corpse hanging from the hook. When she had first seen it she had started but kept a still tongue in her head. She recognised Fortunata; in the circumstances, rather an unhappy name. Fortunata had been a wine-girl, adeptly skilled at filling cups and goblets at this banquet or that. She always wore a low-cut tunic to give the drinkers a good view of her swelling breasts. Much good it would do her now. Her corpse was no more than a slab of meat, the breasts sagging like empty sacks. The lovely legs hung haphazardly, and her face, blue-white, with staring eyes and blood-red mouth . . . Claudia glanced away: Anastasius was still smiling at her but, of course, the deaf mute always smiled. His thin, olive face under tousled, oiled hair seemed to know no other expression; always a smile, with the lips and the eyes, as if Anastasius believed this would disarm the rest of the world. Usually it did.

'Am I in trouble?' Claudia asked. 'Have I done wrong?'

She translated the words into signs. Anastasius' face showed no other flicker of emotion.

'I thought Fortunata had left us? Gossip said that she had been transferred to the Imperial service. To the kitchens of

Divine Augustus.' Claudia coughed. 'Why am I here?' she continued.

She put one sandalled foot down as if to walk away. Anastasius made signs with his hands.

'The guards outside,' he said, 'have orders to kill anyone who leaves before the Divine Augusta arrives.'

Claudia hastily withdrew her foot.

'The Empress!' she gasped.

Anastasius nodded.

'And what does she want with me?'

Even here, in this gruesome, bloody place, Claudia knew the rules. Nothing was to be said, nothing even hinted, not without permission of the Divine Augusta.

'I . . . I have been loyal,' Claudia stammered.

Anastasius made quick movements with his hands: 'Shut up, you silly bitch! You've nothing to worry about!'

Claudia smiled in relief and made herself comfortable. She turned to her left. The piece of beef hanging from the hook looked as if it had been slaughtered some time ago; the fat was white, turning yellow at the edges, the vein-streaked meat compact, slightly glazed. The royal palace, of course, wanted for nothing. Constantine had swept into Rome and everyone had thronged to render loyalty. They provided gifts and comforts for the victorious general who had marched into Rome with crosses lashed to the insignia of his legions. The story had swept the city, how Constantine, before his great victory at the Milvian Bridge, had seen in a vision the Christian sign, with beneath it the words 'In hoc signo vinces', 'In this sign you will conquer'. People speculated on whether it was the truth. Did the Divine Constantine have visions? Or was it the effect of too much wine or one of his epileptic fits? Or even the influence of his Divine Mother the Empress

Helena? She might be the daughter of a tavern-keeper but now she was the mother of an Emperor of the West with secret sympathies for the Christian faith. Sympathy or politics? Claudia wondered. The proscribed faith was now a powerful force in the city: senators, bankers, generals, merchants, not to forget the seething mass of ordinary citizens and slaves, openly supported the cult from the catacombs. The temples to Jupiter and Venus might proclaim their glory but the new order was that of Christ and his followers. It was now fashionable to convert, and a victorious general, not to mention his mother, could never forget fashion.

Claudia heard the door open, the murmur of voices, then it was closed, the latch falling down, the bolts being drawn across, followed by the slap of sandal on the paved floor. Anastasius' fingers flew to his lips as if he had forgotten something; he got down from his stool and scurried through the darkness, bringing back a camp chair, a simple, crude affair, cross-legged with a canvas seat and backing. The woman who followed him into the pool of light sat down, leaned back and crossed her legs. Her hair was carefully coiffed in slight waves with ringlets down each cheek. These were almost hidden by the palla, or shawl of purple silk, which fell down to her shoulders, covering the upper part of the white gown, its fringes embroidered with a lighter purple. She wore no jewellery except for a ring on the little finger of her left hand. The sandals were costly, Spanish leather, the thongs and toes gilded with gold. Her face was long, with high cheek bones, finely shaved eyebrows, and a short stubby nose above lips which, Claudia noticed, could be compressed into a thin, bloodless line or pouted full and sensuous. Her eyes were dark: in any other woman, Claudia thought, it would look as if she'd drunk too deeply of Falernian. They sparkled as if the woman was savouring some secret jest. Whoever she was talking to expected the laughter lines around her mouth to crease in amusement. Claudia knew different. She now knew the Divine Augusta well. Helena was a woman who could act the part with great charm. She could display a deep interest in whoever she was talking to but it was all a mask. Her heart was hard, her will ruthless.

The Divine Augusta looked Claudia over from head to toe.

'Well, my little mouse. What an unexpected pleasure!' Helena abruptly leaned forward, resting her arms on her thighs. 'Isn't it exciting? Dramatic? Why do you think I met you here?'

Claudia pointed to Fortunata's blood-drained corpse.

'Oh, little mouse, you know better than that.'

'Because, Your Excellency, this place is silent?'

'That's right.' The Empress Helena nodded, and smiled as if praising a favourite child. 'The first rule of politics, little mouse: never plot in palaces. The walls have ears, the floors have eyes. You can't even break wind without someone finding out. Some people think the latrines are safe. More men have been executed for what they have said in latrines than whispered in council chambers or bedrooms. Anyway, why didn't you get up and kneel before your Empress?'

Claudia pointed to Anastasius, who still sat smiling serenely at her.

'Good, little mouse,' Helena cooed, clapping her hands. 'Do what Anastasius tells you.' The smile faded. 'Exactly what he tells you and the big cats won't get you, like they trapped poor Fortunata.'

The Empress Helena, the Divine Augusta, sat back on the chair. She did love theatre. She was the mistress of the grand entrance but only as a distraction. Now, through heavily lidded eyes, she studied the young woman opposite. Small, she thought, with soft pale skin. Her shabby short-sleeved tunic hung down to her bare knees. The sandals were good, sturdy, the thongs well tied. She wore no ornament. Helena liked that: the less to attract the better. Mind you, this young woman would find it hard to attract the gaze of any man. Her black hair was cropped close like that of an urchin in the slums, untidy and unwashed, though that was probably on Anastasius' instruction. Her face was plain, with slightly chubby cheeks, a regular nose and mouth and large star-ing eyes under unplucked brows. A perfect mouse, Helena thought. Someone who could scurry along the passageways and corridors and listen to the tittle-tattle of the servants or palace guests. Nevertheless, Anastasius had warned Helena that Claudia's mind was as sharp as her wits. She spoke little and listened a lot. If the priest had had his way, she, not Fortunata, would have been sent to her son's palace. Helena's fingers curled into a fist. She deliberately showed annoyance but Claudia didn't shift. There she sat, hands on her knees, staring down at the ground. If your nose twitched, Helena thought, you would be a mouse.

'Where do you come from, Claudia?'

'From Rome, Your Excellency.'

Helena threw her head back and laughed.

'All things come from Rome, Claudia. Daughter of a cen-turion, aren't you? One who retired and took his pension but didn't live long enough to enjoy it? His wife had three children; one died at birth, so Anastasius tells me. You and your brother remained. What was his name?'

'Felix, Your Excellency.'

'Ah yes, Felix; some story about being attacked? He was killed and you were abused. Do you bear a grudge, Claudia?'

10

'Revenge, Your Excellency; no grudge, just revenge.'

'And your attacker had a chalice tattooed on his left wrist? But I hurry on. You were part of a troupe of travelling actors. After your father died, your uncle became your guardian. Anastasius says you are a good actress, skilled in mime: with your little breasts and deep voice, you can even play the part of a man, be it in the plays of Terence or the farces of Aeschylus. But your manager was a drunkard? Too much wine and too few shows. The bankers closed in: costumes and props cost money so you had to sell your services.' Helena's hand snaked out and she grasped Anastasius' wrist. 'He shouldn't be a priest, you know, Claudia. He can't speak and he can't hear; visible deformity, as the Christian Church says, should be a bar to the Priesthood. Moreover, but Anastasius does like the theatre, an activity specifically forbidden to Christ's priests. But, there again,' she sighed, 'there's such a gap between Christ and his followers, isn't there? Anyway, that's how Anastasius met you.'

'I was pleased to enter your service, Divine Augusta.'

'What service?' Helena snapped.

Anastasius' smile disappeared: Claudia had made a mistake.

'I . . . I am sorry, Your Excellency,' she stammered. 'I am still new to the role. I mean . . .'

'No, no, don't.' Helena smiled and stretched out her hands. 'Clever, little mouse. You've got your lines right. It's a role, it's acting. You are wearing a mask. I wear a mask. Anastasius wears a mask. The bully boys, the generals, the plump senators, the silver-fingered bankers, they all wear masks. When they drink, when they lie head to head, sprawled on their couches, and pass the wine crates around, the mask slips and they chatter. "In vino veritas": wine gladdens the heart and loosens the tongue, Claudia, that's where my little mouse

11

picks up her morsels.' Helena played with the tassels of her shawl. 'Do you know why I call you mouse, Claudia? I mean, it's not very flattering, but people never know you are there. You're not like a fly which hovers over food, or a buzzing bee you hear so clearly the sound seems to grow. No, you glide in and out, scurry here, scurry there. Do you remember two mornings ago? Fat Valeria, the wife of the grain merchant? You brought up a tray of cups from the kitchens. I sent for you deliberately. I made you stand for a while near the door. I dropped one of my hair-pins and made you pick it up.'

Claudia nodded.

'And when you had gone, do you know what I asked fat Valeria?' Helena sniggered behind her fingers. 'I said, "Can you describe the servant girl who just came in?" Do you know, she didn't even know you had been there.'

Claudia turned her head sideways; not even a flush of embarrassment.

'I wonder what goes on in that little head of yours?' Helena added spitefully. 'Oh, stop looking at poor Fortunata!' she snapped. 'She's dead. Rome is full of corpses. No one will miss her. She was stupid. She failed. Will you fail me, Claudia?'

'I am Your Excellency's humble servant.'

Helena watched those eyes and felt a chill of apprehension. She was used to spies. She had been one herself. But this young woman . . .

'Anastasius thinks the world of you,' Helena cooed. 'Of all my mice he says you are the best. And don't say it.' Her voice became clipped. 'I'll say it for you.'

Anastasius raised his hands and made signs with his fingers.

'What is he telling you?' Helena snapped. 'Some of his symbols I know, some I don't!'

'He's telling me to be careful,' Claudia replied.

'Ah yes, so he should.' The Empress opened the palm of her right hand and sniffed at the small sachet of perfume she carried. 'Strange, isn't it?' she mused. 'Blood has an iron tang. This place reminds me of the amphitheatre. The amphitheatre represents life, doesn't it, Claudia? Winners and losers. Spectators who don't care, the rich, the powerful, the poor and the maimed. Each turns up to watch something. I suppose the miserable go to watch someone more miserable suffer at the point of a sword. Do you know why fat Valeria goes? She becomes excited! As if the silly bitch was in bed with a gladiator! The young men pick her up and take advantage of her favours, she gets so carried away. Are you ever carried away, Claudia?'

The young woman stared coolly back.

'No, I don't suppose so,' Helena added drily. 'Are you a Christian, Claudia?'

A shake of the head answered her question. Helena narrowed her eyes.

'You don't believe in anything, do you? Big fat gods or goddesses who thrust out their nipples and raise their legs. There's only one god in Rome, Claudia,' Helena continued. 'That's my son, the Divine Constantine.'

Anastasius shook his head in disapproval.

'Don't be petulant, priest!' the Empress snapped. 'You know all about Constantine, don't you? Your august Emperor?'

Claudia remembered Anastasius' orders: keep still, remain calm, never volunteer knowledge.

'It's a long way from York,' Helena continued dreamily. 'So many Emperors. Now there are only two: Constantine in the West.' She held up one hand clutching the perfumed sachet. 'He defeated his rival Maxentius at the battle of

13

Milvian Bridge and marched into Rome with that tyrant's head stuck on a pole. In the East the Emperor Licinius. Now, I am going to tell you why I am meeting you here. There are two reasons. First, my son intends to become sole Emperor. Oh, he'll swear eternal friendship. However, when Licinius makes a mistake, Constantine will march east, bring him to battle, destroy his army, then kill him. If Licinius has half a brain, he'll try and do the same to my son. They'll smile and exchange the kiss of peace, call each other brother, sign the most wonderful-sounding peace treaties.' Helena lowered her head. 'But we are back in the amphitheatre, Claudia. One of them must die. It must be Licinius. To do that, my son intends to revoke all edicts against the Christian faith.

'Most of Rome is Christian, as are many officers in the army – at least secretly so. Why? Because Constantine claims he saw a vision? I cannot comment on that, but he needs the Christians. They are the second reason I'm talking to you. We have, in Rome, two empires. We have the columns of Trajan, Titus' triumphal arch, the Colosseum, the Forum, but beneath the city run the catacombs, dug out by the Christians to bury their dead and secretly perform their rites. Just look at our city! The monuments are beginning to decay but life in the catacombs is as vigorous as ever. So it is throughout the entire Empire. Now, I don't really care if, three hundred years ago, a Jew called Christus, three days after he was gibbeted on the cross, rose from the dead. What I do care about, and so does Constantine, is that Christianity has become a second empire.' Helena made a snaking movement with her hands. 'It lies beneath the façade, it twists and turns, like those narrow galleries in the catacombs. What am I really saying, little mouse? You have permission to speak.'

Claudia looked at Anastasius, who nodded imperceptibly.

'If Constantine,' Claudia began slowly, 'reached an accord with the Christian Church . . .'

'Very good,' Helena cooed. 'Accord, I like that word. I didn't know you were so well educated. There's a lot about you, Claudia, I'd like to know. But continue.'

'Your son the Divine Emperor will not only unite the Empire in the West but have a path into Licinius' Empire in the East. Licinius is still hostile to Christianity,' Claudia continued, 'but the Church in Asia is very strong.'

'Very good.' Helena clapped her hands. 'I can see you have been talking to Anastasius. Constantine will dig away at the edifice Licinius has built. While that fool gilds and paints the top storeys, Constantine will be weakening the cellars and the foundations. My son will correspond with the elders of the Christian Church in Asia, gently tapping at those officers in Licinius' army who are sympathetic to the new faith.'

Helena sighed. 'But that's going to take time. In the mean time we have enemies in Rome, and enemies watch each other. It's like fat Valeria. She comes to me oohing and aahing but do you think she likes to bend the knee and kiss the hand of a daughter of a tavern-keeper from York?' Helena smirked. 'No! No! She'd love to see my head bounce down the execution steps, and so we return to the fact that we all wear masks: even the Divine Augustus. He'll sit, he'll eat, he'll drink, he'll whore, with men who, six months ago, would have paid dearly to see his head exhibited in the marketplace. So, we come to informers, the Speculatores. They listen to chatter.' She waved a finger. 'To gossip. However, the terrible thing about informers, Claudia, is that they have one precious commodity, the knowledge they collect. They are like hucksters in the market. They'll sell it to anyone for the highest price. Worse, if they can't find information, they'll even make it up. They'll

15

start to tell you what you want to know. You are not an informer, are you, Claudia?'

'I am Your Excellency's most humble servant.'

'No, no, what are you really?'

'I am a member of the Agentes in Rebus Politicis . . .'

'And what does that mean, Claudia?'

'I'm a spy. Your spy, Excellency.'

'And who is your Magister, your master?'

Claudia pointed to Anastasius, who sat, eyes closed, immobile as a statue on its pedestal.

'Good!' Helena breathed. 'My Agentes tell no one who they are. They have no friends, no faithful companions. They can trust no one because they never know who they are talking to. Is the thick-eared oaf in the kitchen responsible for cleaning the slops a servant? There are thousands of them in Rome. Or is he an informer? There are as many as ants in an ant hill! Or a spy? And, if he is the latter, does he work for me, for my son, for one of the great patricians of Rome, or for the police? Even, the Gods forbid, for fat Valeria? It's a lonely life, isn't it, Claudia? You can never say who you really are except to me or Anastasius. To the rest of the world you are a servant, niece to Polybius who owns the She-Asses tavern in those slums near the Flavian Gate. Oh, by the way, he's in trouble.' Helena smiled.

For the first time Claudia let her mask slip.

'He's not in political trouble. He's too bothered about his profits. Do you know Arrius?'

'He's a wine merchant,' Claudia replied. 'A tight-fisted miser. He goes out to his farms and vineyards. After he collects his profits, he always lodges at the She-Asses.'

'Well, he's dead,' Helena remarked. 'I've read the Prefect of Police's report. He had his throat cut at your uncle's

16

tavern and his saddlebags emptied of every piece of silver he carried.'

'Is my uncle a suspect?'

'No, but he's got a lot of explaining to do. We'll worry about him later. You love him, don't you, Claudia?'

'A kind man, Your Excellency. He looked after me and my brother. He can get drunk, sometimes he's too free with his fists . . .'

'A generous man?' Helena smiled. 'Oh, don't worry, Claudia. We've got a great deal in common. My father was a tavern-keeper as well.' Helena put her head back and stared up at the ceiling stained with the smoke from oil lamps. 'It's getting cold in here,' she murmured. 'I told my ladies I wished to go for a walk.' She patted Anastasius affectionately on the knee. 'But don't worry, I've got that cut-throat Burrus on guard outside against any snoopers.' She gazed back at Claudia. 'Doesn't your uncle ever wonder why a well-schooled girl like yourself,' she mimicked Claudia's voice, 'works as a servant?'

'He doesn't really worry, Your Excellency,' Claudia replied. 'After all, one day I might marry a successful general and be mother to an Emperor.'

Helena clapped her hands and rocked backwards and forwards with laughter.

'True, true,' she said, wiping a tear from her eyes. 'The best we women can do, Claudia, is lie on our backs, isn't it? I can't even count the number of ceilings I've looked at.' Helena's face became grave. 'But it was worth it. Constantine is Emperor. So, now we come to poor Fortunata. My son has swept into Rome. He is Augustus, proclaimed by the Senate, the people and the army. However, he is a fool if he thinks he's the master of all. True, he can't be attacked. He's too well guarded and the army adore him. Nevertheless, he can be undermined. My son has had a rigorous campaign. He's too astute . . . how can I put it? . . . to help himself to the charms of Roman matrons and their daughters.' The Augusta stared at her fingernails. 'He doesn't want to offend anyone. Instead, he has enjoyed the company of some of the city's leading courtesans. Three of whom have been found strangled.' She made a sign on her forehead. 'Their corpses have been discovered in different places: one in her bedroom, one in the atrium of a house, dumped there like a sack of pork, and the third in the Gardens of Sallust. All three had been strangled, with a cross etched on their forehead and each cheek. Can you see the danger of this, Claudia?'

'Rome is full of whores, Your Excellency.'

'True, but courtesans are different. They have the same ranking as priestesses, even the vestal virgins. They also have powerful friends, not only because of their charms.'

'But because they know secrets,' Claudia added.

'Continue,' Helena insisted.

'Your Excellency must ask why three courtesans have been killed, particularly after they had been patronised by the Divine Augustus.' Claudia paused to choose her words correctly. 'It could be that they were killed by the Emperor himself, but that would be impossible.'

'Why?' Helena asked.

'There's no good reason,' Claudia replied. 'So, it must be the work of an enemy. Rome doesn't really know Constantine. Constantine doesn't know Rome. The powerful men are going to sit and watch. They might wonder if the women told Constantine secrets and so had to be silenced. Or, it might be that their murders were a mere whim. Rome has a fear of degenerate Emperors; the Gods only know there have been enough of them. People might wonder whether the deaths were Constantine's way of obtaining pleasure whilst the crosses marked on their corpses reflect his vision: the one he claims to have had during the battle of Milvian Bridge.'

'How many people,' Helena retorted, 'would really believe the Emperor would engage in such murders?'

'Ah yes, Your Excellency, but the more he protests, the more they will wonder.'

Helena gripped Anastasius' arm. 'You are correct, Anastasius, she is very sharp. My son is embarrassed,' Helena continued, 'rather than threatened by these murders. I have urged him to be cautious, not to solicit the company of these courtesans, but you might as well tell a bird not to fly! Constantine was always an argumentative boy. He maintains that if he gives up his pleasures, the suspicions will still linger. He does wonder whether there is another reason for their deaths; something we don't even know ourselves.'

'Has every courtesan who visited him died?' Claudia asked.

Helena shook her head. 'Not every one, and so we come to poor Fortunata. Now she is dead I'll tell you. Fortunata was one of my Agentes. I put her in Constantine's household: a wine-server in his palace. She discovered nothing new, then she fell silent. We found the reason why. One of the butchers came here this afternoon. He found Fortunata's corpse hanging from one of the hooks. I ordered it to be kept here. Once darkness has fallen, Anastasius can have it removed, taken out to one of the cemeteries and buried there.'

Helena got to her feet. Claudia was only too willing to climb off the stool; her thighs and calves ached from the tension.

'You will take poor Fortunata's place.' Helena smiled. 'The Chamberlain at the palace, Bessus, is in my pay. He never recruits for my son's service unless he asks me. I know a little about Bessus which, on the whole, he would prefer I didn't.

19

So, you'll pack your belongings, little mouse, and scamper along to the Palatine Palace. Whatever you find, Anastasius here must know.' Her hand shot out like a claw and gripped Claudia's arm. 'I want to find the true assassin. I want to find out why. I want to see the rogue who had the impudence to hang one of my servants on a meat hook take his place there himself!'

Chapter 2

'In this sign you shall conquer.'
Eusebius, *Life of Constantine*, I. 28

Constantine, Augustus, Emperor of the West, stretched out on the purple-covered, gold-fringed couch in the banqueting hall of his royal palace on the Palatine. He licked his lips and looked appreciatively round. The fruits of victory! he thought. The laurel wreath to mark his triumphs! He recalled that rapid march from Milan: the biting-cold winds, the hard rations, wine which tasted like vinegar and a saddle which chafed his thighs and made his arse feel as if it was on fire. Now all was different. Rome lay under his thumb. No more draughty tents and makeshift bothies: the odour of the horse lines, the rank sweat of the men, the fetid taste of the latrines on the morning breeze.

The dining hall was of porphyry marble. On the floor was a precious mosaic, the work of the Emperor Trajan, showing

Bacchus and Ceres smiling over a plentiful harvest. The ceiling was white, displaying dark blue stars around a red moon. The pillars were black streaked with white, their bases of silver, their cupolas of purest gold. Constantine ran his hand along the purple covering of the couch. He felt like closing his eyes, moving the pillow from underneath his right elbow and putting his head down for the deepest sleep. The rigours of the campaign were still with him, clearly visible on his thickset soldier's face, even though he was shaved, oiled, his auburn hair cleverly cropped, with strands combed forward, in imitation of the busts of Caesar and Augustus which stood around the room. The Emperor stretched out his hand for a crater of wine, half-listening to the buzz of conversation around him. It was all so different now. The thongs of his sandals were covered in pearls not tarred rope. His tunic and purple-edged toga were of finest linen. Rings and bracelets, looted from the treasury of the dead Maxentius, now decorated fingers and wrists.

The Emperor eased himself on the sloping couch.

'Your Excellency is tired?'

Constantine looked over at Lucius Rufinus, Rome's greatest banker, Constantine's friend and most fervent supporter.

'His Excellency is not tired,' the Emperor whispered. 'He is just distracted.'

Rufinus scratched his steel-grey hair, and his clean-shaven patrician face broke into a smile. Constantine chuckled as well. He always felt relaxed with Rufinus: a man of wealth and power who ruled a mercantile empire but didn't stand on ceremony.

'I am trying to behave myself,' Constantine murmured.

He looked to his right where his mother, Helena, dressed in purple, her hair coiffed in ringlets, lay on the adjoining couch glaring at him with dark, soulful eyes.

'I am sure if I let her,' Constantine whispered, 'Mother would get up and check behind my ears to see if I've washed properly.'

'I'd box them if I could!' Helena declared.

Constantine grinned and shook his head.

'I keep forgetting she can lip-read,' he whispered to Rufinus.

Constantine burped gently and glanced at the table: gold spoons and toothpicks lay scattered about. Slaves with bowls of rose water were moving around. The cooks had done him proud. Dormice rolled in honey and poppy seed; huge lobsters garnished with asparagus; mullets from Corsica; and their supreme achievement, a large gold plate with the signs of the Zodiac around the edge. Over each of the signs the cook had placed a food that was appropriate: a piece of beef on the bull, kidneys on the twins, and, in the centre, a hare stuffed with spices, its skin refashioned with wings to make it look like Pegasus. The final course was a wild pig standing on a huge platter, two baskets hanging from its tusks, one holding dried dates, the other fresh. Around this were arranged suckling pigs made of simnel cake. The platter had been brought in, preceded by trumpets, horns and the clash of cymbals. When the pig's belly had been cut, thrushes flew out. Constantine groaned slightly and rubbed his stomach. He had drunk deep of the honeyed wine, but remembering Mother's advice, if ignoring her glares, he'd generously mixed his Falernian with water.

The slaves now came in with baskets, scattering saw-dust mixed with saffron and vermillion around the couches. Constantine wished it was a normal evening. Mother would retire and the dancers would come on: particularly those light-bodied Spaniards with their clicking castanets, feet stamping, black hair swirling, breasts, tipped with gold, thrusting out wanting to be grasped. On such an occasion his officers would drink deeply, toast him and the banquet would go on until the early hours. Tonight was different. Business first, pleasures later. In the small cubiculum across the palace gardens Sabina, a courtesan with hair as red as flame and a body white as snow, would be waiting. Constantine looked down into his wine cup and suppressed a chill of fear. Ever since his early campaigning days, he had had a horror of the gruesome diseases which could be contracted from camp whores and prostitutes. If he was truthful, and no wonder with a mother like Helena, Constantine was frightened of women, wary of the sexual act: so much fumbling, sometimes humiliation! His own wife, Fausta? Constantine shook his head: best not think of her! Concentrate on Sabina, he thought: soft and white, like rolling in the costliest silk. No importunate demands, no politicking.

Constantine slurped from the wine, ignoring his mother's loud, dramatic cough. Ever since his arrival in Rome, he had contracted with the Guild of Aphrodite, the perfumed courtesans managed by Domatilla. But now these murders! Constantine glared across at Chrysis, that bald, limp-handed eunuch, master of his secrets. Crafty lump of flesh! He should serve his master better! Constantine bit back his annoyance. Three courtesans murdered and already the whispers were beginning to pass from mouth to mouth, and hadn't there been notices stuck up in the Forum and marketplaces? How did they go? A picture of the Christian symbol, the cross, and beneath it the scrawl: 'In hoc signo occides', 'In this sign you will kill'. A mockery of his great vision before the battle of the Milvian Bridge. Three courtesans dead! The Christian sign carved on their foreheads and cheeks. But why? Why?

'Your Excellency?'

Constantine's head came up. All conversation had died. The Emperor realised he had spoken aloud. Mother was staring at him curiously. Next to her the enigmatic dumb priest Anastasius; Chrysis had his bowl halfway to his lips; even Rufinus looked concerned. Constantine glanced at his guest of honour, a white-haired man with a youngish face, dressed simply in dark tunic and robe: the presbyter Sylvester, personal envoy of Militiades, Bishop of Rome, the real reason for this evening's banquet. Bessus, the Imperial Chamberlain, had now swung his legs off the couch. Constantine blinked.

'Why,' he grinned, 'do mothers always stare at their sons?'

The laughter broke the tension. Before Helena could think of any sharp reply, Constantine raised his earthenware crater and toasted her. The rest of the company followed suit. Helena replied, winking slyly at him.

'Why don't you drink from a goblet like everybody else,' she snapped, 'instead of that earthenware pot which many a man would only use to piss in!'

'I feel comfortable with it, Mother.'

'You were just the same when you were a boy.' Helena pulled herself up from the couch.

'Yes, yes,' Constantine intervened quickly.

Mother had an infuriating habit of suddenly mentioning the most embarrassing circumstances of his childhood to anyone who cared to listen. He loved her deeply, passionately. He'd decreed the title Augusta and harnessed her energy to exploit that great talent of hers, snooping. He allowed Helena, and her priest Anastasius, complete control over the Agentes in Rebus. He had done this for one reason: Helena could be trusted, implicitly and without question. As she had once said, 'No Constantine, no Helena.' It was her motto, her guide to life.

She was now staring soulfully at him. Constantine sighed and nodded.

'We have eaten and drunk enough,' he declared. 'Bessus, have the room cleared, the door sealed and guarded. No one is to enter.'

Bessus, a tall, angular man with a look of constant disdain on his thin lips, hurried to obey. Once all was ready, Constantine raised his cup and toasted his guest of honour. Sylvester, he noticed, had hardly touched his food or wine. He'd just sat staring around, watchful, as if assessing and judging everyone present. He was a small, nondescript man, except for the eyes and the mouth. A generous mouth, Constantine thought, ready to laugh. He noticed the scar on Sylvester's cheek, and recalled vague stories about how, under Diocletian, Imperial troops had hunted this powerful Christian priest. Now he was the envoy and spokesman for the Bishop of Rome. Constantine hid a touch of anger: slaves and common folk! Yet Militiades and Sylvester were just as powerful, even more so, than the banker Rufinus. They could decide the mood of the mob, distract him with their opposition, divide Rome.

'You are most welcome.' Constantine smiled over his cup.

'Your Excellency,' Sylvester answered the toast, 'you do great honour to me and my father in Christ, as well as the Church of Rome. We thank God daily for your great victory. We offer constant supplication for your safety and well-being. No one in Rome, apart from present company,' Sylvester half-smiled, 'is a more loyal supporter of you, Augustus, than Militiades and the Christian community. We give thanks for the edict of toleration.'

'And that will be repeated,' Constantine declared. 'Toleration for Christians here in Rome and throughout the Empire. And more . . .'

Sylvester's head came up with a jerk.

'The restoration of all confiscated property,' Constantine continued. 'The guarantee of civil rights as well as religious freedom, both here and in the provinces.'

Sylvester was taken by surprise.

'And the Bishop of Rome,' Constantine continued, enjoying himself, 'his presbyters, priests and councils will not be troubled. All trials involving Christians will be ended, pardons issued, prisoners released.'

Sylvester's head went down, to hide his tears.

'This is indeed,' the presbyter murmured, 'the day of salvation.' He glanced up. 'The Lord has delivered us. Throughout the Empire, beyond its farthest frontiers, prayers, Augustus, will be offered for your health and well-being.' His gaze shifted to Helena. 'And that of your mother. But, Your Excellency, if I may trespass on your kindness further . . .'

Constantine looked puzzled. 'Is that not enough?' he replied softly. 'One step at a time.'

'Your Excellency, two problems exist. The first, the teaching of Arius . . .'

Constantine suppressed a groan. He found it difficult enough to understand the teachings of Christ: that God became a Jew and allowed himself to be crucified was hard for any soldier to accept. Not to mention Christ's teaching, 'Forgive your enemies.' Constantine suppressed a smile. He was always prepared to do that, once they were dead!

'The arch-heretic Arius,' Sylvester continued, pressing his point, 'disrupts the unity of the Church and, therefore, that of the Empire.'

'How does he do that?' Helena asked.

'By claiming that Jesus Christ is not fully God, of the same divine substance as the Father.'

27

Helena looked as mystified as her son, who shrugged imperceptibly. One day, the Emperor promised himself, he must sit down and really listen to one of these priests. The Christians preached one God but, in the same voice, talked of three persons in that God. He could grasp the symbolism; didn't Jupiter appear in many forms? Yet the Christians meant more than that.

'This matter must wait.' The Emperor intervened quickly before Mother, who positively doted on such finer subtleties, could lead them into conversations he would never understand. 'You mentioned a second problem?' He felt his stomach pitch and heave.

'Divine Augustus.' Sylvester made no apology for giving God-like qualities to the Emperor.

Constantine was pleased. If all Christians were like this priest, a closer rapprochement could be made.

'We have heard,' Sylvester picked up his knife from the table and moved the pieces of pork on the silver dish before him, 'about the murders of three women, courtesans, members of the Society or Guild of Aphrodite.' He put the knife down. 'We are not here to preach, Your Excellency. However, these deaths have caused scandal. Gossips point the finger at you,' he continued, 'even though we know that cannot be true.'

'Scandals and gossip come and go!' Helena snapped.

'Domina.' Sylvester bowed his head in her direction. 'No one is a more ardent supporter of the Imperial house than I or mine. Nevertheless, broadsheets are being posted in the Forum, along the docks at Ostia, in the marketplaces and at the entrances to temples. These broadsheets mock the cross and the Imperial house. My esteemed father in Christ, Militiades, sees this as the hand of the Evil One: to disrupt, agitate, divide . . .'

'But that's not the real source of your concern, is it?' Helena interrupted. She felt both angry and embarrassed. Here was her son, master of the Western Empire, negotiating with this rather plain, nondescript man.

'We are fearful, Domina,' Sylvester replied. 'These murders may conceal deeper currents. Your son's opponents will try to discredit his name . . .'

'We understand your concerns precisely,' Chrysis lisped. 'We have the matter in hand. These murders will end and the traitors responsible will be punished appropriately.'

Sylvester gazed down at the floor, lost in thought.

'I do not mean to cavil or to criticise.' He raised his head and moved, swinging his legs off the couch. 'Divine Augustus has won a great victory. God's hand rests on him. We, the Christian community, will do all in our power to ensure that such Divine favour remains.' He rose and bowed to the Emperor. 'Now, it is getting late.'

Constantine rose to meet him. Sylvester kissed the ring on the Imperial hand, did the same to Helena, bowed to the rest and left. The Emperor heard the door open. He listened intently to the sound of the presbyter's fading footsteps along the marble passageway.

'Twenty years ago,' Chrysis drawled, 'our little priest would have been on a cross or being chased by some lion round the amphitheatre. It proves, Excellency, how fickle Fortune is.'

'That man's master,' Helena replied, 'is spiritual and temporal lord of tens of thousands of Romans in this city and God knows how many more in Italy and beyond. Our friend Licinius is certainly watching and listening at his villa in Nicodemea to see how we deal with him.'

'One day I'll march east.' Constantine lounged back on his

couch, grabbed a jug and splashed Falernian into his cup. 'My legions will meet his and Licinius will be no more.'

'Yes, dear son, and we will need the Christians,' Helena remarked. 'Think of the powerful churches in Greece, Palestine and Asia Minor.' She rose and sat by Constantine, her eyes holding his. 'When you march,' she hissed, 'the Christian symbol will be lashed to your standards and emblazoned on the shields of your legionnaires. And what will the Christian churches of the East think then? They'll hail you as a saviour, God's vice-regent on earth.' She stroked her son's head.

Everyone else sat fascinated. It was as if Helena had forgotten they were there, she, the doting mother with her favourite son.

'You have this matter in hand?' Constantine asked.

'I have it in hand,' Helena replied, warning him with her eyes.

Constantine finished the wine, gently extricated himself from his mother's presence, and clambered to his feet.

'Your Emperor is bored,' Constantine declared. 'He has talked and drunk enough. Now he needs to retire.'

And, spinning on his heel, Constantine left the banqueting chamber. The marble corridors were deserted. The occasional slave scurried across his path. Members of the royal bodyguard, in cuirass and leather kilt, stood in the shadows, holding lance and shield.

'Your Excellency.'

Constantine spun round, fingers going to his dagger as the priest Sylvester slipped out of the shadows.

'I thought you'd left? How did you know I'd be here alone?'

Sylvester's face creased into a smile.

'Your boredom was apparent, Your Excellency. I must say things to you.'

'How did you know?' Constantine insisted, feeling a chill of fear.

'Your Excellency.' Sylvester spread his hands. 'The palace is full of servants and slaves. Very few of them burn incense before idols. Go into their quarters. You'll find our symbols, the Chi and the Rho, the fish and the word Icthus. They have told me about the Lady Sabina.'

'And you've come to lecture me?'

'Your morals, Excellency, are a matter between you and God. At this moment in time they are not my concern.'

Constantine felt afraid. He was, as the others said, master of the West. This was his palace; along the corridors were his bodyguard, those favoured legionnaires who had replaced the praetorians he had smashed at the Milvian Bridge. In the Field of Mars camped two legions at his beck and call; double that number beyond the city walls. Yet this simple priest seemed to be able to go and do as he wished.

'So, why have you come?' The Emperor stared down at Sylvester.

'As I said, your morals are not our concern but your Empire is. We, too, have our spies,' the priest whispered. 'These murders will blacken your name, yet what man in politics has clean hands?'

'You talked of deeper currents in the banquet chamber?'

'Yes, Your Excellency, these murders hide something else. What, we don't know. You were welcomed in Rome as a saviour yet there are many who long for the old days, playing you off against Licinius, making you bid for their favours.'

'And?'

'There are also those of our faith who do not believe we should be negotiating with a state which, for centuries, has persecuted them.'

'Ah!' Constantine smiled. 'Is that why you are here, Sylvester?'

'That and one last word of warning. Trust no one!'

'Not even Mother?'

'Your Excellency, trust no one.' Sylvester bowed and disappeared into the shadows.

Constantine stood for a while then walked on. He opened a door and went along the colonnaded peristyle. The garden to his right was lit by torches and oil lamps, smelling sweetly of the flowers growing there. The flickering light made the shadows of the trees, the laurel, plane and fir, dance and shift. A fountain splashed. Constantine paused and watched the gushing water stream out of the mouth of a marble fish held by Cupid. He remembered Sabina and walked on. The corridor beyond the garden was deserted; the servants had lit lamps and placed them in niches on the walls. Constantine stopped at a door and gently knocked.

'Sabina!'

No reply. Constantine pushed the door open. The chamber inside was opulently furnished. The walls were decorated with motifs and a scented brazier stood in each corner. Their light gleamed in the copper, gold and silver ornaments around the room. The couch was empty; the great bed in the corner was shrouded in a thick mist of gauze veil, a lamp burning on the table beside it. Constantine closed the door and tiptoed across. He pulled back the gauze: Sabina, dressed in a dark mauve gown, lay sprawled on the bed. Even in the poor light Constantine could see the mottled bruises on her ivory neck. The necklace she wore had broken, slipping down between her swelling breasts. Her red hair partially covered her face. Constantine moved this with one finger, revealing the bloody cross on her right cheek. He turned the face slowly: the same on her left and her forehead.

Constantine breathed in to compose his panic. He did not want to run out like some slave girl screaming with fright. He had wandered battlefields where the corpses lay two, three deep. He had watched criminals being executed, soldiers die of the most terrible wounds, but this was different. A beautiful young woman, her eyes now half-closed, her skin clammy cold. He glimpsed a piece of parchment left on the swan-feather pillows. He picked this up. The writing was crude. Constantine recognised a Defixio, a solemn curse. He threw it down and walked to the door. The passageway was deserted. The Emperor hastened across the garden and told one of the guards to bring his mother, Rufinus and the others, before returning to the chamber. He lit more lamps, unshuttered the window and stared out across the garden. When he heard a knock, he didn't even bother to turn.

'Come in!' he shouted.

His mother entered, followed by Rufinus, Bessus and Chrysis. There was no sound, except gasps and muttered curses, as they gathered near the bed. Constantine turned round.

'Strangled!' he declared. 'And the same mutilations made.'

Helena had picked up the parchment.

'What's that?' Rufinus asked.

'A Defixio.'

'A curse!' the banker exclaimed.

'Yes, a solemn curse,' Constantine retorted.

Helena studied it. At the top of the parchment squatted a bearded demon with a flaring torch; beneath this were magical symbols and then the curse itself, a formal consecration of her son to the Gods of the Underworld.

'May burning fever seize all his limbs,
Kill his soul and choke his heart.

33

Oh, demons of the darkness,
Break and smash his bones,
Choke off his breath.
Let his body be twisted and shattered.
This curse has been distilled in the intestines
  of frogs, the feathers of owls, the bones of snakes,
  herbs from tombs and powerful poisons.'

'Nonsense!' Helena snapped and threw it back on the bed.

'Is it?' Chrysis asked. 'Virgil says that a sorceress could draw the moon down from the sky.'

'Well, I've never seen that happen,' Helena retorted.

She gazed narrow-eyed at her son, trying to quell her own fear. Whoever had done this was very clever. Constantine's superstitious nature, the legacy of his father, was well known. She could see that the curse had had almost more effect on him than the murder. Helena also suspected that whoever had done this was close to their circle. How else could a courtesan be murdered in the private quarters of the palace?

'Why?' she demanded.

Constantine sat down on a camp stool and played with the rings on his fingers.

'I thought it would be safer,' he replied, 'if I brought Sabina here and sent her back under guard tomorrow morning.'

'How many people knew she was here?' Rufinus asked, staring down at the corpse.

'If a courtesan arrives in a palanquin, escorted by torch-bearers, not to mention burly ex-gladiators as an escort . . .' Constantine shrugged. 'Half the palace. I thought she'd be safe.'

'How long ago?' Chrysis asked.

34

'About two hours before the banquet began. I visited her myself. We chatted and talked.'

'And you put no guard on her bedroom?'

'Why should I?' Constantine retorted.

'But there was no struggle.' Chrysis spoke up.

'Yes, I noticed that.' Bessus the chamberlain wandered round the room. 'Nothing overturned, nothing disturbed. She should have screamed, struggled.'

'I'll have physicians examine the corpse tomorrow,' Helena offered. She sat on the edge of the bed and turned the corpse over, running her hand through the flame-red hair. 'I can feel no bruise or contusion,' she murmured. 'Nothing to indicate she was taken by surprise or strangled when she was half-conscious. The cuts are slight, made with a thin dagger. A high-class courtesan like Sabina wouldn't allow anyone into her chamber. She'd protest: it must have been someone she knew.'

Constantine went back to the window and stared out into the night. What could he say? Even the priest Sylvester knew she was here, and the curse . . . It was the first time that had happened. And if Mother was correct? Sabina must have known her killer. He glanced over his shoulder at Bessus and caught Chrysis' gaze. Either could have slipped in here. Sabina would not suspect anything amiss: the same could be said for Anastasius. And what about Helena? The palace had been in turmoil before the banquet, servants coming in and out. Any one of these could have come in, but why didn't Sabina resist?

'The second death tonight.' He smiled thinly at his mother. 'I understand a serving wench, Fortunata, was found hanging in one of the slaughter sheds?'

'The assassin is telling you something,' Helena replied. 'You are not safe here in this palace, in your own city.' She tapped the dead courtesan's arm. 'This will be placed firmly at your door. Sabina goes in alive and is carried out dead.'

Constantine wanted to get away. He needed to think, reflect on what had happened. He wished Sylvester was here but, there again, could he trust him? After all, he had been in the palace. Sabina would see him as no threat.

'Where's Anastasius?' he demanded.

'He's seeing to the corpse of Fortunata,' Helena answered. 'It's best if she's taken out under the cover of darkness, and the same applies to Sabina. Quietly, no fuss. We'll send a letter to Domatilla.' She breathed out noisily. 'Yes,' she continued, as if speaking to herself, 'perhaps that's where we should concentrate: Domatilla's spacious villa.'

She wanted to continue, berate her son, ask him to curb his fleshly desires, but this was not the time nor the place. She picked up one of the silk sheets from the bed and drew it up over Sabina's face. As she did so, Helena wondered what her little mouse would make of this.

Chapter 3

'Anger is a brief madness.'
Horace, *Epistles*, I.2

Claudia left the Palatine, following the winding path past marble walls, porticoes and garden houses. She slipped along the shady paths lined by evergreen pines, cypresses, black laurels and ivy. Now and again auxiliaries came out of the shadows to stop and search her. They felt the bundle she carried, the paltry possessions collected from the dormitory. They'd try to grasp her breasts or pinch her buttocks, then let her through. At the bottom of the Palatine hill she passed the Fountain of Fortuna, near the temple of Castor and Pollux. She kept well away from the main concourse, the roads leading to the Via Triumphalis, but skulked in the shadows of the narrow streets which ran parallel to the Via.

The night was cold, the sky clear. Claudia would stop at a corner and peer back to see if she was being followed or she'd examine the skyline, as if interested in the soaring piles of the Circus Maximus, the Column of Trajan, the statues of the Forum or the Basilica Nova of the dead Maxentius. Claudia became more aware of her surroundings. How narrow the streets were, full of different smells; some sweet, others harsh and stale. Always watchful, Claudia spared a glance for the nomads sleeping in the temple porticoes, the fracas caused by a mad dog being cornered, or a mud-spattered sow, a noose round its neck, being chased by a group of screaming children.

She went down the Street of the Saddlemakers into that of the Tanners. The air was thick with the smell of incense mixed with the stink from purple dye stewing in stale urine. On one occasion, concerned at throwing off any pursuer, she lost her way and found herself in an alleyway where Syrian rag men, in their long coloured robes, bivouacked beneath a fig tree. She had to retrace her steps: across the Esquiline cemetery near the Servian Wall where the poor were buried, their corpses hidden under a few shovelfuls of earth. She pinched her nostrils, scaring away the carrion birds who soared up at her approach, feathery wings flapping against the night.

Claudia was certain she was being followed. She twisted and turned, she paused and looked back, but couldn't see anyone. She stopped at a crossroads where huge phalli had been carved as protection against the evil eye. She pretended to be interested in a funeral cortège, preceded by pipers, processing to the sound of flutes, horn and tubae. Torch-bearers ran alongside the gilt-covered coffin whilst the hired women wailed loudly as if they wished to rouse the very dead they mourned. The coffin was followed by a buffoon, imitating some of the dead man's actions. Behind this cortège came a straggle of poor pushing a corpse in a barrow, to take advantage of the glory and pomp of the wealthier funeral.

The streets were still busy, carts, allowed into the city after nightfall, jostling with costly palanquins. Now and again all had to stand aside at the measured tread of the nightwatchmen, the Vigiles, who searched for fires or malefactors. Claudia crossed a small marketplace where, under arches, pedlars sold sulphur matches, cobblers bought and sold shoes, cooks with portable ovens served pease pudding and spicy sausages. A snake-charmer and a sword-swallower were trying to attract the crowd but were facing stiff competition from a monkey-trainer who, whip in hand, did his best to persuade a Barbary ape to hurl spears at a target. Sometimes the street was broad, other times a mere needle cut off by narrow arches which could be blocked by dropped shutters. People watched Claudia pass but the purposeful way she walked, and her stout cane, made them realise she was not some wench lost. A trick Claudia had learned: victims attracted attack, but walk with a swagger, swing a cane and meet everyone's eye and you were left alone. She passed a brothel; on its steps a man was singing:

'Here I had a girl of late,
Bouncing and fine, a good bedmate!'

A group of drunks, sick as snakes which had stumbled into a wine vat, staggered by and knocked him off the steps. The incipient fight was stopped by the appearance of soldiers escorting a slave with an iron ring round his neck, a sign that he had been recaptured and given the name of his owner as if he was a dog. At last, passing through the wealthy quarter, whose spacious houses were protected by walls which ran blind and unbroken, Claudia reached the insula, the great four-storeyed block of flats which housed the She-Asses tavern. This commandeered the bottom floor. A spacious hostelry beneath a creaking sign, its open front was reduced by a counter built into the masonry. On the lintel above the main door perched the Owl of Minerva, whilst on the posts a grinning Hermes squatted with an extended phallus. The tavern seemed deserted. Claudia's heart leaped into her throat. Had Uncle been taken? She went into the main hall, what the rich would call the atrium: Polybius had converted this into a spacious drinking room lit by rush-lights and hanging oil lamps. The air was thick with the fug of tallow, burning meat and fish.

Claudia stood in the shadow of the doorway and smiled. Nothing much had changed! If the police were raiding, the place would be empty. Most of those who frequented the She-Asses had something to hide. It was just rather quiet: men played dice, the board game 'Brigands', or sat, half-drunk, staring into their beer jugs. At the far counter stood the huge ex-gladiator Oceanus: big-chested, pot-bellied, with thighs as thick as tree trunks. He was going bald so he'd finished the job, shaving his head clean. One ear sported a glass ring. The other, bitten off during a match, Oceanus had dried out and kept on a cord slung round his neck. He was glowering, as he always did, little shifty eyes under thick eyebrows, moving from customer to customer, daring them for trouble. His gaze rested on Claudia. He looked puzzled then grinned in the finest display of cracked teeth, as her uncle said, in all of Rome.

'Little one! Little one!' Oceanus waddled across, looking ridiculous in his skimpy tunic. He enveloped her in a hug which smelt of olive oil, herbs and stale sweat.

'Not too hard, Oceanus,' Claudia whispered. 'Where's Uncle?'

'Oh, he's gone along to see the Prefect of the Police.' Oceanus released Claudia.

'He's not in trouble, is he?'

'No.' The ex-gladiator played with the dried ear resting against his sweaty chest. 'The stupid bastard just wants to ask some questions. That's all.' He led her across to a table. 'I've got some fine spiced sausages and fresh bread. Look, everybody!' Oceanus shouted. 'Claudia is here!'

Shadows appeared at the kitchen door but Oceanus gestured at them to stay away. He served a dish of asparagus and chopped sausage and a cup of Falernian wine mixed with water. Claudia ate hastily. She was hungry, but Oceanus would never answer a question until he was satisfied she had had her fill.

'Right.' She wiped her fingers on the napkin provided. 'Polybius is with the police. Where is Poppaoe?'

'Our dusky grape is out in the bird garden with a cold cloth over her face. She claims all the commotion is just too much.'

'What commotion?'

Claudia must not let anything slip to these people: she was a palace servant girl, nothing more.

'That silly bastard, Arrius? He goes out to collect his dues and brings the silver in here? He always rents a chamber, has his dinner then hires two of the girls for bed sport.'

'And?'

'Well, he came here, made himself comfortable and locked the door of the most spacious chamber we have on the first floor. An hour passed. The greedy bugger never sent down for food so off I went, knocked and knocked, no answer. I went out into the garden, looked up but the shutter was fastened. I went back up and peered through the keyhole, The key was still there. I told Polybius.' Oceanus paused to remember. 'That's right, I told Polybius. We forced the door open. Arrius was lying on the bed with a second mouth.'

'He had his throat cut?'

'From one end to the other, mistress. His saddlebags were empty, the money gone. The old bugger was as dead as a nail. Polybius had to call the police. In they came, pinching the wine and the serving wenches. They took one look at Arrius and were about to arrest Polybius when Poppaoe rushed in with a brush. She fair laid about them, I tell you that. Even I was frightened. "Thick heads!" she shrieked. "My husband . . ." He's not really that, is he?'

Claudia shook her head.

'Anyway, she told them her husband had got witnesses: he never went near the room. That made the police really think. So, they bought some wine and sent for an officer. You know, one of those young men who don't want to do a turn in the army. Now, he was really puzzled. You've seen the chamber, mistress. Like a big box: two entrances, one through the window, but that was shuttered, and you know Arrius, the door was locked and bolted from the inside.'

'But the money's gone?'

'Vanished.'

'How do we know he had it in the first place?'

'Because when he came in here, it was fair clinking. The police sent a rider out into the countryside; Arrius had collected his rents and, as usual, brought them in here.'

'It's a real mystery, Claudia.'

Granius, a thin, spiky-haired young man, came over, close-set eyes above mocking lips. He was Uncle Polybius' self-proclaimed manager. Behind him was his girlfriend, the serving wench Faustina. They both kissed Claudia on the cheek, pulled over stools and sat opposite.

'It was a horrible sight,' Granius declared. 'Wasn't it, Faustina?'

The cat-faced serving wench shoved back her long tresses of black hair, a gesture she always performed to make men stare at her.

'Blood all across his chest. You'd think someone had spilt a flagon of wine over him.'

'And he's still there?' Claudia asked.

'Yes. The police have said it's Polybius' concern. He has to send the body out for burial. I hope he hurries back; by tomorrow evening Arrius will be ripe and smelling.'

'We've all been up to see it,' a customer who had been eavesdropping shouted. 'Polybius was charging us to see the corpse.' He stuck his chin close to his chest and twisted his face into a snarl. 'Arrius wasn't the prettiest thing when alive, but just lying there, he looked really angry that he'd been killed.'

'Wouldn't anyone?' Granius quipped.

Other customers now began to group round the table, including Januaria, a buxom wench, soft on the gladiator Murranus.

'He's going to appear in the games, you know,' Januaria said dreamily. 'You know, the Emperor's victory celebration?'

She rested her chin on the heel of her hand as if impervious to everything happening in the tavern. Claudia smiled. Januaria was always in love: Murranus held the record for keeping her attention the longest. Januaria wore her blonde hair parted down the middle, falling in tresses to her shoulders. Whatever the weather, her tunic was always cut low. She had learned how to serve, giving her customers the most generous view, without her plump breasts popping out.

'He says if he wins,' Januaria continued, looking dreamily at Claudia, 'he'll marry me.'

'Fat chance!' Oceanus muttered. 'Here today and gone tomorrow, as Polybius said about his piebald pig which did a runner three weeks ago.'

'He's a Frisian, a good fighter!'

Oceanus breathed in noisily and shook his head. 'Murranus has fought six and won five. The last time he escaped because the crowd felt sorry for him.'

'But that's life.' Simon, a bedraggled, shabby philosopher, spoke up from his stool near the counter. This self-proclaimed stoic spent most of his time in the She-Asses, lecturing anyone stupid enough to listen. He got up and shambled across, his face a picture of misery. 'We are just bladders of wine,' he began, 'strutting about: meaner than flies we are, because flies are good for something! What are we good for?'

'Oh, tell us something happy!' Faustina cried.

Simon the stoic chewed on his gums.

'Crispin the baker's dead.'

'Good riddance!' Oceanus exclaimed. 'He was a man ready to snatch a half-penny out of the dung-heap. He was so randy not even the house dog was safe.'

Claudia watched the doorway, distracted by the man who peered there, a dark, indeterminate shape. Had he followed her here?

Oceanus followed her gaze and got to his feet.

'Welcome, stranger, what do you want?'

'I've swallowed half the dust on the Appian Way.' The stranger came forward, pushing back the hood of his gown: he was old, with a small, wrinkled face under tufts of white hair. He glanced at Claudia then looked away. 'A cup of wine and some fish?' He shuffled over to a corner.

'Well, go on!' Oceanus urged Januaria. 'Serve the man.'

Claudia let the chatter swirl about her. Simon the stoic was in good form: he began to lecture Faustina on her appearance.

'A girl really needs to know how to look her best,' he proclaimed. 'Now, you've got an oval face. So, part your hair down the middle. I understand there are some beautiful blonde dyes from Germany. Have you tried them?'

Claudia watched the stranger. Januaria came tripping out of the kitchen with a cup and platter and put them down. The man sat with his back to her: Claudia waited for a while, then, excusing herself, walked to the doorway. When she came back she stopped at the table. The stranger had put his finger in the wine and drawn a fish above the number IV. Claudia went back to her stool. Faustina had now regained her wits and was screeching at Simon the stoic about his unsolicited advice. A fight would have ensued but Oceanus intervened. Januaria began to moan loudly about the whereabouts of Murranus.

'Oh, don't worry about him,' Granius declared spitefully, narrowing his eyes. 'He's probably trying out some little filly, making sure it shakes its head and raises its legs.'

'I wish you'd go!' Januaria leaned across the table. 'I wish you'd piss off back to where you came from, some kennel in Marseilles!'

'I will be leaving soon.' Granius winked at Faustina. 'Isn't that right, my dear?'

'Where?' Claudia asked curiously.

'Oh, perhaps north. Maybe go to Milan. See some of the world.'

'Join the army,' Oceanus declared. 'You'll see the world then, my boy.'

'No thank you,' Granius replied. 'I don't fancy chasing some bare-arsed barbarian through the mist.'

'You wouldn't know how to hold a sword!' Januaria riposted. 'You have difficulty enough with your dick!'

'Don't you go up there!'

Claudia looked round. Poppaoe had come in from the garden. Dark, juicy and jovial as a little plum, her black hair piled up and kept in place by a silver comb, Poppaoe stared round the eating hall. Claudia got up and Poppaoe's plump face creased into a smile, followed by screams of delight, hugs and kisses. Simon the stoic, who had been creeping up the stairs to have another look at Arrius' corpse, slunk back into the shadows.

'It's good to see you, Claudia.' Poppaoe held her at arm's length.

'Very good indeed!' a voice thundered from the doorway.

Polybius was back. He swaggered across, his heavy, dark face twisted into a grimace. He wiped the sweat from his balding pate and plucked at the tendrils of hair which circled his head like an imperial wreath. He ignored the others, and for once that day, Polybius smiled. He kissed and hugged his niece, then squeezed one of Poppaoe's breasts.

'Questions, questions, questions,' he grumbled, ushering them all back to the table. 'The Prefect of Police is a cantankerous bastard. He kept asking me the one question: if I didn't kill and rob Arrius, who did?'

'And what did you reply?' Claudia asked.

'I told the bastard I was an innkeeper with a good cookshop, restaurant and clean rooms. He's the so-called Chief of Police, not me!'

'What's his name?' Poppaoe asked.

'Saturninus. I kept calling him Arsinus. It took the thick clod an hour to realise I was making fun of him.'

'And?' Poppaoe demanded.

'Not for the moment.' Polybius stood up. 'I want a cup of unwatered wine.'

Claudia noticed the stranger had now disappeared, his meal

half-finished. Her uncle made her stand up and looked her over from head to toe.

'So, a serving-girl in the Imperial Palace, are we?' His lips curled in disdain but his eyes were soft and gentle. He stretched out a hand and cupped Claudia's cheek. 'It's good to see you,' he murmured. 'I get so worried.' He ignored the rest. 'Every time I look at you reminds me of your mother.' He blinked quickly. 'Lovely lass, Claudia, with a smile to lighten my day. If your father hadn't married her . . .' Polybius wetted his lips, lost in his own reverie. 'I've been out to Felix's grave.'

'Hush now! Hush now!' Claudia stroked the back of his great hairy hand. 'You've got troubles enough.'

Polybius snatched the wine cup from Oceanus and half-drained it.

'But business is good now the Greasy Pig has gone up in flames. You remember sly old Cassius, kept a filthy tavern two alleyways away? A born fraud, he could turn red wine white and white wine red. Anyway, he was roasting some thrushes, drunk as one of the pigs he resembles. The entire place went up in flames.'

Claudia refused to be distracted.

'Arrius!' she insisted.

'Ah well,' he breathed. 'You've got sharp eyes. I might as well show you: the rest stay down here.'

Claudia followed her uncle across the hall and up the stairs. She was always fascinated by the apartment block. Polybius owned the three floors facing the front: the rest was a rabbit warren and smelt like it, though Polybius kept his part clean. The stairs and walls were scrubbed, with flowers placed in pots. He'd even put some carvings on the walls.

Polybius had also served as a soldier in the Second Augusta

and fought in both Germany and Britain. Claudia knew little else of his previous life, but loved him for what he was: a man who pretended to be miserable and hard but was really kind and gentle, except for his fierce hatred of the local police. True, Polybius was also a rogue with fingers in many pies. Claudia suspected that he liked this apartment because there were so many stairways, exits and entrances; it would take an entire legion to organise a thorough search. As they mounted the stairs, Claudia recalled the quiet knocks on the door in the dead of night; Polybius meeting people out in the hall or the garden; carts, their wheels covered in rags and straw, delivering goods at the most surprising times.

'You are well, Uncle?' she called out as they reached the passageway.

Polybius paused, his hand on the latch of the door which had apparently been forced. Great splinters of wood had been gouged out and lay scattered on the floor.

'I was until this bastard turned up. Come in!'

The chamber was dark, the shutters still drawn close. Claudia smelt the stench of death: a nasty, fetid taste. Cursing and muttering, Polybius threw open the shutters and, using a sulphur match, lit the lamps. The chamber was box-like. It contained a few sticks of furniture, bench, stools, table, a large earthenware chamber pot and some hooks on the wall. Arrius' corpse lay on a bed in the alcove with a horse blanket tossed over it.

'Behold our sleeping beauty!'

Polybius, holding the lamp, pulled the blanket away. Someone had made a pathetic attempt to accord Arrius a little dignity by straightening his legs. He was a scrawny old man with cropped white hair, streaky moustache and beard. His chin seemed to have sunk into his chest and so he appeared to be looking at them from under his half-closed eyes. The dark blue tunic was soaked in blood, as were the sheets and blankets. Claudia inspected him carefully. She had seen death in so many forms. She had knelt and wept beside her brother's corpse. What further horrors could be inflicted? Death was the end. A lump of flesh cruelly treated.

'This is peculiar.' Claudia inspected the weather-beaten panniers at the foot of the bed. 'There's nothing in here at all. I mean, he must have carried more than a few bags of coins? And look, Uncle, though he's lying on the bed,' she tapped the dead man's leather boots, 'he didn't even take these off.'

'He always was an inconsiderate bastard,' Polybius growled.

Claudia noticed Arrius' cloak was still draped round his shoulders, the chain which held it secure also stained in blood. She walked round the bed and stared back at the door. The bolts had been forced, the lock splintered, the key still in it.

'So?' she asked. 'Arrius came up here?'

'Yes, Granius brought him up. My noble assistant asked him if he wanted anything to eat or drink. Arrius, miserable as ever, sat on the bed and said not for the moment, so Granius left him. He heard the bolts being drawn and the lock being turned.'

'Was that customary?'

'Oh yes.' Polybius pointed to a sycamore box with special clasps. 'Arrius put whatever he had in there, kept the window shuttered and the door locked.'

'He must have eaten and drunk?'

'Oh, he paid well: on previous occasions food was taken up to him on a tray. When he'd finished, he'd open the door and call down. Granius would go up and collect the tray and arrange for some girls to visit him. Mind you, Arrius wasn't

49

popular! He only paid the asking price and the wenches always said they had to work very hard.'

'But this time it was different?' Claudia was now concerned. The bravado Polybius had shown below had now disappeared. He sat on a stool scratching his stomach, a common gesture whenever he was highly anxious.

'Yes, this time it was different. Granius left. He met Faustina at the top of the stairs. She also heard the bolts being drawn and the lock turned. Down they come. Time passes, darkness begins to fall. Oh, aye, I think, the miserable bastard hasn't ordered any food. Oceanus went up and knocked, no answer. He went out into the garden but the shutter was closed so he alerted me. Soon we had half the neighbourhood on the stairs. Granius fetched a wooden bench. Oceanus and I broke down the door. We smashed the lock and this is the sight which greeted us.'

'And what did the police say?'

'Well, they've got no proof against me or anyone else, but the Prefect is threatening to close me down for a month, maybe even two, so he can carry out a thorough search.'

'And Arrius was . . . ?'

'A wine merchant. He went out every month to collect his dues. He lived the other side of the city. A bachelor. I think he liked to lord it here for two or three nights, have his pleasures and go his miserable way. I'd do anything,' Polybius moaned. 'I'm not too sure if the Prefect was angling for a bribe, but if I'm closed down, Claudia, it would be a fate worse than death. I wish I had followed Poppaoe's advice,' he continued, lost in his own misery of woes. 'She advised me to buy a wolf's beard and tie it to the door post to fend off ill-luck.'

Claudia half-listened as she went round the bed. The straw mattress had been covered by a sheet. She noticed this was tucked in at one corner. She lifted it up and saw the tawdry yellow parchment sheets beneath. She took these out and unrolled them.

'No one thought of looking there,' Polybius said.

'What's this?'

Claudia suppressed her own unease. The parchment was of poor quality, rather greasy. At the top were the Christian signs: the Chi and the Rho. Beneath, scrawled in dark red ink, as if it was blood, the crude letters 'In hoc signo occides'.

'What's all this?'

Polybius snatched it out of her hands.

'Oh, shit! Something to do with the Christians, is it? I recognise those signs. They are appearing all over Rome.'

'I think I should take them,' Claudia offered.

'I should give them to the police!'

'I don't think so,' Claudia replied. 'They were being carried by Arrius. The Prefect might say they belonged to you.'

Polybius was clearly agitated.

'It's best if I take them,' Claudia reassured him. 'If these were found in your possession you might be accused of something more serious.'

Polybius strode across the room and closed the shattered door. He turned and leaned against it.

'What do you mean, Claudia?'

'There is a new Emperor in Rome; the tavern gossips say the Christians are to be tolerated.'

Polybius walked across and grasped her shoulders.

'How do you know all this? Look at you, Claudia, with your cropped hair, your pale face and those eyes. You are nothing but a slip of a girl. Yet sometimes you act as if you're much older than you claim. I've seen you in the hall below: watching and listening. You never speak about what you do. Here and there, always busy.' Polybius grasped her face between his great callused hands. 'I am sorry about Felix. I always tend his grave. I'm sorry what happened to you. I should never have let you go there!'

'It wasn't your fault.' Claudia gently took his hands away.

'But you haven't forgotten, have you?'

'No, Uncle. One day I will find the man who attacked me and killed Felix.'

Claudia's face was so pale, her dark eyes so intent in their gaze, Polybius wondered if her wits were safe.

'I'll catch him and I'll kill him, Uncle.'

'Hush now, girl. Don't say things like that. Why don't you come back here? You could manage this place for me. My brother gave you the best of educations. He was so proud of you. "Listen to my Claudia," he'd boast. "Virgil, Cicero . . ." ' Do you remember the day, you must have only been twelve, you stood on a table in the eating hall and recited from memory the opening of Cicero's speech "Pro Milone", followed by Virgil's description of Aeneas' flight from Troy.' He smiled. 'None of those thick buggers knew what you were on about but they were impressed and I was proud. Then you were off with that acting troupe. Oh, I wish that drunken bugger had never come here!'

'Valerian said I was a born actress.'

'I know that,' her uncle grumbled. 'I've seen you imitate some of the customers downstairs. What else are you, Claudia? I am not a stupid man. You slide away in the dark, you run errands round palaces. You are not an informer, otherwise the police would be swarming all over me.' He studied her sadly. 'I am just worried.'

'And I'm worried about you,' Claudia retorted. 'Carpe diem, Uncle. Carpe diem! Seize the day!' Claudia held up the sheaf of parchment. 'These, I'll take care of. You'll remove the corpse?'

'Tomorrow morning.'

Claudia got up and walked to the door. The bolts were damaged, the simple lock so shattered she could clearly see the primitive wheel which held the key-clasp.

'One step at a time,' Claudia murmured. 'Come on, Uncle. Show me to my room.'

Chapter 4

'Leave the rest to the Gods.'
Horace, *Odes*, I.9

Claudia lay on her bed and stared up at the ceiling. From the cookshop below came shouts and laughter, and the sound of a tambourine, which meant Januaria was planning to dance. Her room was a simple one. She glanced at the wall where previous customers had scrawled graffiti:

'Theophania is a good ride.'
'Pornus has got a nasty mouth.'
'Quaestus is a public utensil.'
'Forget the republic, go for the pubic.'

Underneath, a more cultured quotation from Virgil:

'Silent they fell, each man of them.'

55

Claudia breathed in and pinched her nostrils at the smell of boiled cabbage. She watched the oil lamp in its black jar rise and fall with the breeze seeping through the shutters. She kept remembering Polybius' face and felt an ache at her own sad loss. Mother was gone, Father dead, and then little Felix. They called him her shadow: where she went, Felix always followed. She blamed herself for his death. They had gone down to the Tiber, searching the mud flats for precious objects, a coin, a ring. Felix had loved doing that. How long ago? More than a year? That terrible shadow stepping out of the darkness. Felix's life snuffed out like a candle. His murderer over her, thrusting away while he held a knife to her throat. Claudia would always remember his smell: incense, oil and wine. His face was hidden by some form of mask but she'd glimpsed the chalice tattoo on his wrist. She'd heard of similar attacks in the same area.

The days following had been a nightmare. She never cried but lay by Felix's bier and went to sleep with him as she had when he was alive. Then it had all changed. Valerian swaggering into the tavern; she was standing on a table quoting from one of Terence's plays. He'd asked her her age, felt her breasts and burst out laughing when Claudia imitated him back. So accurately, so shrewdly, or so he told her later, he'd offered her a job. Polybius had been furious but she had gone with Valerian and his troupe, wandering for months up and down the roads of Italy, oblivious to the tramp of armies, the crash of empire. In Milan she had seen the priest Anastasius watching her intently during some piece by Proteus. She had been using the sign language and so it had begun.

Claudia rolled over on her side. Valerian always drank too much. He'd gone bankrupt in Rome by late summer; within days Anastasius had visited the tavern. He communicated swiftly, moving his fingers in quick, bird-like movements. The following evening she had met him outside Rome and been drawn deeper and deeper into his world. She had been recruited to the household of Helena in Milan and been with Constantine when he had marched south.

Claudia had acted as both spy and informer. She prided herself that she betrayed no one but traitors. Anastasius had given her his solemn promise. Not just money to lodge away with the bankers but, one day, the life of her attacker.

Claudia heard a burst of laughter: Oceanus was bellowing a crude doggerel of a song. And this business? Claudia wondered The slaying of courtesans? What did it matter if the Emperor took his pleasure? But why kill them? To blacken his name? Perhaps. There must be other pieces to the puzzle. Claudia fell asleep wondering what would be said in the dark catacombs the following morning.

She was up early, just after dawn. She washed and dressed in a new blue tunic Poppaoe must have brought into the room during the night. Then she put on heavy thonged sandals, grasped her walking stick and went downstairs. The tavern was still quiet. Out in the streets all was noise and bustle: the clanging of hammers, the scurry of school children, the meandering of wealthy clients to the wealthy mansions of their patrons, the clattering and grumbling of servants. Along the streets, slaves, armed with brooms of intertwined tamarisk, heather and myrtle, were scattering sawdust on steps before sweeping it into heaps. Two drunks staggered about, blinking furiously against the sunlight. Shutters were coming off shops, wares being taken out to the stalls, braziers lit against the cold morning air whilst the barbers were already busy with early customers.

Claudia kept an eye on the upper storeys along the narrow

streets: this was the hour of the chamber pots, when every type of filth and dirt was tossed out on the streets before the Vigiles began their rounds. Claudia was soon out of the area that she knew so well and into the marketplaces. The colonnades were busy: shoemakers and cloth merchants, sellers of copper vessels, vendors of hot sausages, boys offering bread and cakes, women hawking fruit and vegetables, scribes offering pen and parchment. Stalls displayed fried dates, black pudding sausages and small pots of stew. Wine-sellers shouted that they were the best. The further Claudia travelled, the busier the city became. Matrons in their chairs, a fat man being trundled along in a wheelbarrow by his two sons. Important officials lounging in their litters, either reading some parchment or bellowing at their slaves to find a quicker way through the crowds.

Claudia ran on, going south against the drift of traffic swarming in from the countryside. Beggars clustered like flies, cheap-jacks wandered around looking for mischief. She kept her hand on her purse, fastened to a cord round her waist, and pulled the hood of her cloak close about her. She stopped at a cookshop for some bread, dates and watered wine. As she hurriedly ate and drank, Claudia studied the surrounding crowd closely. She then hastened on. Just before she reached the main road down to the Appian gates she stopped, bought a spiced sausage and sat on the steps of a temple. She ate the hot sausage, once again looking round, searching for any face she had glimpsed before. A drunk staggered up and lifted the hem of his tunic. Claudia raised her staff and poked him playfully in the stomach.

'Wrong time, wrong place, wrong woman!' she said tartly.

The drunk swayed. Claudia could see he wasn't acting.

'Go home,' she murmured, 'and sleep it off.'

58

She got up, pushed by him and soon reached the city gates, where auxiliaries in their red cloaks and blue shields, helmets beside them, lounged against the sentry house picking their teeth and whistling at the girls. Claudia hastened by. At first she had to stop; here the carts thronged, unloading their provisions to be taken in by barrows or slaves to the many markets. At last she was through them. The way became more deserted and she reached the great sprawling cemetery, the city of the dead which stretched out as far as the eye could see on either side of the Appian Way: mausoleums, statues, crude headstones, a veritable Necropolis.

Claudia entered this, following a path which wound through the burial mounds, the faded splendour of the patrician tombs, the tawdry imitations of those less fortunate. The deeper she went, the more silent it became, except for the occasional bird call or the scurry of some animal through the long grass. It was early spring; the sun was strong but the breeze would remain cool until at least midday. Claudia paused and, using her staff, climbed on top of a tomb, looking back the way she had come: nothing. In the far distance she could see a throng of travellers on the Appian Way, but she was alone; no one had followed her into the cemetery.

Claudia clambered down and followed the path to an open stretch of wasteland. Even in the morning light it looked gaunt and desolate. This had once been used as an execution ground. Here, according to legend, the Christian officer Sebastian had been shot to death by arrows. Across the heath she glimpsed the derelict tomb, the entrance to the catacombs below. Claudia always felt uneasy here. One night she had come here and, by chance, had stumbled on two ugly old women with bare feet and dishevelled hair, their faces deathly pale due to the white paint smeared on them. They had been wrapped in black, chanting their spells with mournful howl-ings. Claudia had hid. Witchcraft and sorcery were common in Rome, which was why she was so rarely summoned at night. This was a common place for wizards to invoke the shades of night, to tear up the earth with their nails and pour into their makeshift trenches the blood of a black lamb or some other animal. On that particular night Claudia had had to wait, hiding behind a tombstone until the old women had either finished their rite or become exhausted.

Now the heathland was deserted, though she could see the scorched grass where night fires had been lit. She walked slowly across. Something in the grass caught her eye: the feathers of a black cock, beside them whitened bones. Claudia closed her eyes, made the sign against the Evil One and reached the tomb. She bent down and entered, taking great care, for the steps plunged abruptly into the darkness below. She walked carefully down and paused, peering into the gloom. No sign of any light. She must be the first. Claudia carefully felt the wall just above the bottom step. She sighed with relief as her fingers touched the oil lamp and sulphur matches. She lit the lamp, fingers shaking, and gazed round. The catacombs were hollowed out of the porous rock which ran around the city of Rome. They had begun as graves for the poor but the Christians had taken them over as hiding-holes, cemeteries and even places of worship. Men, women and children who'd died barbarously in the arena were brought here secretly by night for burial. Some even had the reputation of being what the Christians called saints: by their sufferings passing immediately into Paradise. Despite all this, Claudia recalled the bogey-man stories told her as a child: of the Mormo, a terrifying woman with donkey's legs, or the Lamia, bloody-mouthed ghouls, who prowled around devouring children. The narrow catacombs, ill-lit, narrow and dank, were a fitting place for such nightmares.

Claudia, carrying the lamp, went deeper into the darkness. Now and again she would stop to light another. She carefully followed the marks etched in the wall, arrows in the form of fishes. The catacombs were dangerous, easy to enter, but if she became lost in their labyrinthine passages, it could mean interment for life Every so often she stopped and checked she was going in the right direction. At last the passageway debouched into a small cavern. She glimpsed the marble bench, stolen from one of the mausoleums, which lay beneath the grave of the martyr Philomena.

Claudia went across and sat down. To her right stretched another tunnel. She had been carefully instructed: if danger emerged, this tunnel would take her out across the cemetery. Claudia smiled to herself. What danger? She wasn't a Christian. Even so, the Christians had nothing to fear in Constantine's Rome. She had been told to be here at the fourth hour and she reckoned she was in good time. To calm her agitation, she got up and walked around, staring at the tombs and their various inscriptions. She heard a sound, a slither in the passageway. She doused the lamp and stood in a corner watching the entrance. A figure emerged. Claudia sighed with relief as the priest Sylvester, a lamp in his hands, walked into the antechamber.

'You are here, Claudia?'

'I am here.'

Claudia went across to meet him. She rekindled her lamp. Sylvester lit others in the wall niches and sat next to her on the bench.

'Why here?' she began. 'I hate these places. You've got nothing to fear.'

'We have everything to fear,' Sylvester replied tartly. 'Constantine has promised us the earth, but will he keep his word? You shouldn't fear the dead, Claudia. They are with God. It's the living who pose the threat. I won't waste your time.' He turned to face her squarely. 'They say you are like your mother, Claudia, except for your eyes. I always see your father there!'

'What was he like? I can hardly remember. A man in a tunic with close-cropped hair and shrewd eyes.'

'You always ask the same question, Claudia. I always give the same answer. Julius was one of us. A very good soldier. He commanded the auxiliaries in the Third Pannonian. A decent man, he would have been proud of you, even though you have not accepted baptism.'

'I have no difficulty accepting your God,' Claudia replied, 'as a concept. I am more concerned that He allows some rich sot to murder a young boy and rape a young woman.'

'I have no news of that,' Sylvester replied. 'You believe your assailant was Christian?'

Claudia nodded.

'Well, he wasn't. Perhaps a soldier? Possibly a priest of the Dionysiac rite?'

'What guild of priests is that?'

Sylvester half-smiled. 'To me, Claudia, one is very much like the other. Dionysius, Aphrodite, Bacchus. There's a whole horde of them, all fervent in their support of Maxentius. So, yes, this rogue could be in Rome, he may be in hiding, he may have turned Christian, or he may even have fled east to Licinius. Time will tell. I could advise you,' he added, 'to put your trust in God. But you have no God, do you, Claudia?'

'Look around you, priest!' Claudia retorted. 'They call this the City of the Dead. Will all these come back to life? Be resurrected?'

Sylvester bowed his head. 'In time, Claudia. Whatever, you have my word about the man with the chalice tattooed on his wrist . . .'

'But we are not here for that.'

'No, no, we are not.'

Sylvester rested his hands on his thighs and leaned forward as if speaking to himself.

'This is the beginning of a new era, Claudia, for the Christian Church. There will be no more persecutions, proscriptions, violent deaths in the amphitheatre. In the East, Licinius squats in Nicodemea and plots; all the world watches. There is unfinished business. Constantine or Licinius will emerge as the master of the Roman world. We pray Constantine wins. He is favourably disposed to us. We regard his mother as one of our most powerful friends.'

'And the murder of these courtesans threatens all this?'

'Yes, they come from the House of Domatilla. They call themselves the Guild, or Society, of Aphrodite. Girls from high-ranking families, with powerful friends.'

'But they are not the only courtesans in Rome?'

'No, they are not. Constantine has picked girlfriends from other quarters and nothing has happened to them.'

'What made him choose Domatilla's?'

'She's a friend of the Augusta Helena. It's one way that Constantine's mother can keep an eye on her boy. Now,' Sylvester continued wryly, 'the personal morality of the Emperor used not to concern us; now it does. There have been three, possibly four, murders.'

'Another one?'

'So our spies in the Imperial Palace tell us. A girl called

Sabina was brought there last night and later found murdered, bloody crosses etched on her forehead and cheeks. A Defixio was also left by the corpse.'

'A solemn curse?'

'Yes, Claudia, a solemn curse. Now, true,' Sylvester waved a hand, 'these deaths are not to our Emperor's credit. They create an unease, disquiet, offend people's susceptibilities. They pray the bad old days are over, that Rome will never again be ruled by a Nero, a Diocletian, a Caligula or an Elegalbus.'

'The bloody crosses also discredit your faith?'

'Yes, they do, Claudia. In some places Christianity is still regarded as a blood-thirsty, deviant movement, its real purpose cloaked in secrecy. People might argue that these murders prove that neither Constantine nor Christianity can really be trusted.'

Claudia told him about the murder at the She-Asses, and the handbills she'd found.

'Well, that at least proves a point.' Sylvester tapped his sandalled foot. 'The murders are meant to create unease and unrest, raise mockery against Constantine and us. Arrius was a wine merchant, wasn't he?'

'Yes.'

'He may,' Sylvester explained, 'have been working for an agent of Licinius; someone close to Constantine, who is trying to discredit the Emperor and us by these murders.'

'So, Licinius is behind it all?'

'Yes, Licinius and a traitor at Constantine's court.'

'But I can't imagine that,' Claudia replied. 'Every time a whore is slain, the murderer is risking his own life. I mean, to kill the likes of Sabina in the heart of a royal palace?'

Sylvester shook his head. 'Think of Licinius as the hub of a wheel. He's in Nicodemea wishing to bring about Constantine's discomfiture; his agents in Rome are the spokes.'

'And the rim of the wheel?' Claudia asked.

'The murderer himself, someone close to Constantine.'

'But you have not answered my question. If it was Bessus the chamberlain, even Constantine's own mother, found standing over a courtesan's corpse, knife in hand . . .'

'The deaths would have been easy enough,' Sylvester replied. 'One was killed after leaving the baths, the second in the atrium of a house on the Esquiline, the third in public gardens and the fourth in the palace itself. Now the courtesans live their own lives. They keep secrets; that's part of their stock-in-trade, to be discreet. So, if the powerful patrician wants to have his pleasure, he'll meet the woman of his choice in places well away from the public eye.'

'So?' Claudia asked.

'The murderer could be the one who invites the courtesan. Or, more probably, he just stalks his victim till he's ready to strike.' Sylvester sighed. 'Although I admit, last night's murder would have been more dangerous to carry out than the others.' Sylvester paused and listened into the darkness.

'What's the matter?' Claudia demanded.

'Nothing, I thought I caught a sound. Oh, it could be anything.' He paused, finger to his lips. 'Have you ever heard of the Sicarius?'

'Chatter and gossip. It means "Dagger Man", doesn't it?'

'Yes, it's also the name of a professional killer: a man who accepts a contract to carry out murders.'

'But Rome is full of them. There are as many killers as there are rats in a sewer.'

'No, this man, or woman, whoever the Sicarius is, is special. You want an assassination carried out and it's done.'

'How?'

'I don't know.' Sylvester shook his head. 'There's a tavern down near the Tiber called the Horse of Troy. It's mean, squalid and rambling. It's owned by a witch, a poisoner, a whore-mistress called Locusta. She is twisted and wicked with it. The only thing I know is that the Sicarius demands high payment. When he's hired, the name of the intended victim is left, somewhere or somehow, at that tavern.'

'Then why don't the authorities close it down?'

'First, they have no proof. Secondly, why should the authorities close down something they've probably used themselves? Finally, if the police raided it, all they'd capture is the cage not the bird itself.'

'So, you are saying that Locusta will take the name of the victim and hand it to the Sicarius?'

'So it seems, and it would be difficult to trap him. Let's say I went in there and gave your name.' Sylvester playfully pinched her arm. 'He would scarce accept it. Indeed, I would be putting myself at risk. He would want to know who I am and where I come from. It has been known for the Sicarius to carry out private executions against those who trouble him.'

'But the Emperor or the Augusta could intervene by force or bribery?'

'It's possible, but would it be successful? Vermin like the Sicarius accept a task and work for one master. Now he is committed, the assassin would smell a trap.'

'And you think this Sicarius killed the whores?'

'Possibly.'

'What proof do you have?'

Sylvester rose and stretched.

'How much did the Empress Helena tell you?' he asked.

'Not as much as you are going to.'

'We know,' Sylvester smiled, 'that five years ago this Sicarius was given a task to track down and kill one of our elders. He was successful and the Sicarius left his own individual mark: a penny thrust into the dead man's hand. A macabre joke, so his victim can pay Charon, the God of the Underworld, when he crosses the river Styx.'

'And these pennies have been found near the courtesans?'

'Certainly in the hands of the first two, but then it stopped, or the coins weren't found.'

'And all the victims were from the same house? Could it be that their murderer has a grudge against Domatilla? And if so, why doesn't she leave Rome?'

'According to rumour,' Sylvester replied, 'she wanted to, but no less a person than the Augusta herself forbade it. Apparently, Helena argued, it would look as if Domatilla no longer trusted the Emperor; it would cause public outcry and draw more attention to these murders.'

'Could Domatilla herself be responsible?'

'Domatilla, fat and pleasure-loving? I doubt it. She lives for her perfumed milk, silk sheets, gossip and the patronage of the powerful and famous.' Sylvester rubbed his hands together. 'She owns a most opulent villa and gardens near the Esquiline. During the civil war, when Constantine was marching on Rome, Domatilla, together with Lucius Rufinus, was Constantine's most powerful adherent. When matters reached a crisis, Maxentius and his henchman Severus began to lash out. Domatilla and her ladies fled Rome. They took a boat down to Ostia, then a ship to Milan. Severus took over Domatilla's villa. First, because of its opulence; secondly to help himself to any treasure Domatilla had left; and thirdly, to search the villa to see if any treasonable documents could be found.'

'And what happened to Severus?'

'Well, as you know, Constantine smashed Maxentius' forces at the Milvian Bridge and marched into Rome. Severus, like everyone else, decided to change sides. However, late one evening, he was visited by a young woman. When his servants went to rouse him in his bedchamber, Severus was dead, a dagger straight to his heart, and of the young woman there was neither sight nor sound. Constantine marched into Rome, carrying Maxentius' head before him, Domatilla moved back, and all was sweetness and light till these murders began.'

Claudia stared at the flickering oil light Sylvester had placed on the ground. She had to take stock of what was happening, ask herself was this too dangerous? Sylvester was right. There was more to this than just the murder of young women. Quietly, Claudia marvelled at how much this powerful Christian priest knew. No wonder Constantine and Helena were showing favour to such an organisation with its myriad spies and informers across the city and Empire.

'Your thoughts, Claudia?'

'What if,' Claudia replied slowly, 'these murders have nothing to do with Licinius? Oh yes, he'll be pleased to hear of them, be ready to dabble in troubled waters. But what if Constantine has a secret enemy, a man, a woman or a group who fiercely resent him? Who would like to take the Empire for themselves? No, no.' She shook her head. 'That doesn't make sense. Constantine controls the army, the troops adore him. So, what if,' she continued her speculation, 'the murders have really nothing to do with Constantine; more with Domatilla and her villa? Yes,' she went on excitedly, 'what if Severus left something there, hidden away?'

'What makes you say that?'

'What if someone wants Domatilla out of Rome? To frighten

her away? Either because she knows something, or because her villa conceals something the murderer wants?'

'I see.' Sylvester smiled. 'That makes sense. The inconvenience shown to the Imperial family and our Church? Well, it's something . . .'

'More like a sideshow in a circus,' Claudia retorted. 'After all, it's Domatilla and her girls who have been punished, not the Emperor.'

'And the murderer?'

'Someone who has something to hide as well as someone who intensely dislikes Constantine. This murderer is the master of the dance; the Sicarius is his agent, who organises and threatens people, like the dead merchant Arrius, to bring broadsheets into the city and distribute them.'

'Yes, that would be logical.'

'Which brings me to one death,' Claudia declared, 'which no one seems concerned about. The girl Fortunata, who was killed then hanged on a meat hook in the Imperial Palace. Now the marble corridors of the Palatine are full of informers and spies. Servants are prepared to sell tidbits of information. So, why should one girl be singled out, unless she knew something? But what?'

'That you must find out,' Sylvester replied. 'We want these murders to end, the perpetrator to be unmasked. If you do that, Claudia,' he grinned impishly, 'you'd not only have the support of the Emperor and his august mother, but the personal patronage of the Bishop of Rome.'

'And the man with the chalice on his wrist?'

Sylvester got to his feet.

'If you do that, Claudia, there'll be no hiding-place for him. If he's alive, you will have both justice and vengeance. Now I must leave you. I understand you are moving to the Emperor's own household. When you do, seek out the girl Livonia, ask her about Fortunata; she may be able to help.'

The priest stopped at the mouth of the passageway and sketched a blessing.

'In a while, follow me.'

Then he was gone.

Claudia sat and waited, so engrossed in her own thoughts her eyes grew heavy. When she woke, she immediately wondered if it was just the cold of this dark place, or a sound she'd half-heard.

Chapter 5

'Everything in Rome comes at a price.'
Juvenal, *Satires*, I

Claudia got to her feet, grasping her bundle and staff. She walked down the passageway and paused, rooted to the spot. The catacombs were an empty, sprawling place. She and Sylvester always followed the same ritual when leaving. He would go first, she would follow, extinguishing the small oil lamps. Now these had gone out. The one to her left as well as further up the cavernous passageway. Sylvester would never have done that. Someone else was here, an intruder waiting in the shadows with knife or garrotte string. Claudia recalled an incident on the outskirts of Constantine's camp months earlier. On the orders of Anastasius, Claudia had gone out to meet a spy from Maxentius' army. No one, the Imperial priest had informed her, would take notice of a little mouse, a serving girl, going out to pleasure her boyfriend who had the misfortune to be on picket duty. That night had proved different. Their spy had been caught and executed. A paid killer had been waiting in his place. He did not give the pre-arranged signal. Now Claudia felt the same stomach-clenching fear she had experienced that cold October night. Death was waiting for her: someone had followed her into the catacombs. He would not, dare not, attack Sylvester, but a serving-girl? Claudia walked forward.

'Who's there?' she called out harshly.

'Claudia!' The reply was low and throaty. 'Claudia, come here!'

She stepped back.

'Shall we play cat and mouse?' the voice mocked. 'Up and down amongst the graves? Shall I catch my little mouse? Look at the walls, Claudia, full of recesses. I'll lay your corpse among the faithful departed and no one will ever know.'

Claudia tensed; the voice was nearer. Was it male, female? Young or old? She wiped her hands on her dark blue tunic and cursed; it was her best. Her mouth turned dry as she peered through the darkness. She carried a small dagger and a staff.

'Let's play cat and mouse,' she taunted back. 'And remember, he who hunts can become the hunted.'

Then Claudia fled back into the cavern she had left and down another passageway. She paused in a recess and heard the quiet slither of a sandal. On she fled, now and again pausing, whenever a shaft of light from some crack in the ground above illuminated the gloomy passageway.

'Always bear left,' she had been told. 'Follow the sign of the fish.'

She did this, but although her pursuer was moving cautiously, there was no doubt he was gaining on her.

'Claudia!' The voice was now importunate. 'All I want to do is talk. Why not rest a while?'

She hurried on, her skin clammy, her chest beginning to hurt. She knew she had not to become lost, yet there was still no sign of an entrance, and even if she got out, wouldn't her pursuer continue the hunt? She would not be safe until she reached the Appian Way, became lost in the crowds thronging into the city. The staff slipped in her hand. She rounded a corner and sobbed with relief. The light was stronger. She looked back at the narrow entrance she'd come through. On the bottom, at each side, rose a small cleft of rock. She placed her staff across these and listened intently. Her pursuer was close.

'I've run the race and I've won!' she mocked into the darkness. 'Soon, I'll be gone!'

Grasping her bundle, Claudia fled down the passageway. She heard a crash behind her and grinned. Whoever was following had tripped over her staff.

'I'll know who you are,' she taunted, 'with your bruised ankle and hobbled gait!'

Then she was up the steps into the sunshine at the far side of the cemetery, not far from the Appian Way. She raced around the decaying monuments and raised tombs, the ivory funeral jars, the weather-beaten headstones. Across a ditch and she almost stumbled into a surprised group of farmers pushing their wheelbarrows up towards the gate.

'I'm sorry,' she stammered, 'but my boyfriend is most persistent.'

The farmers laughed and made salacious comments. One offered her a wineskin, another a rather crumbling oatcake. Claudia accepted these. She looked back but she could see no sign of any pursuer. She followed the farmers back through the gate and into the city. She thanked them and paused outside a cookshop to buy some meat and a cup of watered wine. Only then did she begin to tremble, her stomach heaving at her narrow escape. She watched the people pass into the city but recognised no one who acted suspiciously. An old man hobbled by but he was bent, his face dirt-stained. Apart from him, no sign of anyone who had sustained an injury. Claudia sighed and continued. She called at a woodcutter's to buy a new ash cane and, following the crowds, made her way deeper into the city.

At a tavern she paused and tried to tidy herself up, but there was little she could do about her tunic. It was torn and stained with dirt and green slime where she had brushed against the catacomb walls.

When she presented herself in the servants' quarters of the Imperial Palace at the Palatine, a chamberlain looked her over from head to toe and smirked.

'You are not much of a catch, are you?'

'I am not a catch!' Claudia snapped. 'I am a serving-girl hired by the household!'

'So you are,' the fellow retorted spitefully. 'But we only hire clean ones.'

He clicked his fingers and a kitchen boy took Claudia off, through porticoes, across gardens, to a dormitory behind the palace, no more than a long room above the stables. It housed two rows of beds, each with a small cupboard and stool. One of the servant girls was sick and thrashed about. A leech sat beside her, holding a bowl of colt's-foot root, telling the girl to breathe in the fumes. The dormitory was ill-lit: windows, no more than slits, provided light; the air reeked with the stench of stale sweat, urine, cheap oil and tawdry perfumes. At the far end was a lavarium, where bowls stood on a wooden shelf with pitchers of water. Claudia filled one of these with the ladle provided, washed her face and hands and walked back along the dormitory. The kitchen boy was already trying to undo her bundle. Claudia raised her ash cane threateningly. The boy bent down, lifted his tunic, farted noisily in her direction and fled.

Claudia quickly changed her own tunic. Rolling up her new blue one, she thrust it into the cupboard along with a few keepsakes. She wasn't frightened of theft. She had worked in these places often enough. The unspoken rule of such dormitories was that girls never stole from each other. What they filched elsewhere, however, was up to them.

'Are you Claudia?'

A tall, rangy girl stood in the entrance to the dormitory, dirty blonde hair tied tightly at the back of her head. She had a broad, weather-beaten face, and her voice was guttural.

'I'm Clatina. You are working with me in the kitchens.'

Claudia walked forward. Clatina looked foul-tempered, with narrow blue eyes and tight lips. Her hands were clenched, the skin raw and peeling. They studied each other closely. Again the game was being played out. Claudia knew that Clatina was thinking the same as she: who are you? I mean, really, who are you? An informer? A spy? Do you have a powerful patron? Or some bully-boy friend amongst the guards? Are you to be appeased or frightened?

'Are you German?' Claudia asked.

'No, Helvetian.'

Claudia nodded.

'And you?'

'My father was a Roman centurion, my mother British.'

This time Clatina nodded, her eyes studying Claudia intently.

'Why are you here?' the woman asked.

Claudia shrugged. 'I worked in one household. Now I am transferring to another. I am free-born.'

Clatina forced a smile. Claudia knew she had made a decision. The newcomer was not to be punished or pummelled, bullied or beaten. No mean tricks in the kitchen. No pretend accidents with a pan of boiling oil.

'You'll find me a good worker,' Claudia assured her. 'I keep my mouth shut and my head down.'

Clatina's eyes smiled. Again she made a decision. This new girl knew the rules, the hierarchy of the pack.

'You can work alongside me,' Clatina offered. 'It's not bad. The cooks are bastards, the kitchen boys will try and nip your bum. The soldiers think they are the Gods' answer to womankind. Whilst the rest . . .' Clatina shrugged off the courtiers, flunkeys, hangers-on and visitors. 'Just make sure you are never alone with them! You've worked in palaces before, haven't you? The great ones come and go.' Clatina's smile faded and she bit her lip: such a comment could be construed as treason. Her eyes took on a pleading look.

'I understand.' Claudia smiled. 'The great ones come and go every day. But we've got to stay and work from morning till night.'

Clatina extended her hand. Claudia took it.

'I think you'll do very well,' Clatina murmured. 'But come on. The chamberlain said you should have been here at day-break.'

So began Claudia's service in the kitchens and corridors of the palace. A humdrum routine, running here with bowls of water or jugs of wine. Hours spent in the kitchens, where the heat swirled and smoke rose like clouds, or the press room, where the oil was ground and poured into storage jars. Tables had to be washed, floors scrubbed. Quick meals of eggs, butter and goat's cheese snatched amidst the clatter of dishes or carrying bundles here and there. In the main, Claudia was confined to the working part of the palace. Now and again she would have to cross to where the Sublime Ones lived along their marble corridors and sun-washed colonnades. She kept to herself; probing hands were slapped away, malicious gossip listened to but never responded to. At first she was noticed, but eventually ignored. On one occasion she passed Anastasius in a corridor. He winked and passed on. She learned the palace routine and, more importantly, who Livonia was: a stocky, blonde-haired girl who worked in the laundry room. Claudia bided her time until one afternoon when she and other servants were eating in a sun-washed courtyard of the palace. She managed to sit next to Livonia, who was greedily bolting her food. Claudia watched in pretended amazement.

'Here.' She passed across her wooden plate with portions of bread, grapes, cheese and heavily spiced diced meat, the remains of some banquet.

'Aren't you hungry?' Livonia replied, eyes rounded in astonishment.

'Not as much as you.' Claudia smiled. 'You remind me of my friend Fortunata.'

Livonia gulped her food and swallowed hard. She looked at Claudia, brown eyes rounded in amazement.

'You knew Fortunata?'

Claudia smiled, wondering if Livonia was as stupid as she looked or just pretending. In the palaces of the Caesars, nothing was ever as it seemed.

'We served together, here and there,' Claudia replied. 'But then she disappeared, ran away with a sailor, I suppose?'

'Not Fortunata,' Livonia scoffed. 'Clever as a snake she was!

Had great pretensions to being an actress. You should have seen her when Zosinas' troupe came here. You've heard of him? He owns a theatre down near the baths of Diocletan.'

Claudia nodded. Zosinas was a well-known impresario, who hired troupes and staged plays, both in Rome and elsewhere.

'What makes you think Fortunata would go to him?' Claudia asked.

'Well, a couple of weeks before she disappeared, the troupe visited the palace. Fortunata was full of it, kept talking about Paris, one of the leading actors.'

'Now, I've heard of him,' Claudia intervened.

Actors in Rome had a reputation all their own: Claudia had a keen interest in the meteoric rise and fall of this actor or that. She had heard Paris' name mentioned in the She-Asses and had seen his name in graffiti around the city.

'Smitten, she was,' Livonia declared, 'like a real bitch on heat, but she may have been watching the wrong mousehole.' She laughed loudly at Claudia's puzzlement and nudged her with a red-raw elbow. 'You know these actors? Buttocks up!'

'Of course, yes.' Claudia laughed. 'So, Paris didn't respond?'

'I don't know. Fortunata was much smitten, but whether she did anything about it or not, I don't know.'

'But why Paris?' Claudia asked.

'Well, he's a show-off. There was a play put on for the high and mighty. Afterwards, the entire cast came into the kitchens to be fed. I believe Fortunata filled Paris' wine cup.'

'Did she go to meet him?' Claudia asked.

Livonia tapped the side of her podgy nose.

'Ask no questions, get no lies. Anyway, I thought you were her friend, you should know.'

'I've been away,' Claudia explained. 'And when I came back looking for her . . .'

78

'Strange you say that.' Livonia finished off the food. 'Someone else was asking about her. Don't ask me why or who. Just some tittle-tattle, gossip. Look, thanks for your food.' She thrust the wooden plate back.

Claudia leaned back against the wall and stared up. As she did, a window closed, very quickly. It could have been anyone, but she was certain she and Livonia had been carefully observed.

The following afternoon Claudia slipped out of the palace. Clatina had told her she could take the afternoon off, and Claudia was determined to visit the actor Paris. The day was surprisingly warm, a touch of spring freshness in the air. The great patricians and their ladies, followed by their retinues of slaves and servants, promenaded for their neighbours to see. The streets were busy with litters and palanquins, hucksters and traders, squads of soldiers swaggering down to their barracks. Claudia walked as she always did, quickly, keeping to the alleyways and narrow lanes. Occasionally she stopped, but she could detect no one following her.

She found Zosinas' theatre across a small square, overawed by the soaring masonry of the Diocletian baths; a circular building with satyr heads set in the stonework above the main door. She slipped down a corridor; no one stopped her. The orchestra pit was full of workmen and musicians, people sweating and shouting as the scenery was changed for a new play. Claudia immediately felt at home: the paint, the sawdust, the strange perfumes from the make-up booths, the screech of musical instruments as lutists and harpists tried their hand. People shouted rather than talked in an air of frenetic excitement. Stage managers swaggered about, bawling orders or dictating to harassed-looking scribes. Young girls scampered hither and thither in painted masks and costumes:

boys returning from the cookshops with bowls of steaming food, baskets piled high with bread and fish.

Claudia sat on the edge of a tier of seats looking down at the orchestra. A girl came up.

'Are you here for a rehearsal?'

'No, I am here to see Paris.'

'Aren't we all?' The girl grinned mischievously.

'What are you getting ready?' Claudia asked.

'Oh, Zosinas' next great productions: two plays by Terence, Ovid's *Medea* and *The House of Fire* by Ferinus.'

'All together at the same time?' Claudia quipped. 'I once worked in Valerian's troupe.'

'Did you now?' The smile faded. 'So you are looking for a job?'

'No, I am looking for Paris.' Claudia opened her purse and took out a coin. 'I bring him urgent news. Someone he knew has died. I promise you, that's the only reason I wish to see him.'

The girl looked at the money and licked her lips.

'It's yours,' Claudia offered, holding it out, 'if you bring Paris to me.'

The girl scampered off. Claudia moved to sit in the shade as the sun was growing stronger. The heat brought the frenetic industry to a pause as workmen, painters, artists and actors sought shade and solace. Eventually, the girl reappeared.

'Paris will be with you. In fact, he is closer than you think.'

Her eyes strayed beyond Claudia; she whirled round and stared at the young man smiling down at her.

'You are Paris?'

'That's what everyone says.'

Claudia had never met anyone so handsome: smooth olive

face, dancing eyes turned up at the corners, a straight narrow nose above full, sensuous lips. He wore a clean dark tunic; his black hair was curled, specially coiffed with feathery curls down his cheeks.

'Give the girl her coin,' he lisped.

Claudia handed it over. Paris climbed across the seats and sat next to her. He put one arm round her shoulder, his light grey eyes full of laughter.

'And you are?'

'Claudia,' she stammered. She was used to actors, their false friendships, ecstatic greetings which meant nothing. In the theatre, people hugged and kissed you, yet an hour later would totally ignore you.

'And you were an actress in Valerian's troupe? The drunken braggart who went broke?' Paris snapped his fingers and pointed one manicured finger at her. 'I've heard of you, Claudia. You weren't so good at spoken lines but brilliant at mime. I think I saw you once? In a show at Capua?'

'I have been to Capua.'

'And now?'

'I am in service. As you say, Valerian went broke. My uncle owns the She-Asses near the Esquiline Gate.'

'And you are looking for a job?'

'No.'

'Good!' Paris flapped his hand languidly. 'Stage managers are such bitches,' he lisped. 'They are nothing but a bunch of silly tarts. They promise you the world but all they really want is a handsome profit and a feel of your buttocks.'

Claudia studied the smooth, almost beautiful face, the long eyelashes, pencil-thin eyebrows, and that glorious shock of black hair. Paris leaned back, swung his legs up, lithe and strong, glistening with oil, and tapped his sandals together.

'Well, the other darlings are eating, drinking or fornicating. Whatever they do. The girl told me someone I knew had died, but people are dying all the time, darling, aren't they?'

'Fortunata's dead!'

Paris swung his legs back and withdrew his arm.

'I am sorry,' he murmured. 'She was a merry lass, dancing eyes and pert mouth. She wanted to be an actress. I upset her.' Paris' eyes filled with tears. 'She was too old to start. Yet she seemed to be in good health.'

'She was until she was murdered.'

'Murdered!'

'Her throat was cut, her corpse slung up on a meat hook.'

Paris turned away to retch. When he controlled himself, his eyes were watery, his face pale.

'Jupiter's cock! Who'd do that?'

'I don't know. That's why I came to see you, as Fortunata did, remember?'

'Yes, yes, of course I do. We went to the palace. We put on some plays and a show, miming and singing. Afterwards, as is customary, we were given a meal in the servants' quarters. Fortunata approached me; she looked a comely little poppet.'

'Did you sleep with her?'

'Oh, you are a naughty girl,' Paris cooed. 'But yes, I did. We became great friends. She came down here to the theatre and later dined in a restaurant. She was,' he pulled a face, 'a little mysterious.'

'And?'

'One day she just stopped visiting.'

'Did she say anything?' Claudia paused. 'Anything unto-ward?'

Paris shook his head. 'Gossip from the palace about other servants. How she would like to be away from it all.'

'Did she talk of marriage? Was there anyone else?'

'Yes, there was. A gladiator, one of those Frisians. You know, the big, beefy sort, who like to wear gorgeous helmets and small tight pants and do the dance of death in the amphitheatre. Ah yes, Murranus!'

Claudia hid her surprise. Wasn't Murranus Januaria's sweetheart? Though there again, gladiators were noted for their love affairs.

'Was she sweet on him?'

'Darling, I don't know what she was sweet on. She was very good to me and I was very good to her. I said I would mention her name to Zosinas. No, no.' He raised his hand. 'I didn't promise anything for favours received. I just mentioned her name to get her a job in the theatre or a place in the chorus line. There was something else.' He paused and stared down at the orchestra. 'They are never going to get the stage right. Do you know that? I told the silly bastards not to go for anything too complicated, but,' he waved a hand languidly, 'you might as well talk to the trees.'

'Fortunata . . . you said she was mysterious?'

His hand slipped behind her.

'Will you come for a meal with me, Claudia? I get so tired of theatre types.'

She grinned. 'I am not too struck on them myself. But yes,' she added hastily, 'if you can help me.'

'There's a lovely restaurant just off the Forum.' Paris kissed his fingers. 'Oysters in the most ravishing sauce. You can hire your own table. It's up above the main eating board so you can watch all the other tarts poncing about.' He sighed. 'Anyway, Fortunata! I thought she was a quiet little thing. Well, except in bed, where she proved she had a good voice. But one day she was late and, of course, no one is ever late for Paris! So

I became petulant and stamped my foot. I wouldn't forgive her until she told me where she had been. Well,' he rolled his eyes expressively, 'you could have knocked me down with a feather! The silly little tart said she had been down to the Horse of Troy tavern near the Tiber.'

'The Horse of Troy?'

'You know its reputation. I wouldn't go there with a company of gladiators. That's when she mentioned Murranus, said he'd kept her company. I must admit, after that, our relationship cooled a little. I mean, I know the eating-houses and taverns of Rome: the Horse of Troy is a place you steer well clear of.'

'Was she secretive?'

'Yes, she would chatter like a sparrow but I always felt her mind was elsewhere. Sometimes, even in bed, you could tell she wasn't thinking about me.' Paris breathed in noisily. 'And you know what acting's like, Claudia, you have got to keep your mind on the job.' He gave a dramatic sigh. 'But hung up on a meat hook? If I were you, dear, I'd have words with Murranus. That's the sort of thing gladiators do.'

'And where could I find him?'

Paris seized her shoulders. 'Not too fast, little bird. Give me a kiss.' He pursed his lips and closed his eyes.

Claudia kissed him lightly.

'Don't you have enough girlfriends round here?' she teased.

Paris laughed, a shrill neigh.

'Look at me, Claudia. And don't be such a bitch! I have a good voice and what Zosinas calls a presence.' He bared his lips. 'My own teeth. Now you know what happens to actors . . .'

He didn't even finish the sentence, for Claudia knew full well what he was hinting at. Actors had a notorious reputation with women. Even in Valerian's little troupe it had been a common occurrence for bully-boys to be waiting for some actor who had ploughed a field that wasn't his, or so Valerian put it. An actor with broken fingers, a limp or a shattered mouth found it hard to perform, and once an actor slipped, he usually kept falling.

'I am no different, Claudia, to the men you worked with, you know that. It's all very well being picked up by a grand lady in a litter, but sooner or later, you pay the price.'

'So, it's girls like me and Fortunata?'

'Yes, girls like you and Fortunata. Now, where do you work? In the palace?'

Claudia smiled. 'You can always find me there.'

He tapped her on the nose. 'Then I'll find you there.'

He got up and was about to saunter away. Claudia noticed his ankles were unblemished and he walked with no limp, though she quietly admitted it was hard to imagine a man like Paris haunting her along the dark passageways of the catacombs.

'Where can I find Murranus?' she called after him.

'Oh, don't be such a tart and make me jealous!' he shouted back. 'Where do you think? Go to the amphitheatre. Like the other butchers, he's preparing for the great games in a few days' time.'

Claudia watched him go. She knew he had told her the truth. Fortunata was a spy, a member of the Agentes in Rebus, but her private life was her own. Paris would not consort with theatre girls. Such relationships caused chatter, gossip, jealousy and division. It was natural he would choose a girl like Fortunata and understandable that she would respond: a casual alliance which gave pleasure and profit to both. But why would Fortunata go to the Horse of Troy? And what was her relationship with Murranus? Claudia moved on the seat. For Fortunata to go down to such a tavern meant that she had discovered something. Locusta, its owner, had an evil reputation, while according to Sylvester, the Horse of Troy was where the Sicarius could be hired. Claudia sucked on her teeth as she followed her argument through. Fortunata must have seen, heard or learned something. Or was she just making enquiries, hence her brutal murder? Was Murranus involved? Claudia quietly cursed Augusta and her own Magister, Anastasius. As usual, they had told her as little as possible. She wiped her hands on her tunic.

'If you sit there much longer I'll charge you.'

Claudia glanced round. One of the burly door-keepers was towering over her.

'I am going.' Claudia smiled.

She left the theatre and walked across the square full of stalls, in between which petty pedlars and hucksters thronged, shouting and screaming what they had to sell. Claudia pushed her way through and went into a cookshop on the corner of the alleyway. It was dirty, the tables grease-covered, but the spiced sausages she bought were hot and tasty, though sticky to the touch. She ate these quickly and made her mind up. If Fortunata had known Murranus, then Murranus might clarify some of the mystery. She finished her food and went out down an alleyway.

'Mistress! Mistress!'

She turned round. An urchin was running towards her, carrying a stick. Claudia recognised the ash cane she had left in the catacombs. The dirty, gap-toothed boy pushed it into her hands.

'I was told to give you this.'

Claudia went cold. She crouched down.

'By whom?'

She seized the little boy's thin wrist, quickly fished in her purse and held the coin up.

'He gave me one as well.'

'Who did?'

'The soldier.'

'Which soldier?'

The boy looked over his shoulder.

'He's gone now!'

Chapter 6

'Honesty is praised and left out in the cold.'
Juvenal, *Satires*, I

Claudia grasped the walking cane and let the urchin go. She glanced back down the alleyway and across the square. So, she had been followed! She hurried on, round to the main thoroughfare, which would take her down to the gladiators' school near the Colosseum. Claudia knew such haunts, built all over Italy, were of a standard kind: curtain wall, dominating gatehouse and, beyond it, the drill ground and barracks of the gladiators. Some of these were slaves, others free men: their skill and courage, their constant dancing with death always attracted hangers-on. Today was no different. Young women thronged at the gates, trying to peer round the guards. Pie-sellers had set up small booths. A cart from a local tavern served cups of ale and wine. Claudia pushed her way through. The captain of the guard, an old gladiator, seized her by the shoulder and thrust her back.

'No one comes in,' he growled, blinking his good eye. He was tall and thickset, dressed for the part in leather loin-cloth, greaves on his legs, a battered helmet on his head.

'I've got to see Murranus,' Claudia declared. 'He's expecting me.'

The fellow pursed his lips but grinned in appreciation as Claudia pulled a coin out of her purse.

'Tell him I come from Fortunata. If he lets me in, I'll give you this.'

The captain disappeared. A short while later he returned, grasped Claudia by the shoulder and pushed her through the cavernous gatehouse into the sun-drenched arena. Claudia felt as if she'd entered a battlefield. The drill ground was hemmed in on either side by a shadowy portico. At the far end must be the drill hall for bad-weather training. On benches outside it, men lounged drinking and eating, all eyes on the drills being carried out. The air was close and reeked of sweat, blood and oil.

The gladiators, under the instructions of the 'Doctores', the specialists in every form of fighting, lunged and parried at each other with imitation weapons or circled the post, practising blows and cuts under the harsh commands of their masters. Claudia stared, fascinated. The young men, of various nationalities, were like dancers, their slim, compact, oiled bodies rippling: they moved to a rhythm as if listening to some invisible music.

'Attack!'

The men shuffled forward with shield, wooden sword or net.

'Defence!'

The men drew back; a liquid movement, arms thrusting out, heads going down. The rhythm was heart-catching: the stamp of feet, the sharp orders, the swift intake of breath, the movement from side to side, the fixed gaze of the gladiators. Claudia had drunk and eaten with such men. They all said the same. 'Never lift your gaze from the enemy, even if his face is visored. You will always know what he plans next. Forget the weapons, the net, the trident, the shield, the sword. Watch the face. Note the chest. Is your opponent tired? Is he beginning to flag? Does he breathe easily?'

Gladiators lived in the shadow of death. On one day they could be victors, showered with flowers, gifts, coins, the soft embraces of beautiful women. The next they could be lying prostrate on the sand, hands raised, beseeching the crowds, only to hear the mob scream back: 'Hoc habet! Hoc habet! Let him have it! Let him have it!'

Some fought for years: a few emerged as rich men in their own right. Most died, choking on the sand in some amphitheatre. A few, like Oceanus, recognised the signs in time: the slowing-up, the confusion. As Oceanus had once told her: 'You just get tired of the killing, Claudia. The amphitheatre is not a place for the tired or frightened.'

Claudia studied the gladiators. The Samnites in their heavy armour. The Fish Men with their strange garbed helmets, nets and tridents. The simple swordsmen with small, round shields who depended more on their agility than on strength or armour. She noticed how all the gladiators crouched in a half-stance. In fact, Oceanus constantly stood like that. Some had their heads shaven. Others tied their hair in a queue at the back. A few wore jewellery, an earring in the left lobe or a medal, some keepsake from an admirer, around their neck.

'They would eat you alive, little one.'

Claudia started. The man standing behind her was tall, slim-built, with cropped red hair. A square face, clean-shaven, with light blue eyes, almost child-like. He had thrown a simple sleeveless tunic over him. His legs, smooth and muscular, still dripped with sweat; his leather sandals were covered in dust.

'You are Murranus?'

'And you?'

The man bent down and smiled at her, wiping the sweat from his face on the back of his hand.

'I am Claudia.'

'And you knew Fortunata?'

'No.' She smiled. 'I didn't. I told a lie.'

The light blue eyes blinked.

'I am glad you told me the truth, little one. Fortunata never mentioned any Claudia. So, why are you here?'

'I knew Fortunata, vaguely,' she stammered. 'I was appalled at her murder.'

Murranus took her by the arm and led her off the drill ground, into the shadow of the colonnade. He sat her down on a bench then went and filled two earthenware cups from a water jar. He came back, thrust one of these into her hand and raised his.

'We who are about to die salute thee!' He looked sadly across the arena. 'We have the games in a few days,' he murmured. 'The Emperor wishes to celebrate. All the gladiator masters are fielding their men. There'll be no sham fights or fixed contests. It will be to the death.' He glanced at her. 'Strange, isn't it? Some of those lads are my best friends. We eat, drink, sleep together; we share the same whores, but in a few days' time, I'll try and kill one of them and he'll try to kill me.' He sipped from the water. 'I would like to catch Fortunata's murderer. I would love to do the same to him. She was a kindly girl.'

'How well did you know her?' Claudia asked.

Murranus laughed and put the cup down.

'Better than you, apparently. She was my half-sister: same father, different mothers. Fortunata's was from a city in Gaul. We were born free. Father was a soldier; bought a small farm. And, of course, hated every minute of it. What he grew he drank. Fortunata entered service. I thought of joining the army, but I remembered Father, so I became a gladiator.'

'Did Fortunata talk about her life?'

'I didn't ask, she didn't tell me. True, I was suspicious. She seemed to have more silver than she should but she laughed that off. She was comely enough to other men. You remember her?'

Claudia recalled the blood-drained corpse hanging from the hook in the slaughterhouse.

'She was attractive. She caught the eye of the actor Paris.'

'I met him on a few occasions,' Murranus murmured. 'If he wasn't a man, he'd be a very good woman. Paris likes both male and female. He sometimes saunters down here to watch us fight. Why are you interested in Fortunata?'

'Coincidence,' Claudia replied. 'We have a lot more in common, Murranus, than you think: I bring you fond greetings from Januaria.'

Murranus' jaw dropped. He peered closer at her.

'Of course, Claudia! You are Polybius' niece.' He grasped her by the shoulder and kissed her on the forehead. 'Why didn't you say? I know Polybius, Poppaoe and Oceanus. I've heard about you.' He grinned. 'Is that why you're really here? Spying on me for Januaria, finding out who Fortunata truly was?'

'In a way,' Claudia replied glibly. 'But it is strange that we know each other through other people. I was curious, about both you and Fortunata.'

'And I'm certainly curious about you.' Murranus turned on the bench. 'Sometimes I wonder,' he continued, leaning closer, 'what girls like Fortunata and you really do. My sister was no whore and neither are you. I can tell that by your eyes. You haven't got that sly look.' He grasped her wrist and squeezed. 'Like her, you scurry about here and there, asking questions.'

'Mere coincidence,' Claudia repeated.

'Bollocks!' he retorted. 'It's no coincidence. Watch this.' He turned. 'Crixus!' he shouted to a gladiator further down the colonnade. 'What do you think of the She-Asses?'

'A good tavern,' the fellow bellowed back. 'But you have got to watch out for Oceanus. If you're drunk, he'll bore you to death!'

Murranus thanked him and turned back.

'You see, Claudia, Rome might be the centre of the Empire, a great sprawling city, but people like ourselves know each other: the tavern-keepers, their girls, the likes of Paris. We all cluster together, except you and Fortunata. You keep well away from the herd.' He dabbed at a cut on his lip. 'I once asked her if she was a spy, an informer. She just laughed. I wager, if I asked you the same question, I'd get the same reply, wouldn't I?'

Claudia smiled at him.

'And now we come to Fortunata's death,' he continued. 'Who'd kill a poor servant girl like that? Cut her throat and hang her up on a hook? That's what the palace chamberlain told me, even though the embalmers had done a passable job before they handed the corpse over.'

Claudia tensed. Murranus was sharp-witted.

'If someone murders the likes of you, or Fortunata,' he declared, 'your throats are cut and you're tossed in the Tiber or down a sewer hole. But Fortunata's corpse was left as a warning to someone else, wasn't it?' He patted her on the knee. 'I see you are not going to tell me the truth. At the same time I mean no harm. So, what do you want to know? Come to the point, I've got to get back.'

'Did Fortunata tell you anything untoward?' Claudia asked.

'We hardly met.'

'But you did take her to the Horse of Troy tavern, down near the docks?'

Murranus' face became more guarded.

'She came and saw me,' he replied. 'Asked if I would accompany her there. Now, I was a little bit more wary. I've been there myself, but as you know, you hear stories, gossip.'

'What stories?'

'How can I put it?' He stared across the drill ground. 'If you want a potion or a philtre or you have found a jewel in the street which you would like to sell. Or you want to get someone out of Rome without the guards noticing. It's popular enough with the rogues and footpads, but they don't like strangers. If I went there now, they wouldn't give me a second glance, but you or Fortunata? Strange faces draw attention. I told her that but she was insistent.'

'Why?'

'She said she wanted to sit and watch. I'd be the gladiator and she my girlfriend, out for the night, looking at the sights. She was so insistent I agreed. Down we went – this was about two or three days before she disappeared. We hired a table in the eating hall: Fortunata and I pretended to be drunk.'

'And was there any trouble?'

'None whatsoever. After two hours I got bored and said we'd have to go, so we left.'

'Did Fortunata ever mention the Sicarius?'

Murranus looked anxiously over his shoulder.

'I've heard the name myself, but she never referred to it.' He spread his hands. 'That's all I can tell you.' He tapped the ash canes where Claudia had left them. 'You should buy yourself something heavier.' He smiled. 'You must go now, but leave one of these here.'

Claudia, mystified, obeyed. She got to her feet, clasped Murranus' hand and made her way back through the gates. She walked purposefully away from the crowd then stopped as if to fasten the thong on her sandal.

'Claudia!' Murranus was hastening towards her. 'You forgot this!' he called out. He reached her and handed the ash cane over. He chucked her under the chin with his finger then kissed her roundly on the lips. 'Don't tell Januaria about that.'

Claudia, acting the part, smiled back.

'Tell her I'll see her soon and she must be at the games! And remember this.' Murranus' eyes were no longer smiling. 'I'll tell you here, where no one can eavesdrop. You mentioned a certain dagger man. I think Fortunata was hunting him. She went down to that tavern. I saw nobody I recognised but Fortunata, just as I left her near the palace gates, claimed she had seen something interesting. I asked her what. She just laughed and said we must have another date. That was the last time I saw her alive.' He lifted her hand. 'Fare thee well, Claudia.'

She watched him stride back through the crowds, stopping to kiss a woman or raise his hand in greeting as someone shouted his name. Then she tapped the ash cane against the ground. If her brother had quick wits, Fortunata had been even quicker. Somehow or other she had realised the Sicarius was involved in the murder of the courtesans. Had Fortunata discovered who he was? Was that what she had seen in the Horse of Troy tavern?

'You have been busy, Claudia,' the Empress Helena cooed.

Claudia sat on a small chair and stared at the ever-smiling Anastasius. She had returned to the Palatine Palace for her usual duties and been despatched with a jar of water to the Dolphin Chamber, a small council room in the Imperial quarters. The floor was of white and blue marble with silver dolphins leaping above red-gold waves. Similar motifs decorated the walls, whilst the ceiling had been painted a dark blue with a gold sun in the centre. A circular room, no outside windows, only one door, which was protected by a narrow passageway: the ideal place for princes to sit and plot. The Augusta sat at one end of a purple couch, its arms covered in gold, carved in the likeness of leaping lions. At the other end lounged Rufinus, elbow on the arm-rest, fingers covering his mouth, watching her intently. Claudia did not answer the Empress's question. She had to be careful. Everything she had learned must come from her talks with the likes of Murranus or Paris. She must make no reference whatsoever to her visit to the catacombs, the confidences of Sylvester or that murderous chase through the darkness.

'Have you been busy?' Anastasius' fingers clawed the air, making the signs, emphasising the question mark.

'Don't answer similarly!' Helena snapped. 'I really do wonder what you two say to each other. What have you learned, Claudia?'

Claudia glanced quickly at Anastasius, who nodded, warning her with his eyes to be honest.

'I have not been all that busy,' she replied. 'But Fortunata was.'

She quickly gave a pithy summary of what she had learned from Livonia, whom she described as an acquaintance, and from Paris and Murranus. She hinted that the little she had learned about the Sicarius came from them. As she talked, their expressions became more sombre. Anastasius, in particular, grew agitated.

'My belief,' Claudia concluded, 'is that Fortunata did not concentrate on the victims but on the Sicarius.'

'I don't believe it,' Rufinus murmured. 'I find it difficult to accept.'

'Then you'd best tell her why,' Helena replied.

Rufinus leaned forward, hands joined.

'How much do you really know about the Sicarius?'

'Very little except what Paris told me about the Horse of Troy. Gossip from my own uncle's tavern. And what others hinted at.'

'This Sicarius is a professional assassin,' Rufinus said. 'He doesn't work for anybody. He remains well hidden.'

'Why don't you,' Claudia countered, 'send troops down to the Horse of Troy? Arrest Locusta and put her to the question?'

'You mean torture her?' Rufinus scoffed. 'On what evidence? We send troops into the slums, ransack a tavern, arrest the keeper, who certainly won't tell us anything, and we will never get our hands on the Sicarius.'

'That's not the entire truth, is it?' Claudia asked.

'Clever, little mouse!' Helena intervened. 'What do you think is the truth?'

'That you've used him!'

Helena clapped her hands but agreed.

'We've known about the Sicarius for months. When my son, the Divine Emperor, was planning his march on Rome, we used his services to have a certain opponent quietly removed.'

'You mean Severus?' Claudia asked. 'Maxentius' Keeper of Secrets?'

'I mean Severus,' Helena answered.

'But he was killed by a woman.'

Helena stared at her. 'How do you know that?'

Claudia could have kicked herself.

'Rumour, gossip.'

'Ah yes, rumour and gossip. But you see, little mouse, that's the problem: at the time we didn't know whether the Sicarius was man or woman.'

'So, who in Constantine's party,' Claudia asked, 'sent the message for Severus to be killed?'

'I did,' Helena answered. 'A simple letter with my seal attached and, of course, the necessary money, neatly tied in two leather bags. One of our spies, a merchant, left the little parcel at the Horse of Troy. He nearly got out but he was captured. Maxentius' soldiers crucified him. Poor man!' She sighed. 'They say it took him two days to die.'

'So, this Sicarius will only act,' Claudia asked, 'if he has proof of the person hiring him? Isn't that dangerous?'

'Well, he can't blackmail us, can he?' Helena riposted. 'Killing Severus was part of the game.'

'But murdering those courtesans?' Claudia retorted. 'Whoever is slaying them is mocking Christianity and threatening the Emperor. The same person is having placards and bills posted all over the city: that's definitely treason.'

'I know what it is.' Rufinus stirred on his couch. 'But we have no proof the Sicarius is involved, no evidence. The same could be said of any other traitor left in the city who's accepting gold from the Emperor's enemies to cause discomfort and chaos.' He tapped his embossed silver sandal on the floor. 'Fortunata's task,' he snapped, 'was not to go hunting assassins!'

'Hush now!' The Empress Helena held her hand up.

Claudia stared at the patrician. His narrow face was twisted in annoyance, but then he remembered himself, smiled at her and held up his hand.

'I meant no insult.'

Claudia accepted his apology. Yet for a patrician even to offer it was a sure sign that he regretted what he had said.

'Let us say,' Claudia spoke up, 'that this enemy of the Emperor's is plotting and, for the sake of argument, that he has hired a professional assassin. Therefore, the assassin must know the identity of this enemy. If you follow Fortunata's logic, you trap him and also snare the man who hired him.'

The Empress bowed her head and laughed behind her fingers. Anastasius smiled but Rufinus looked furious.

'Augusta!' the banker snapped. 'What is so amusing?'

She lifted her head. 'There goes my little mouse, scurrying about the corridors. I can wager what you're thinking, Rufinus: why wasn't I told about all this before, eh?'

'Your Excellency, the thought did cross my mind.'

Helena turned to Anastasius. 'Bring in Burrus!'

A short while later the Empress's bodyguard swaggered in. A blond-haired German mercenary, he looked gigantic in his gladiatorial helmet, corselet and leather kilt; the sword in his scabbard was a huge, two-handed affair. He had no eyes for anyone but his mistress: he would have fallen on his knees before her, but Helena snapped her fingers. The look on Burrus' face was one of pure adoration.

'Don't be a silly boy, Burrus: just stand beside me.'

The German did as he was told, and Helena caressed his hairy hand, still smiling at Claudia.

'I paid,' she explained, 'for Severus to be executed. I sent his name on a piece of parchment with my seal to the Sicarius. The agent who took it was crucified but Severus was assassinated. Later, I became angry. I wondered if the Sicarius hadn't played both ends off against the middle, carried out my assignment but made sure my agent was captured. So,' she sighed, 'last October, when my son's legions swaggered into Rome, I offered a bribe to meet the Sicarius, a simple invitation to discuss matters.'

'And you killed him?' Rufinus broke in.

'I killed him, or rather Burrus did. He followed him out, took the gold I had given him, slit his throat and tossed his body into the great sewer. I really couldn't have a man swaggering around Rome, could I,' Helena's face became hard, 'believing he had duped the Emperor's mother? The person responsible for managing the Agentes in Rebus.'

'And what was he like?' Rufinus asked in astonishment.

'A young man, not as bright as you think, claimed to come from Dalmatia.'

'But you are sure it was he?'

Helena pulled a face. 'True, the Sicarius might be two people, but I doubt it. He knew about Severus and he could provide great details about that bastard's death. He liked his wine, a bit of a boaster. Now his tongue is silenced. His mouth can't clack, can it? So, little mouse, you've been wasting my time.'

Claudia hid her fury. The Augusta could have told her this: she glared at Anastasius; he had been no better.

'But why was Fortunata killed?' Claudia demanded.

'I don't know,' the Empress retorted. 'That's for you to find out. Perhaps she went poking her nose into business she shouldn't have.' Helena looked up at the German mercenary. 'You remember killing Severus, don't you?'

The mercenary nodded, blue eyes glowing. Claudia wondered how many people this personal bodyguard of the Empress had despatched.

'There, you are a good boy! Now, go and stand on guard outside!'

Helena waited until the door closed behind him.

'I still believe these courtesans have been killed to discredit my son. I want the murders stopped. I want the villain caught.' She rose to her feet and stood over Claudia. 'I think you are wasting your time here. Tomorrow,' she glanced at Rufinus, 'the games begin. Domatilla and her girls will be there. Rufinus, you can introduce our little Claudia, say she is now a member of their household.'

'Will she object?' Rufinus asked.

'Do you think she will object, Claudia?' Helena smiled.

'No, Your Excellency.'

'And why not?'

'Because, Your Excellency, Domatilla is also in your pay.'

Helena stroked Claudia's cheek.

'Clever, little mouse.'

And, spinning on her heel, with Rufinus behind her, Helena walked out of the chamber.

Anastasius never moved. He sat still and carefully arranged his robes. Only when he was sure they were alone did he rise and pull his chair closer so he sat with his knees almost touching Claudia's. He stroked her gently on the cheek, dark eyes watchful. Claudia felt her heart skip a beat. It was always the same. Whenever she faced this enigmatic priest, with his soft face and gentle eyes, she thought of Felix, who would sit for hours staring at her. But Anastasius was not Felix. The face was a mask for a cunning brain and very sharp wits. Claudia wondered if Anastasius knew about her relationship with Sylvester. But, there again, wasn't the Christian faction beginning to divide? Strange sects like Arians and Gnostics. There were those of the East and those of the West. Some, like Anastasius, believed the Church and the Empire had a great deal in common. Others saw Rome as a scarlet woman. A few trod the middle path: Sylvester and Militiades, the Bishop of Rome, who believed an accommodation could be sought.

Sylvester, surely, wouldn't betray her? The link between them was her father, and if Sylvester had told her the truth, the priest owed his life to him. She made the signs.

'You look sad, concerned, Anastasius?'

He kept staring at her.

'Am I in danger?' she asked.

He nodded and replied, using hand signs. Claudia shook her head.

'You move too fast.'

She couldn't understand, so he repeated it.

'You are in danger, little mouse. You seem to know more than you should about the Sicarius whilst you've made little progress.'

Claudia tightened her lips in annoyance. She'd been summoned to this meeting unexpectedly. Yet that was her life: she must always be ready for the unexpected.

'What I learned came from Livonia, Paris and Murranus. Moreover, Fortunata did go to the Horse of Troy.'

Anastasius shook his head. 'You've been followed,' he replied with the fingers of one hand.

'I'm always followed.' She smiled.

'Are you working for anyone else?'

Claudia gazed round the chamber. They were well away from the door but she could never be sure. She tried to hide her relief. The Empress Helena controlled the Agentes in Rebus.

103

They were hand-picked by her and this priest. Others, of course, resented this. Men like Bessus and Chrysis. They, too, had their legion of informers. They sometimes tried to bribe those who worked for the Empress; that was what Anastasius suspected.

'I am not working for anyone else,' she replied wearily.

'Be careful,' Anastasius warned her.

'Do you think the Sicarius is dead?' Claudia whispered. She spoke slowly, not making any signs because Anastasius could also lip-read.

'If the Empress says he's dead,' the reply came, 'then the Sicarius is dead.'

He wagged a warning finger at her, rose and left the chamber.

Claudia grasped the jug she had brought and followed him out. She returned to the kitchen and sat by herself on a bench, watching one of the cook's boys build a fire in the hearth. She idly wondered what was happening at the She-Asses and smiled at the thought of working in one of the most expensive brothels in Rome. Had Fortunata gone there? If the Sicarius was dead, why had the girl gone to the Horse of Troy? What had she seen which provoked her own savage death? If Helena was correct, the Sicarius no longer had a trade. Or was there more than one? Had he left a successor?

Chapter 7

'Remember in difficult times to keep a level head.'

Horace, *Odes*, II.3

Claudia busied herself about her duties. She was surprised later in the evening, just as the oil lamps were being lit and the guards changed, to be once again summoned by Anastasius, this time to the Empress's private quarters. Claudia expected opulence but found a chamber almost as stark as any soldier's tent. The walls and pillars were of dark marble. Beautiful sycamore furniture, tables, stools, chairs, was the only concession to luxury; no decoration on the walls. Claudia glimpsed locked coffers and chests. Two of these were open: one was packed with small leather purses, the other with rolls of vellum and parchment. The windows overlooking the Imperial gardens were thrown open; the chamber was perfumed with heavy scent from the alabaster jars and capped braziers which stood in the corners. Helena was sitting behind a huge desk on a throne-like chair, tapping a scroll of parchment against her cheek. She was dressed completely in white, though her mantle and robe were trimmed with a narrow line of purple. Her black hair was piled up but unadorned. In the light of the oil lamps Claudia could see how once she must have been the great beauty who captivated the Emperor's father. She also wore an expression Claudia had never glimpsed before: fearful, wary.

'It is good of you to come, Claudia,' Helena declared softly, as if her visitor was some great noblewoman.

Anastasius pushed forward stools for himself and her.

'Sit down. Sit down.' Helena scratched the back of her neck. 'Earlier I treated you harshly, little mouse. What do you really think about this matter?'

'I find it difficult to believe the Sicarius is dead.'

'And what else?'

'The signs on the faces of the corpses. True, the assassin is mocking the Emperor, but he is also mocking the Christian Church.'

Helena glanced at Anastasius.

'Continue, little mouse.'

'The deaths themselves. These are courtesans, high-class ladies. They were killed in the parks and quiet places of Rome. But one was killed here in the palace itself. Surely that death would be easy to investigate?'

Helena nodded. 'It was investigated. No one is allowed into the private quarters of the Emperor without a pass. The guards remember people coming and going. Some they recognised, some they didn't. They certainly recall Sabina arriving in a litter. And, listen to this, another woman, beautiful and veiled, smelling of perfume. The guards remember her coming in but cannot recall her leaving.'

'That would be the assassin,' Claudia replied.

'But if it is that woman,' Helena declared, 'the only way out is by a window and across the gardens, yet they are always patrolled by guards.' The Augusta shrugged wearily. 'There was no alarum that night, and now we have this.' She handed the scroll over. The writing was large, the letters well formed.

'They are quotations?' Claudia asked.

'Read them, little mouse.'

'The first is from Sallust: "Just to disturb the peace seems a great reward in itself."'

'And the second?'

'By the same author, from his book on Jugurtha: "Every war is easy to begin but difficult to stop. Its beginning and end are not in the control of the same person."' Claudia moved the piece of parchment to catch the light from the oil lamp. 'The remaining two are from Juvenal's satires.'

'I know what they say.' Helena leaned back in the chair. 'The first is: "Everything in Rome comes at a price"; the second reads: "Quis custodiet ipsos custodes?" "Who will guard the guards?" Each of these quotations could be seen as a warning to me.'

'It would fit with the mind of the murderer,' Claudia agreed. 'Those quotations from Sallust about creating chaos just for the sake of it, and saying that those who start wars do not necessarily finish them.'

'And Juvenal's epigrams?' Helena asked.

'They are more threatening. The writer says that anything in Rome can be bought. The final one is a hint about your guards.'

'Very nearly the truth,' Helena agreed, taking the parchment back. 'The scroll was handed in late this afternoon. The

Sicarius is not dead. Or, if he is, someone has picked up his mantle and is now wearing it. You see, the last quotation: "Who will guard the guards?", is the same riddle I posed to the man I thought was the Sicarius. He sat and laughed with me, offered his services.' She waved a hand. 'Of course, I pretended to agree. Before I sent him away, I asked the question again: how could I trust him? Who will guard the guards?' She paused. 'What do you think, little mouse?'

'I believe the Sicarius wasn't killed. He or she sent someone in their stead, as a pretence, to find out what would really happen. It would be easy to bribe someone to step out of the shadows, pretend that he was the Sicarius; to give him assurances that he would be in no danger. That he might even win the protection and favour of Rome's new rulers. Indeed, Your Excellency, if you hadn't killed him, the Sicarius would have done.'

'A cat's-paw?' Helena asked.

'More a mask, Excellency. The Sicarius is a consummate killer, sly and cunning. On the one hand, he'd be eager to meet you, but on the other, nervous that a new power was in Rome.' Claudia dropped her gaze. 'Those in power need people like the Sicarius.'

'But the cunning fox didn't trust me,' Helena smiled, 'and sent someone else. Now he's back for vengeance. But why doesn't he strike directly at me? Why choose his victims from Domatilla's house?'

'More importantly, Your Excellency,' Claudia ignored the hand signals made by Anastasius to be careful, 'how did this Sicarius manage to obtain Imperial passes? He would need one to enter the Emperor's private quarters and kill Sabina.'

'The seals are held by scribes, priests, high-ranking officials,' Helena snapped crossly. 'There are bound to be traitors here. Men who are prepared to sell the seals for a price.'

Anastasius tapped Claudia on the shoulder and made her look at him. He moved his hands quickly. Claudia knew why: Anastasius could hear very well and usually communicated with his mistress by writing. Nevertheless, Helena was sharp; she must, over the years, have learned some of the skill herself. Now and again Claudia asked Anastasius to repeat certain gestures.

'What's the alarm, little mouse?' Helena demanded. 'Your keeper looks more agitated than I do.'

'He says that you should not have killed the Sicarius, that he now wages war against you and will do great damage if he can. Anastasius believes the Sicarius is being used by someone close to the Emperor.'

'He's told me that before.'

'Yes, Your Excellency: he's asking, is it possible the Sicarius is being used by the Emperor himself?'

'Nonsense!' Helena retorted. 'Constantine is as troubled by these murders as I am. It is the Sicarius,' she emphasised. 'We sat and spoke for some time. I told him of my great dream: to win the favour of the Christian Church, to go east and find the true cross on which Jesus died. According to my spies it lies buried outside Jerusalem.' The Empress leaned forward, eyes sparkling. 'Can you imagine, Claudia? What a coup! What a great gift, to render thanks for my son's vision before his victory at the Milvian Bridge.'

Claudia sat in amazement. She could tell from Anastasius' eyes that he knew something of this dream, and wondered if Sylvester did.

'That will explain the crosses on the faces of the courtesans,'

Claudia declared. 'Your Excellency, I think you should have told me this.'

'And there is more. I met the Sicarius in Domatilla's house, shortly after my son's troops entered Rome.'

'Was Domatilla party to the Sicarius' supposed death?'

'Oh no, in fact he chose the villa himself.'

'But that could explain the attacks on Domatilla's ladies.'

Claudia studied the Empress closely. She, Anastasius and the Augusta had often sat like this, in darkened chambers or weather-stained tents during the hurly-burly days when Constantine had marched south to seize the purple. She wondered if Constantine knew about everything his mother did. Or did he trust her enough to leave everything in her hands? Had he now changed his mind? Was Anastasius correct? Was that why the Sicarius could produce an Imperial pass to enter the palace? After all, the history of Rome was peppered with occasions when the Emperor's mother had been given considerable power only to have it seized back. Nero and Agrippina, even the old Emperor Diocletian now in exile, not to mention a host of others. Sometimes the Emperor–mother relationship lasted till death. Others collapsed in a bloody palace brawl.

'What was this cat's-paw like?'

Helena pulled a face.

'Young, dark-haired, narrow-faced: one of those half-educated bully-boys from the slums. He knew all about Severus' death, claimed to have paid a whore to kill him: he later strangled her. I discovered little about my mysterious guest.'

'One way of discovery,' Claudia offered, 'is to send troops down to the Horse of Troy. Arrest Locusta and bring her back for questioning.'

Helena laughed softly. 'We have already considered that.'

The Augusta looked at her priest. 'I think it's best if we bring our visitor in.'

Anastasius rose and walked quietly as a shadow to the door. He returned, a dark figure behind him. The priest stepped aside. Claudia could see his companion was a woman; tall, severe-faced, sharp nose and harsh mouth, iron-grey hair under the mantle she now pushed back. She sank to one knee, hand out, in a gesture of salute.

'Sit down, Locusta,' Helena murmured. 'You are amongst friends.'

'Am I now?'

Locusta's eyes slid to Claudia: she reminded Claudia of a mosaic in Milan depicting one of the harpies, with that hooked nose and those cruel eyes. A ruthless woman, Claudia considered, twisted and dangerous to cross.

'Why am I here, Your Excellency?'

Her voice had a nasal twang. She sat, one shoulder slightly forward, hands resting on her knees. At first Claudia had thought her dress shabby; now that she looked closer, she realised it was of dark pure wool. A silver chain hung from one wrist. Precious stones sparkled in the rings on her fingers.

'The Sicarius?' Helena demanded.

'I know of no such person.'

'Come, come, Locusta. I can issue a warrant for your arrest and you'd disappear.'

'Then, Your Excellency, I would disappear,' Locusta mocked. 'But I have friends, senators and lawyers, who would demand why an innocent woman had been arrested and confined without trial. I am a Roman citizen.'

'You know who the Sicarius is?' Helena demanded.

'I know of him: an assassin who carries out silent executions for the great ones.'

'And he frequents the Horse of Troy?'

'If he does, Your Excellency, then I know nothing of it.'

'I can be your friend,' Helena murmured. 'If you had my friendship, Locusta, you would not need senators or lawyers.'

'The Sicarius is dead,' Locusta declared wearily. 'Yes, he used to visit my tavern. He paid me well. We would meet at his command, in one of the outhouses. He chose it deliberately. It has a side door and windows, a difficult place to trap a man. It looks out on a crossroads of alleyways.'

'And you would meet him there?'

'People would come, shadowy figures. A purse would be left, a piece of parchment tucked inside. On it the name of the victim. I would hand it over.'

'You're lying!' Claudia retorted.

Locusta's eyes rounded in amazement.

'And who may you be, little girl?'

'A servant of the Emperor's.'

'Are you now? Are you now?' Locusta sucked on her teeth. 'You should come to the Horse of Troy and call me a liar.'

'I think the Sicarius worked for one man,' Claudia interrupted. 'The late usurper Maxentius; either for him or for his Master of Secrets, Severus.'

Locusta sniggered. 'You are right. Severus called himself by many names: the Sicarius only worked for him.' She half-smiled at the Empress. 'Except in the last days, Augusta. Someone came to the Horse of Troy. He brought a letter carrying your son's seal: this time Severus' name was on it.'

A muscle twitched high in Helena's cheek, a sure sign that she was controlling her famous temper at this woman's impudence.

'But the rest is true. I would meet the Sicarius in the

outhouse, give him a purse and the name. He would pay me, then he would be gone.'

'And you never knew who he was?'

'If I did, even if I pretended to, I doubt if I would be alive now.'

'Was the Sicarius male or female?'

'I don't know.'

'And what happened,' Helena asked, 'in the last days of Maxentius, when all was hurly-burly?'

'It was, as you say, Your Excellency, all hurly-burly. We heard of Severus' death.' Locusta raised one eyebrow. 'The armies marched, your son entered Rome. Since then I have had neither sight nor sound of the Sicarius.'

'He's disappeared?'

'As you say, Excellency, he has disappeared.'

Claudia studied this evil woman. She sat poised and calm, but Claudia suspected she was still telling lies.

'So, why should Fortunata die?' Claudia asked.

'Fortunata? Fortunata? Who's Fortunata?'

'She visited your tavern with her half-brother, the gladiator Murranus.'

'Ah, Murranus I know.' Locusta pulled a face. 'But I do not keep a tally of who comes in and out of the Horse of Troy. Everyone is welcome.' She smiled. 'Even you.'

Claudia turned to Helena. She could sense the Empress's exasperation. Locusta was holding firm to her story: she had helped the Sicarius in the days before Constantine assumed the purple, but since then, nothing. Helena's hand dropped beneath the table. When she raised it, she held a small leather bag of coins which she tossed and Locusta expertly caught.

'Your Divine Excellency,' Locusta bowed, 'shows me great favour. I am, and I shall always be, your most loyal servant.'

'Quite, quite.' Helena forced a smile. 'And a loyal servant should be rewarded. I thank you, Locusta.'

The tavern-keeper rose, genuflected and left. Helena leaned back in her chair, and her eyes slid towards Claudia.

'And what do you make of that, little one?'

'Nothing, your Excellency, except that Locusta takes to lying as a duck to water.'

Helena angrily made a sign with her hand.

'You are dismissed!'

Claudia walked out of the chamber and up the silent marble pathway. On either side the walls depicted scenes from the lives of the Emperors: Trajan crossing the Danube; Diocletian in the East fighting Persian cavalry. The murals were set in stone, elegant testimony to the Emperors' achievements and victories. Claudia walked on. She thought of what she had learned but she could see no way through the tangled lies. Was the Sicarius dead or alive? Somehow she suspected that Helena's murderous attack upon the professional assassin had stirred up this present hornet's nest. But how or why remained an enigma. Nor was there any solution to the killer's identity: male or female? Noble or common? How had the Sicarius got into the Imperial palace? Or had this most elusive of assassins sent someone else?

Claudia entered the servants' quarters: the walls were shabby, the windows close and narrow. She was about to cross a courtyard when she heard her name called. Paris stood in the colonnade, one arm against a pillar. He was dressed elegantly in a tunic and a robe which looked like a toga: Claudia wondered if he had the right to wear it. She walked across. Paris' hair was oiled and coiffed, his handsome face shaved and burnished with oil. He stood like an actor about to make a speech. Dark brown boots high above the ankles provided a telling contrast to his elegant garb, as if he wished to be all things to all men. The refined Roman and yet a man of susceptibility, aware of the desires and lusts of those who crowded into the orchestra to watch him perform.

'What speech are you preparing?' Claudia asked. 'You look like Hermes come to deliver a message from the Gods, an invitation to join them in Olympus.'

Paris dropped his poise. 'I've come to ask you to go for a drink. Let's go to a tavern, one of the cookshops. The evening is still yet young.' Paris' beautiful, lustrous eyes widened, twinkling with mischief. 'Some fish or poultry? White wheat bread, a glass of wine?'

'How did you get in here?' Claudia immediately regretted the harsh question: anyone could enter the servants' quarters.

'I told the guards I'd die if I didn't see you.'

'Why the friendliness?' Claudia asked suspiciously.

Paris clapped his hands and crowed with triumph.

'Your uncle said you'd say that.'

'Polybius?'

'I went to see him.' Paris walked forward. 'Rome is a dangerous place, Claudia. I had to make sure that you were what you claimed.' He sighed and dropped his hands. 'Do you blame me?'

On reflection Claudia couldn't. In fact he had done the logical thing. She had turned up at his theatre asking questions. He had happily obliged, so it was only natural that he should seek confirmation of who she really was. She noticed the key slung round his neck on a silver chain.

'What is that?'

'My heart.' Paris grinned. 'But,' he raised a hand, 'I bear messages from your uncle.' His face became grave and Claudia's heart skipped a beat.

'Why?' she stammered. 'What is wrong?'

'Not here,' he murmured, looping his arm through hers. 'Let me show you the grandeur of Rome, Claudia.'

'I am not ready. I haven't changed.'

He winked. 'You look comely enough to me. But, seriously.' They walked on through the colonnade which led through the gardens of the Imperial palace. 'I had to make sure who you were, and Uncle Polybius is a garrulous man. He's apparently very worried. The Prefect of Police has been back, breathing threats . . .'

'And?' Claudia asked.

'Your uncle could face closure for a month . . . something about the murder of a merchant?'

'Arrius,' Claudia explained.

As they walked, she relaxed and told this popinjay of an actor everything that had happened. By the time she had finished they were halfway down the Palatine.

'I can see the problem,' Paris confided. 'Arrius is a fairly powerful merchant. He is killed and his silver taken; the police would draw the line at that.'

'Why did my uncle tell you all this?'

'Oh, I went in as bold as brass and introduced myself. Now, some of them knew me and I knew them. I had seen Januaria before, and that big oaf Oceanus, he is no stranger to me either . . .' Paris grasped her hand and stroked it. 'I told a few lies, but your uncle took me for what I am.' He smirked. 'An honest fellow.'

Claudia laughed. She felt at ease with this actor steeped in self-mockery. On the one hand honest; on the other, like many of his kind, careful and cautious.

'I met Granius and Faustina, even Simon the stoic.' Paris paused. 'Natural evils,' he took away his arm and stared

116

sorrowfully at Claudia, 'steal on us quietly. The eye and ear have no warning. Evil comes in many forms: sword and fire; heavy chains or ravenous wild beasts ready to tear out your guts.' Paris' eyes rolled heavenwards. 'Picture to yourself,' he intoned in accurate imitation of the stoic, 'the prison, the cross, the rack, the hook and the stake. They hold horrors to shatter a man's life . . .'

Claudia laughed. Paris' imitation of Simon was so accurate, the voice so clever in its intonation, that if she closed her eyes, she could almost believe the philosopher was beside her.

Paris clapped his hands. 'A miserable bitch, isn't he? Such an old tart! He kept looking me up and down as if he wanted to get his hands under my tunic.' His face became grave and once again he linked his arm through Claudia's. 'But your uncle is worried. He must produce the murderer or face closure and a heavy fine. Poppaoe, your aunt, spends most of her time in the garden baying mournfully at the moon. Yet it's all quite simple.'

'What is?' Claudia asked.

'Well, it's a matter of logic.'

Paris steered her into the mouth of an alleyway. Claudia wondered where they were going, but she found the actor interesting and, more importantly, the bearer of news.

'Well, I listened to your uncle's sea of troubles. Apologies aside, Claudia, but he chatters like a squirrel. The solution is quite simple. Arrius was killed in a chamber where there are no other entrances: the window was barred so the murderer must have come through the door.'

'Yes, but that was locked and barred.'

'I know. That's the problem.' Paris paused and held her hand. 'Think of it as a play, Claudia, a scene from some drama. You know the window was barred and shuttered. You know there are no secret entrances. True?'

Claudia nodded in agreement.

'But do you really know that the door was shuttered and locked?'

'My uncle had to break it down.'

Paris scratched the back of his head.

'Yes, but was it truly locked and bolted?' He wagged a finger. 'Think about that.'

They walked quietly down the alleyway: it smelt of refuse, rotting vegetables, urine and the other stale odours from the houses clustered around. They passed a tavern, its doors and windows thrown open. Claudia peered through: a group of men sat round a table littered with platters, dishes, wine jugs and cups.

'Gladiators,' Paris explained. 'The games begin tomorrow, so for some of them it's the last supper.' He raised a hand in imitation. 'Those who are about to die salute thee. But do so,' he added in a whisper, 'drunk as pigs with full bellies!'

'Do you like the games?' Claudia asked.

'I went once,' Paris replied. 'I vowed never again. They had a prisoner lashed to a pole fixed on a trolley. He was pushed towards a ravenous bear. The beast opened his stomach with one swipe of his great paw and the entrails came spilling out. I was sick for days.' Paris pushed his face closer. 'But keep talking,' he whispered, 'and hang on to my arm as if I am a veritable Hector and you are one of my admirers.'

Claudia felt a shiver of fear.

'Why?'

'Don't look so tremulous,' Paris replied. 'You are more than a servant girl, Claudia, I can see that. But I've drunk and eaten with informers before. What's more important, we are being

118

followed.' He touched Claudia's face and held it tight, pressing his fingers so she wouldn't turn. 'Only when I tell you,' he whispered, 'look quickly up the alleyway then laugh and turn away.' He smiled and removed his hand. 'Now!' he ordered.

Claudia glanced back to where they had come from and glimpsed the shadows flitting from doorway to doorway.

'They are either following you,' Paris added drily, 'or they are secret admirers of myself. But come.'

He walked quickly. They entered a house with grotesque figures carved on the lintel, Hermes with a huge red phallus. The corridors smelt of cheap perfumes, oil and spilled wine. She glimpsed graffiti on the walls and realised they had entered a brothel. She passed a small room and looked inside: a stone couch along one wall with cushions and mattress. A girl was sitting there, her half-dressed customer red in the face and gaping. The passageway led into a main hall with a huge candelabrum hanging from the ceiling. Five cells opened out, their doors ajar: girls lounged naked and chatting. Some wore red or white shoes, their hair and necks decorated with roses. They passed a stairway where the keeper stood in a screened recess, then they were out into the garden: across that, through a wicket gate and into another alleyway. Paris pushed her along this and into a spacious tavern-cum-restaurant with a large stand where ales and wine were sold. Beyond it, up a small flight of stairs, a large eating hall. Paris took her in, shouting greetings to those who called out his name. The greasy-looking keeper came up carrying a slate listing the main dishes of the day. Paris ordered some racks of lamb cooked in a sauce, vegetables, fresh white bread and watered wine. Claudia felt nervous but enjoyed the actor's attention.

'What's the real reason for this?' she asked tartly as the meal was served.

'I told you. I like girls who are not attached to the theatre.'

'You are not sharing my bed tonight,' she replied sharply.

Paris laughed. 'No.' He raised his hands. 'I went to see your Uncle Polybius. I brought messages and that's the end of it.'

They ate in silence. Now that the excitement of their meeting and the news Paris carried had receded, Claudia felt uncomfortable. She usually kept men at arm's-length, believing she had not time for dalliance. She glanced up. Paris was watching her expectantly.

'You know the city?'

He nodded.

'Have you ever seen a man,' she bent her right hand, 'with a tattoo of a chalice, purple in colour, etched on the inside of his wrist?'

Paris swallowed what he had in his mouth.

'I've seen a few,' he replied quietly. 'There's a guild, or fraternity, dedicated to Aphrodite.' He looked gravely at her. 'But what do you want with that decadent bunch?'

'Decadent?'

'Yes, decadent. They like little girls, children. Even the city rakes take pride that they are not one of them.'

'And where do they gather?'

'Oh, they have no temple or fixed sanctuary.'

Paris looked at the drinking room below. Claudia followed his gaze. A group of men thronged in the doorway, shabby, half-cloaks over their shoulders, the cowls pulled up.

'I'd like to take you to the theatre.' Paris smiled. 'You should come and see me perform. During the recent troubles I was away, but now I am back, I want to make my name famous.' He drained his cup. 'However, I don't like the company who keep following us.' He grinned. 'I think it's time I saw you home.'

Claudia rose to her feet. She thought they were going to go down the steps but Paris took her by the hands and pulled her towards the back of the room.

Chapter 8

'We who are about to die salute thee.'
Acclamation of gladiators
before the games

'They either want to see me or have words with you, Claudia,'
Paris declared once they were out into the back streets. He
pulled her closer. 'Who are you really? What are you doing?'

'My business, not yours!' she retorted sharply, drawing
back.

'One final drink,' Paris murmured. 'But in a place I know.'

They threaded through the alleyways. Claudia realised they
were going back towards the Palatine by a circuitous route.
Against the starlit sky she could see the monuments and
pillars, though here there were only shabby, dirty houses.
Prostitutes, decrepit and aged, stood in doorways, leering out
at them.

'I'll do you and your friend!' one of them called out.

Paris turned, made a filthy gesture and pushed Claudia into the Oil Lamp, a small eating house. The air was savoury and sweet, the floor of its dining hall clean, with spacious drinking booths and a gallery above them. Paris was immediately greeted, people coming over to shake his hand. He smugly accepted their plaudits. Mine host showed him and Claudia to a booth and brought them two cups of what he called the best wine from Campania. A young man came swaggering up: thin-faced, with blubbery lips and popping eyes under close-cropped blond hair.

'Paris!' he drawled and sat down.

Claudia recognised Iolus, a famous actor until he drank too much and made a fool of himself on stage.

'I know you,' he slurred, pointing at her. 'So, brave Paris is back.'

'What?' Claudia queried.

'When Maxentius ruled the city,' Paris explained, 'I performed a mime at the theatre. Severus didn't like it; he thought I was mocking his master. So I had to flee. I spent most of my time hiding in a cellar. I didn't return until Constantine arrived. Aren't I glad there's been a change in government!'

'You were never one for knives and blood.' Iolus sipped from Claudia's cup. His face became serious. 'Can you use your influence, Paris? I'll take any job.'

'I have one for you at the moment.' Paris pushed a silver coin across the table. 'We are going to leave by the back entrance. Claudia, our guests have arrived!'

A group of thugs were now elbowing their way towards them. She glimpsed unshaven faces, hard eyes. Paris grabbed her by the hand and was pushing her towards the door. Iolus immediately created a disturbance to distract their pursuers. They reached the alleyway by an outside staircase.

'Come on!' Paris was no longer the arrogant, carefree actor. In the dim twilight he looked pale and anxious. Claudia obeyed. This was not the first time she had fled assassins, and it followed the same pattern, slithering and slipping, avoiding pot-holes, turning and twisting. The further they fled, the more Claudia became aware of how frightened Paris really was. Now it was up to her to grasp him by the wrist and urge him on. Then, like the end of a race, they reached the main thoroughfare leading up to the Palatine. She glimpsed guards and horsemen. She and Paris stopped by a fountain and stared round: their pursuers had disappeared.

'That's the last time,' Paris gasped, his face coated in sweat, 'I invite you for a cup of wine. Next time you can join me in the theatre.' He leaned over and kissed her on the brow.

'Paris?'

He was about to walk away but came back.

'Why did you come to see me tonight? Where were you when Fortunata was killed?'

He sighed in exasperation. 'Claudia, I didn't single you or Fortunata out: both of you came to me. Yes?'

Claudia agreed.

'I was curious about you, I had to check you out. Yes?'

Claudia smiled.

'I'm an actor,' Paris continued. 'I hate bloodshed and I couldn't give a fig about Emperors. I fled Rome long before Maxentius and Severus died: I liked Fortunata, but I've been away from Rome for days. Fortunata was alive when I left. Oh yes.' Paris grinned at Claudia's embarrassment. 'Zosinas sent me to his villa in the Alban hills, near enough to Rome, but too far away for me. I returned the same day you met me.' He tapped the key round his neck. 'This is to my strong-box; all

125

I want is to be rich.' He squeezed her hand and disappeared into the darkness.

'Are you all right?'

The centurion in charge of the guard sauntered across, his corselet gleaming in the torchlight. He crouched down, his raw-skinned face kindly: for a moment Claudia thought he was her father.

'Yes, yes,' she said. 'I am well. All I need is a good night's sleep.'

By the time she had reached the servants' dormitory Claudia was too tired to reflect on the evening's happenings. She splashed water over her hands and face, rolled on the bed and was fast asleep in minutes.

She woke early next morning, and quickly washed and dressed, packing her possessions into a bundle. She broke her fast in the refectory on some stale bread and rancid stew, then made her way down to the palace courtyard, where Rufinus would be preparing to leave for the games. The sky was now seared by flashes of red-gold: as if all of Rome had woken and, in one breath, recognised that today the games would be staged. Everyone, from the meanest slave to the Emperor's own ministers, would be present to see the pageant of blood and death. Claudia could sense the excitement when she arrived in the courtyard. Syrians in tunics of red sat around the great carved palanquin, its curtains pushed back, in which Rufinus would be carried to the Colosseum. Negroes clothed in white would precede the litter, and on either side would be a small military escort under an officer to keep the sweaty mob well away from Caesar's minister.

Claudia made her way through the throng of servants and hangers-on. Bessus the chamberlain caught her eye, clicked his fingers and summoned her over.

'You are to walk beside Rufinus' litter,' he announced pompously.

'I'll walk beside Rufinus' litter,' Claudia repeated dolefully. 'Do I have to go to the games, Bessus?'

'Of course you do, my girl!' The fat lips pursed in annoyance. 'You are to enter Domatilla's household. What a splendid place to work!' He stomped away.

Servants came round with food: cheese, grapes, beer in cups. The sky grew brighter.

'I wish he'd hurry up!' one of the Syrian bearers muttered. 'The streets to the Colosseum will be crowded and it's going to get hot. I wish the bugger would move!'

At last, after another hour's wait, trumpets sounded: Rufinus came down the steps looking resplendent in his white toga, his iron-grey hair neatly combed, his thin olive face wreathed in smiles. Slaves on either side carried fruit, wine and parasols. Rufinus climbed into his litter. He glimpsed Claudia and winked.

'You could join me,' he whispered, studying her closer, 'but if my wife found out it would take months of explanations. If you are going to sin, Claudia,' he added, 'always sin in secret.'

The bearers formed up. The palanquin was lifted and the procession began its triumphant way down the hill and into the city streets. Here the excitement was tangible. No markets, no stalls, no booths were open. Shops and taverns were closed. Everyone was going to the games. A noisy, happy throng, the experts loudly proclaiming certain gladiatorial skills, gamblers shouting out wagers. Some of the combatants had followers; these had fashioned huge, garish banners proclaiming their idol's virtues. A group of school children were chanting an ancient syllogism: 'My donkey has got ears. You have ears. Therefore you are my donkey.'

127

The corps of guardsmen cleared a way. The noise and din became deafening. At one point the entire crowd came to a standstill. Rufinus, who was reading some papers in his palanquin, pushed his head through the curtains.

'Claudia, be a poppet, go and see what's wrong.'

She ran through the crowd, dodging past the soldiers, pushing her way through. She stood on the edge of the great open expanse which surrounded the Colosseum and stared in horror. Imperial guards were holding the crowds back from their first sight of blood that day. Carts holding criminals, men condemned to die at midday in the Colosseum, now stood in a long line. The prisoners squatted inside, hands tied behind them. One prisoner, however, unable to bear the tension, unwilling to die for the pleasure of others, had somehow escaped from his cart and committed suicide by sticking his head between the spokes of the cart in front. His corpse still lay twisted in the wheel, blood pouring out onto the dirty cobbles. Claudia's hand went to her mouth. She turned and hastened back. Rufinus just nodded when she told him.

'It will whet the appetite,' he sighed. 'The crowds will love it.'

'Will the Emperor stop the games?' Claudia asked.

Rufinus' eyes rounded in amazement, and his finger went to his lips.

'Hush, girl! There are already rumours that the Bishop of Rome and his coterie are not happy.' He smiled. 'After all, in my lifetime, the only occasion the Christians went to the Colosseum . . .' He left the sentence unfinished.

The captain of his guard came swaggering back and told them they would be moving. The palanquin was lifted. They crossed the open expanse. Claudia glanced quickly at the cart. The slave was still wedged there. A soldier was drawing his sword to sever the cords of the neck. Claudia was only too pleased that the crowds were moving quickly, their guards forcing a way through for Rufinus' litter.

The Colosseum soared above her, its white brickwork emphasised by the dark shadows of the arcades. The façade itself rose four storeys, each carved in a different manner. Huge statues dominated the many doorways, seventy-six in all. Each entrance had a number carved above it. Anyone who wished to gain admission had to produce a ticket which bore the numbers of the entrance, the tier and the seat. Rufinus, however, went through the Imperial entrance dominated by a huge colossus of Nero, though of course succeeding Emperors had changed its face so it reflected theirs.

Rufinus climbed out of his litter. The Master of the Game, the stewards, the Lanistas, the owners of the gladiatorial schools, met him in the shadow of the entrance. Cups of wine were distributed, toasts made, compliments exchanged. Claudia stood in a corner, holding her bundle and ash cane. She thought the banker had forgotten her, but just before he was led up to his seat he snapped his fingers.

'You are with me, Claudia!'

They climbed some steps, up a slight ramp and into the amphitheatre itself. Claudia paused in amazement. She was aware of banners, standards, flags and pennants snapping in the early-morning breeze; the boxes of the wealthy, shaded and draped with costly cloths; the sand dyed a strange orange colour; and above all, the crowd. Even though it was early, a sea of faces and the chatter of thousands made her feel dizzy. Rufinus kindly took her hand and she followed him into the shaded box next to the Imperial podium. Looking to her left, Claudia glimpsed where the Emperor and his entourage would sit in throne-like chairs edged with gold, small tables before them.

'The Emperor will not come till this afternoon,' Rufinus whispered. 'His place will be taken by the Editor of the Games.' The banker mentioned the name of some nobleman.

Claudia gazed at a number of chairs placed on steps inside Rufinus' box.

'They are for Domatilla and her ladies,' Rufinus explained. 'I am afraid you will have to stand.'

Claudia nodded, went to the edge and looked over the sea of faces. Her uncle, Poppaoe, all the servants from the She-Asses would be there. The tavern would be closed and locked, guarded by some bully-boy. Oceanus would also be present, loudly advising everyone on what to look out for. She tried to pick out single faces but this was impossible.

The Colosseum was filling up fast. Hucksters and traders were moving along the aisles offering water, wine, beer, spiced sausages, bread soaked in chicken gravy, honey-cakes, tattered sheets of parchment bearing the names of the gladiators who would fight. Book-keepers, distinguished by their huge parasols carried by scribes bearing wax tablets, went along taking bets. The sun had now fully risen. Over some parts of the Colosseum the great water-soaked awnings would be pulled out on cords and pulleys manned by sailors to protect the crowd from the worst effects of the heat.

In the amphitheatre huge trestle tables had been set out bearing the weapons of the gladiators: these would be formally inspected before the games began. Already marshals and Lanistas, pompous, self-important officials, were moving along the tables, picking up shields, checking helmets, licking their thumbs to feel the sharpness of the swords. The sand was being raked smooth. A group of musicians tried to rouse the crowd to some song, only to be ignored. Already soldiers and auxiliaries were taking up position with shield and sword near the gate from which the gladiators would enter. They would guard the escape route, with strict instructions to kill any gladiator who panicked and fled. Beneath the hum of the crowd echoed the roar of the lions and tigers penned in their cages beneath the amphitheatre. Claudia shivered. She hated the games, she didn't know why. She had seen battlefields littered with corpses. It was something her father had said, quoting a poet . . . how did it go? 'At the games, death is so cheap, so common.'

Claudia heard ecstatic squeals and screams and whirled round. Domatilla and her ladies thronged in to be greeted by Rufinus. Claudia was aware of beautiful young women of different nationalities: Negroes, Saxons, Dacians, Illyrians, Germans and Gauls; hair perfectly coiffed, ears, throats, wrists and fingers glittering with jewels; their soft, perfumed bodies covered in silks, gowns and shawls. Faces expertly painted, eyebrows plucked, eyelashes emphasised. Rufinus greeted them all with kisses and hugs. They were ushered to seats; cups of iced sherbert were served. Rufinus escorted their leader, the Lady Domatilla, to a chair at the front of the podium. Their arrival had been noticed by the crowd, who greeted them with cat-calls and whistles, salacious comments and jibes. Beneath this rose a low chant: 'In hoc signo occides! In hoc signo occides!' Domatilla's podgy face creased in concern at this eloquent testimony to how well known the murders were in Rome. The chanting grew. Thankfully the Editor in the Imperial box came forward, hands extended, to be greeted by wild applause. Domatilla sighed in relief and slumped in her chair.

'The Gods be thanked!' she whispered hoarsely, and, taking out her fan, waved it vigorously.

Rufinus called Claudia over and introduced her. Domatilla seized her by the shoulders and, in a gust of exotic perfume, kissed her roundly on both cheeks. She was a plump, pleasant-looking woman with glossy black hair, quite clearly dyed, and an inch of paint on her face.

'So, you'll be joining us at the villa,' she cooed, looking Claudia over from head to toe. 'You are not pretty but you look interesting. You can wait on me. Just keep in the shadows, but remember, what people don't pay for, they don't get.' She twisted her mouth primly, her eyes hard.

Claudia suspected Domatilla knew who she really was.

'The Divine Augusta has already sent me a message. She calls you her little mouse, and there are so many cats, aren't there, Claudia?'

Claudia just smiled. Rufinus, sitting alongside Domatilla, winked mischievously.

'I'm going to watch the games now,' Domatilla confided. She withdrew her hand, the nails painted a deep scarlet, the fleshy fingers covered in precious gems. She rattled the bracelets on her wrists. 'I hope the games are good,' she murmured. 'It's time the city returned to its pleasures, isn't it, Rufinus?'

Claudia took that as a sign of dismissal and stood back in the shadows of the box. She glanced sideways. Some of the courtesans were looking at her sly-eyed, whispering and laughing amongst themselves. Servants now came in bearing silver trays to serve white wine and specially cooked delicacies. The air became hot and thick with the smell of perfumed robes. All the chatter and the giggling died on a shrill blast of trumpets. The games were about to begin. However, the Editor must have been busy elsewhere because he failed to respond to the trumpets' blast. The ladies went back to their chattering. They were full of a story about a criminal who had killed himself.

'I heard,' Domatilla cried, 'that there have been other suicides! A German went to a latrine and choked himself by plunging down his throat a piece of wood and sponge which is used for the vilest purposes.'

Her statement brought cries of horror from the rest.

'And three of the Saxons strangled themselves . . .'

Again the trumpet blast. The Editor came to the edge of his box and lifted his hand. He was greeted by a thunderous roar. The gladiators filed in from the chambers beneath the amphitheatre: Thracians, Samnites, Net Men. The Colosseum fell silent as if the collective mouth of the crowd had been stayed by some huge hand. Sixteen gladiators in all, bodies glistening with sweat. Some were bare-headed, others wore ornate helmets: carrying large shields or small round ones, they lined up in front of the Imperial box, weapons raised.

'We who are about to die salute thee!'

The Editor raised his hand in acknowledgement and the crowd roared its approval. On the warm morning air they could scent blood. The arena was now cleared, all the pomp and circumstance disappeared. The crowd began to shout out its favourites' names; some of the women threw flowers: the Dance of Death was about to begin. Claudia watched the gladiators leave, trying to distinguish Murranus from the rest until she realised that he had stayed. He'd be one of the first to fight. His body, apart from his chest, was covered with pieces of metal and leather. He wore a loin-cloth of red linen supported round the waist by a sword belt. Both legs were protected by greaves, his left arm covered by a leather sleeve reinforced with metal scales. He carried a small shield and a curving, sickle-like sword. Murranus was a Thracian; he would have to depend on skill and strength. He put his helmet on, a huge affair shaped in the form of a boar's head. His opponent, a Samnite, carried a small shield and a long stabbing sword. He wore a loin-cloth, belt, and leather guards on his wrists and legs. He would depend on speed and agility. Another trumpet blast. The arena was cleared, the Editor made a sign. The crowd gave a collective sigh, followed by murmurs of appreciation as the two men separated. They hardly moved; they would conserve their strength: the parrying and feinting began with sword and shield. Abruptly, as if they sensed the impatience of the crowd, both men were drawn into vigorous, violent fencing: sword and shield moving, each of them turning, seeking the advantage. Claudia watched, fascinated. The Samnite, Murranus' opponent, withdrew, crouched, flexing his arm, bringing his small shield forward, his sword next to it. He moved to the right, Murranus moved with him. The Samnite feinted, Murranus struck, trying to beat his opponent to the ground. Their blades zig-zagged, their shields see-sawed in a harsh clash of metal. The contest became prolonged. Both men seemed impervious to the scorching heat, then Murranus didn't move fast enough. He was sent flying, his sword knocked from his hand.

'He's had it! He's had it!' the crowd roared.

Claudia clutched her stomach.

'Mitte! Mitte! Send him off! Send him off!'

The crowd was showing their appreciation of Murranus' skill. Murranus moved whilst his opponent was distracted by the crowd: he rolled over in the sand, picked up his sword and sprang to his feet. The combat was renewed but to a different rhythm. Murranus seemed determined to finish it. The Samnite lost his shield, Murranus sliced his arm and the

Samnite broke away. He threw down his sword and raised one finger of his left hand towards the Imperial box, a sign that he could not continue the combat and was begging for mercy. His outstretched arm now streamed with blood; the wound had been deeper than anyone thought. The Lanistas, armed with whips and swords just in case both gladiators decided not to fight, now entered the arena. They came between Murranus and his defeated opponent. The Editor rose and leaned over the edge of his box. The Samnite was now kneeling back on one heel. He had thrown his sword down and bowed, hands extended. The crowd were divided. They had enjoyed the fight but now they turned against the Samnite. The mob thought he should have fought on. The cry grew.

'Cut his throat! Cut his throat!'

The cry rose to a roar. The Editor stretched out his right hand, thumb extended. The roar grew. The Editor turned his thumb down: no clemency, no mercy, the Samnite would die! Murranus took his helmet off, put aside his shield and advanced, sword in hand. The Samnite drew himself up. He gripped Murranus' thigh just above the knee to steady himself. Murranus said something to him. The man's head came up. Murranus plunged his sword straight into his opponent's unprotected throat. The Samnite fell back; he remained half-seated and then tipped slowly on to his side. The crowd fell silent. Murranus, overcome with exhaustion, also slumped to the sand.

Strange creatures now appeared in the arena, led by a grotesque clothed in close-fitting tunic and long boots of supple leather. He wore a bird-like mask over his face. In one hand he carried a mallet, in the other a burning iron. He and his followers went up to the dead gladiator. The iron was stamped on the Samnite's chest to make sure he was really dead, before

135

his head was struck with the mallet. Ropes were attached to the dead gladiator's heels and he was dragged off through the Gate of Death with the grotesque, posing as Charon, Lord of the Underworld, dancing a jig before him. Murranus now staggered to his feet and, arms extended, accepted the plaudits of the crowd. As he left, the rakers hurried on, turning the sand over to hide the blood and collecting fallen weapons. The games continued.

Claudia sat deeper in the shadows of the podium. She was glad Murranus had won, that Januaria would not weep into her food, yet she felt sick and agitated. She watched the other ladies. Some were clearly excited, hands slipping beneath their robes, between their legs. Two were sitting close, arms about each other, hands running over legs, arms and breasts. Domatilla slumped, open-mouthed, like a woman who had drunk too much. Rufinus, although pretending to watch the contest, was secretly reading some documents laid out over his knee.

The morning drew on; the fights continued. Sometimes the gladiators were reluctant; others pleased the crowd and both were allowed to leave alive. At last the first part of the day's festivities was over. All available awnings had now been pulled across and the wandering food and wine sellers were doing a roaring trade. Some of the crowd left their seats to seek shade and refreshment. Others, however, stayed for the fun: the wholesale execution of condemned slaves and malefactors. Five or six of these were driven into the arena and three massive bears released. At first animals and men kept well apart. Eventually, the bears were urged on with whips and burning irons. Driven to fury, one of them charged the prisoners, knocking them aside like skittles. The other two, sensing blood, joined in. One of the prisoners broke free of his bonds and began to flee, pursued by a bear. The crowd forgot their lunch and roared with laughter at the poor man's antics. Claudia turned away. She sidled to the door and slipped out. The crowd on the benches around her were in a holiday mood, mouths full of food they had either bought or brought with them. They only had eyes for the miserable criminal, who had now run himself to exhaustion and was surrounded by all three beasts. Claudia tried to ignore the roars and the screams of the mob. She felt her tunic tugged and turned round. A grubby-faced urchin, mouth smeared with honey, stared owl-eyed at her.

'Are you Claudia?' He stumbled over her name.

'I'm Claudia.'

'Uncle Poly . . . Uncle Polyb . . .'

'Polybius,' Claudia finished for him.

'He said you must come. The man with the chalice on his wrist. He's gone down. He's in the animal dens.'

Claudia's stomach lurched. She had searched for this man! Now he was here, in the searing heat of the Colosseum, the air thick with grease, oil and blood, the crowd screaming with laughter at some unfortunate. Claudia stared at the boy.

'Uncle Polybius saw him. You must come! You must come!' He waved his little hand.

Claudia felt strange, slightly faint with the shock. The crowd seemed to move and turn. She steadied herself by stretching out a hand, touching the man who sat on the edge of the tier.

'You can put it a bit further down if you want, dear!'

Claudia drew a deep breath. The boy was already scampering up the steps, dirty bare arse clear of his skimpy tunic. Claudia had no choice but to follow. They came to the entrance to the pits. The guards were busy watching the arena. The boy was halfway down, his pale face clear and distinct in the murky darkness. Claudia felt her strength return, a tingle of excitement in her stomach. She clattered down. The passageway ahead of her was long, stretching into the darkness. The air smelt stale, fetid, of dung and straw, that feral smell of wild animals kept in pens.

Claudia had been here once before, years ago, with her father. They were on holiday and he had taken her down to see a tiger, snowy white with green eyes. Each of the doors down the passageway led to a whole series of parallel corridors with wild animals caged on either side. The boy opened a door. Claudia stepped in. The passageway was dull, lit by a torch fixed in a niche at the far end. She was aware of cages on either side. The one on her right was empty, then she screamed as a huge lion, with thick heavy mane and tawny coat, suddenly flung itself at the bars on her left. It reared up on its hind legs, lips curling to reveal great white teeth.

Claudia turned to the door but it had been locked behind her. The lion had now dropped to all fours and was staring at her, fury raging in its amber eyes. Claudia looked at the bolt on the gate. It was drawn fast. She had nothing to fear. Again the lion roared, head back; its cry was taken up by other beasts in cages along the corridor. Claudia tried the door again. It was locked from the outside. She pressed against it, hammering with her fists. Again the lion roared and all along the corridors she could see shapes crashing against the bars. She took a step forward. Again the lion charged. It was like being in some antechamber of the Underworld. The air was sour, and she was aware of straw under her feet. The torch above the door at the far end beckoned her forward. She had been so stupid! Was this some form of cruel joke? The boy had led her on, some urchin given a coin and a message to learn. But why?

Feeling sick, she leaned against the door, drew in her breath and calmed herself. This door was bolted, but the other? The lion was studying her curiously as if puzzled itself. Suddenly it sprang, one great paw thrust through the bars, scything the air.

Claudia ran. She was aware of bars, the air rent by roars and snarls, manic eyes blazing out at her. She kept to the gallery along the centre. With a sob she reached the far door, pulling up the latch. It was stuck fast. She hammered on it. The door at the other end was now being opened. Was this some sadistic game? She whirled round and stared in horror. Someone had come in at the far end of the passageway: the door was closing but the latch of the lion cage had been pulled up and was swinging open. Claudia stared in horror. The lion padded out, stretched its forepaws, roared, then turned, a monstrous, massive shadow at the far end. Some other beast screamed defiance. The lion padded forward, head going down. Claudia felt in her girdle for a dagger or knife; there was nothing. She turned to her right, but all she could see was a dark shadow in a cage; to her left, a bear sprawled out on the straw. Claudia wondered if it was wounded. The lion had paused. Claudia climbed up and took the torch from its iron niche, jarring and scoring her elbow as she did so. Then she turned, holding out the pitch-soaked fiery brand. The lion was puzzled by its new-found freedom. Claudia was prey: it would attack, but the torch held it at bay. It tried one short charge, then paused. Claudia could hear screaming, someone kicking at the door. She realised it was her: the heel of her left foot was bruised. The lion moved closer. Claudia waved the torch about. It turned and slunk back, going down on all fours in a crouch. The beast would watch and wait, then come in a rush, leaping the torch as it would a fence. Something hard struck Claudia's head. The door had been opened. The lion was moving. She threw the torch at it just as she was picked up and dragged through the door, Murranus kicking it closed and slamming the shutter down.

Chapter 9

'Who stands to gain?'
Cicero, *Pro Milone*, XII

Claudia was aware of torchlight, gladiators in half-armour, their torsos smeared with oil. Murranus had a sword in his hand, his hair tied back in a queue. He lowered her gently to the floor, where she crouched like a dog and vomited.

'By Apollo's penis!' he swore. 'And all the cocks of the Gods! What happened, Claudia?'

He knelt down, one hand on her shoulder. She retched again. Murranus shouted something to his companions. One of them brought a small earthenware bowl of water mixed with wine. Claudia smelt the myrrh which tinged it and shook her head.

'I don't want to sleep,' she gasped. 'I came down here looking for someone. It was deserted.'

'Of course!' Murranus snapped. 'It's noon, everyone is

out watching the poor bastards in the arena. Only animal trainers, armed with whips and torches, go down those corridors.'

Claudia wiped her mouth on the back of her hand.

'Where's Polybius?'

'Feeding his face.' Murranus touched her cheek gently with his finger. 'You look like a ghost from the Underworld. Claudia, what in the name of all the Gods were you doing? How did the guard let you by?'

'I was looking for someone. A young boy brought me down. He . . .'

'He'll be gone now,' Murranus muttered. 'Back into the slums. Someone tried to kill you, didn't they? It's not the first time this has happened, Claudia. Is it, lads?'

The other gladiators were indistinguishable in the murky glow but she heard their grunts of agreement.

'It's a sick joke,' Murranus explained. 'You lure someone into the animal corridors, then do what the trainers do when the animals are to be released. You pull back the latch of a cage, either with your hand or a hook. The animal bounds out.' He pointed down the corridor towards the pool of blazing light which marked the entrance to the arena.

'I came down here,' Claudia repeated. 'I was looking for someone. I made a mistake.' She leaned her head back against the wall. 'I thank you, Murranus. What were you doing here?'

'That's the Claudia I know.' He grinned. 'Never mind the danger or the rescue, straight back to the questions.' He touched the tip of her nose. 'Little bright-eyes, with your doll-like face.'

Claudia felt her heart skip a beat. She could smell the blood and sweat from this gladiator, yet he was gentle. He'd saved her life.

'I know what you are thinking,' Murranus said quickly. 'You saw me fight?'

Claudia nodded.

'I looked up towards the Imperial box. I could have laughed. In the one next to it I saw this little face staring down at me, eyes as big as Athena's owl. I came up looking for you. I watched you go down the steps but the crowd was so packed I couldn't get through. I saw the boy leave, like a rat from a hole. I came down, the door was locked, but I heard you scream, so I collected some of the lads and came along the other side.'

He hoisted her to her feet. Claudia studied his face. In the half-light he looked very handsome. He reminded her of her father; the way he used to stand over her, study her closely as if mystified by how small she was.

'You'd best get back,' Murranus said gently.

'I . . . I can't do that.' She shook her head. 'Could someone please present my compliments to the Lady Domatilla? Tell her I have urgent business. I'll join her household tomorrow.'

'Crixus!' Murranus shouted to one of his companions. 'Take this young lady home.'

'To the She-Asses,' Claudia whispered. 'Near the Flavian Gate.'

'Go on, man! Take her home! You've fought your fight. You'll get a bellyful of wine there.' He tapped Claudia on the shoulder. 'I'll see the Lady Domatilla about your possessions.'

Claudia seized him by the leather wrist-guard.

'Murranus, I thank you. I really do. I am glad you won your fight.'

Murranus' eyes filled with tears. 'So am I. The poor bastard shouldn't have begged for mercy. He was a new lad, fast on his feet but not much between his ears.' He bent down, his face only an inch away from hers. 'Do you know, Claudia, there are times when I hear the crowd bay; when I see those fat bitches and their husbands screaming for a gladiator's life, and I wish the mob had one throat so I could cut it with my sword.'

He paused as he heard shouts and roars from the door they had left further down the corridor. He grinned.

'It appears the trainers have realised there's a lion loose. You were lucky, Claudia: that beast had been fed this morning. Some of the cats I have seen just charge, not one whit frightened by fire or sword.' He paused at the roar from the arena. 'The bears have finished,' he whispered. 'It's time we got out of here.'

Murranus walked away. Claudia was aware of Crixus, a small, thickset man with a squashed nose and cauliflower ear, close-cropped hair, one eye half-closed under a ripening bruise.

'If Murranus wants you back at the She-Asses,' he muttered, 'then that's where we'll go.'

Claudia didn't resist. She left the Colosseum like a sleep-walker. The streets of the city were deserted, no stalls or shops open. Soldiers and police stood on corners or, in full ceremonial dress, around the monuments, temples and entrances to basilicas. Crixus was chattering but Claudia hardly recognised what he was talking about. Now and again he paused to exchange greetings or good-natured abuse with some acquaintance. At one time Claudia felt giddy and swayed on her feet.

'Steady there, lass,' he muttered. 'It's not every day you are chased by a lion.' He grinned in a show of chapped gums. 'I know how you feel. At Tarento I was in the amphitheatre; I had won the fight but the sick bastard allowed two lions into the arena. The first thing I knew about it was the howl of the crowd and those massive buggers charging towards me.'

'What did you do?' Claudia asked curiously.

'Same as you, ran like the wind out of the amphitheatre. I didn't stop until I was five miles from the city.'

Claudia laughed. She allowed Crixus to hold her hand, and before she knew it they were at the entrance of the She-Asses. Januaria came clattering down the stairs and opened the door.

'The place is closed. Oh, Claudia, it's you.' She looked at Claudia, then Crixus. 'Murranus!' she gasped.

'Ah, don't worry.' Crixus pushed her aside and dragged Claudia into the eating hall. 'He'll be back here, cock aloft.' He leered at Januaria. 'And ready for a different fight.'

Januaria closed her eyes and put her face in her hands.

'Oh, God be thanked, and you, Lord Christus!'

'I didn't know you were a Christian,' the gladiator said.

'I'm not.' Januaria took her hands away. 'But I'm thinking of becoming one. Claudia, what's the matter, where are you going?'

'To my room. I don't want anything to eat or drink. I just feel tired.' Claudia stopped at the foot of the stairs. 'Crixus will drink my portion.'

She climbed the stairs; the windows at the top were open, the afternoon sun pouring through. She stood and watched the dust motes dance. She used to do that when she was a child, and wondered if they were little gods. She went along to her own chamber, pushed the door open and went in. Polybius always kept the room for her. Sometimes, when the tavern was crowded, he allowed the occasional traveller to rent it. Claudia sat on the floor and pulled out the old box from underneath the bed. The clasp was broken, the lid loose on its leather hinges. She threw this back and took out her doll, a battered, tattered thing; it was supposed to look like a Roman matron, made out of cloth and soft wood filled with sawdust. The paint had now faded, and one glass eye was cracked. She put the doll on the floor and took out a wooden horse: one of the wheels was missing. She sat for a while rolling the horse up and down. Other possessions came out. Some belonged to her, others to Felix, mementoes of their childhood. She went back to that night along the banks of the Tiber, searching for precious things in the mud: that terrible shadow, the man dressed so elegantly, his spice-like perfume, the purple chalice emblazoned on his wrist. The pain and humiliation which had followed. Felix's corpse growing cold, his poor eyes staring sightlessly up at her.

Claudia began to cry: for herself, for Felix, for her father, for the way things were rather than how they should be. She recalled Murranus' soft touch, yet what did that mean? She could stand no man close to her. Anastasius knew that, cunning as always. He had tracked her, watched her, offering her a post before sweetening the dish with the prospect of vengeance. Claudia dried her tears: that would be enough. The mistake she had made today she would never repeat. She had walked into a trap like some dim-witted peasant from the countryside. A man with a chalice on his wrist! What had the boy said? Something about Polybius? So, whoever had lured her down there knew her history, but then that wouldn't be hard. Everyone at the She-Asses knew about her brother's murder. Her Uncle Polybius had even posted a reward, giving the man's description, describing the tattoo. Claudia's temper blazed. How cunning the assassin had been, but how easy it had been for him. He'd just waited and watched. If she hadn't left the box, the boy would have knocked on the door and delivered his message. The assassin could have been anyone: the Emperor, the Augusta, Rufinus, Domatilla. She could search for the boy but that would be useless. Even if she found him, there would be little chance that he would be able to describe the person who had concocted the fictitious message.

Claudia got up, walked to the door and opened it. Januaria was sitting downstairs, laughing with Crixus, sharing a jug of wine. Claudia walked to the window and stared out. The garden below was Poppaoe's work: vegetable patches, flower beds, a round wall with a painted stucco. On top of that, the bird-trap, a wooden structure of curved latticework: a hemp net shrouded it to keep the birds in. Poppaoe prided herself on raising plump pigeons or magpies which could be taught to speak. Claudia stood for a while, calming her mind. The attack beneath the Colosseum was finished. The assassin had failed, but why had he struck in the first place? Because she was getting closer to him? Claudia went and lay on the bed. She let her mind float, summoning up the pictures she wanted.

'What have I learned?' she asked the ceiling.

Claudia closed her eyes. A few months ago, Rome and its Western Empire had been ruled by Maxentius and his chief minister Severus. In Nicodemea, Licinius ruled the eastern half of the Empire. Constantine had marched south, defeating and killing Maxentius at the Milvian Bridge. In Rome, the likes of Domatilla and Paris had fled the city. Severus, Maxentius' chief minister, had taken over Domatilla's villa, and warrants had been promptly issued for the arrest of Paris, who had been foolish enough to satirise Maxentius' rule. In the city, a professional assassin, the Sicarius, worked for Maxentius.

Claudia opened her eyes.

'I do not really know,' she whispered, 'if the Sicarius was male or female.'

She returned to her meditations. The Sicarius was undoubtedly responsible for the murder of Severus. He had been hired for that task by the Augusta Helena. In the end, Constantine had swept victorious into Rome but Helena had done something very stupid. She had lured the Sicarius to a meeting and arranged his murder. In reality the Sicarius had probably sent someone else, a stooge who would play the part. The Sicarius had escaped, vowing vengeance on both Helena and Domatilla.

'Yes.' Claudia rolled to the side of the bed and stared at the toys still littering the floor: that would make sense. It also explained the murders. Domatilla was being punished; so was Helena, by the Sicarius striking at what she loved most: her son Constantine. The corpses were deliberately disfigured with the Christian symbol, which, according to Helena, had been responsible for Constantine's great victory. Helena retaliated by despatching the girl Fortunata as a spy to her son's household. Now Fortunata was linked to both Murranus and Paris: both maintained she had visited the Horse of Troy tavern. A short while later, Fortunata was executed and her corpse hung up in the slaughterhouse of the Imperial Palace. Why? Because she had learned something untoward? Claudia scratched her cheek: how many of these conclusions could be verified? Locusta, that harridan who owned the Horse of Troy, maintained that the Sicarius had disappeared.

So, was the Sicarius really dead? Were there two of them? Had someone else inherited his mantle? All the murders could be dismissed as an act of vengeance, a settling of scores, but why was the Roman priest Sylvester so interested? Were he and his master fearful that Constantine's position would be weakened? After all, the crowd in the Colosseum knew there

148

had been murders, whilst Arrius, killed in this very tavern, had brought broadsheets into the city advertising the murders and mocking Constantine. Who had organised that? More importantly, the assassin had shown that Imperial palaces and bodyguards meant nothing to him. He apparently had authority to move directly into the Emperor's private quarters to kill the courtesan Sabina.

There was also the attack on Claudia herself, both in the catacombs and under the Colosseum, not to mention those thugs who had followed her and Paris the previous evening. Was this the work of the Sicarius, and who was he? Paris? Claudia shook her head. The actor was a fop. He had been with her when they had been pursued the previous evening, and like many of his kind, he had a hatred of the amphitheatre. He was a well-known figure. If Paris had approached the Colosseum, he would have been recognised and hailed by those who had seen him on the stage. Moreover, he had been out of Rome when both Severus and Fortunata were killed. The same was true when Claudia was attacked in the catacombs: her assailant would have badly bruised his ankles, and Paris bore no sign of that.

So who else? Domatilla? Severus had been killed by a woman. On the night Sabina had been murdered, Domatilla could have disguised herself and entered the palace. Sabina would certainly have allowed her into her own chamber. Or was it Murranus the gladiator? A born killer? Was Claudia's escape from the lion simply Murranus trying to protect himself? Disguise his true nature? How had Murranus known where she was? Why didn't he express any surprise that she was now working for Domatilla? And how did he know she had left her possessions in Rufinus' box, unless he'd been following her? Or was the Sicarius someone else? Helena?

Was she telling the truth? Burrus, her mercenary, would do anything she wanted. Or Rufinus the banker?

The list was endless. Claudia's eyes grew heavy. She drifted in and out of sleep, listening to the laughter of Januaria and Crixus. She wondered wearily how Uncle Polybius would fare over the allegations laid against him. Suddenly a hand was across her mouth. She thought she was in that nightmare, back along the mud-flats near the Tiber. She opened her eyes and struggled, lashing out. The figure bending over her was cowled and cloaked. She glimpsed something silver round his neck, then the hood was pulled back.

'Hush now, Claudia!' Sylvester was smiling down at her. 'I will release my hand. I mean you no harm.'

He sat on the edge of the bed and Claudia pulled herself up.

'Why are you here?' she hissed.

'I have to see you, urgently. There wasn't time to meet in the catacombs.'

'I wouldn't have gone there anyway,' Claudia retorted.

She was about to tell him what had happened, but he put a finger to his lips.

'I knocked at the front door; it was off the latch.'

Claudia cursed Januaria.

'I could hear laughter from the garden so I came up the stairs.'

'We must be gone,' Claudia whispered.

She slipped her feet into her sandals, grabbed her cloak and cane and hurried down the stairs.

Thankfully the alleyway was deserted: the occasional crone squatting in a doorway sucking her gums, some children playing with a hoop. At last the alleyway debouched on to open wasteland. In the centre stood a derelict temple once dedicated to an Egyptian god. Its plaster columns were flaking, the steps were chipped and cracked, and some had fallen away. Claudia climbed up and walked through the doorway. A beggar came lurching out of the gloom, milky-white eyes, toothless mouth, saliva dribbling down his unshaven chin, claw-like hands stretched out. Claudia neatly avoided him. She seized his wrists and thrust a coin into his palm.

'Get yourself something to eat and drink, Father. Go on, old man, I wish to be alone!'

'No, you don't.' The fellow cackled. He sniffed the air. 'A girl and a priest friend, eh? I can smell the incense. It will be slapping of buttocks!'

'Go, old man!' Sylvester ordered. 'Or we'll take the coin away.'

The fellow scuttled out. Claudia went over to a far corner. Some daylight was provided by windows high in the wall. These lit up the strange carvings and paintings, the crumbling statues.

'I used to play here once,' she said, 'with Felix, my brother. We called this the entrance to the Underworld.' She pointed across to the far corner. 'There are steps going down to the cellar. We thought all sorts of demons and beasts lived there.'

'It probably is a house of demons,' Sylvester replied, coming over. 'My Church believes such places should be purified and hallowed. Sacrificing to bulls and birds . . .'

'Oh, I think demons own more comfortable places than this.' Claudia sat down on a plinth. 'You came to see me, it must be urgent. Why?'

'You work for Helena, the Divine Augusta?'

'You know that,' Claudia snapped. 'I also work for you, because of what you promised and because of my father.'

'And because we have high hopes of you, Claudia.' Sylvester

smiled through the gloom. 'When the new order comes into being, the Church will need its eyes and ears.'

'At the moment these eyes and ears are very bruised,' Claudia retorted. 'I am also tired and hungry, not to mention frightened.'

She told Sylvester exactly what had happened.

'We know about Murranus,' Sylvester declared when she had finished. 'We sometimes wonder whether he is what he claims to be.' He chewed on the corner of his lip. 'He's attended some of our assemblies. We don't know whether he's a spy or a genuine seeker of the true way: whether he works for the Empress or for someone else.'

'And Paris?'

'Paris is a butterfly.' Sylvester laughed. 'I remember during Maxentius' reign, when he fled Rome, he sought help from Christian friends who smuggled him out. They say he was gibbering with terror.'

'And the others?'

'Everyone,' Sylvester confided, 'is suspect. The Empress Helena, although she protests her friendship. Bessus, Rufinus, Chrysis. They've all realised the wind has shifted.'

'And what does this wind blow?'

Sylvester scratched his thin, greying hair. He sat on the plinth like some schoolmaster, hands on his knees; a dark brown gown covered him from neck to sandalled foot. Claudia was always intrigued by him. She also had a genuine fondness for this rather humble man who wielded so much power.

'Can Anastasius be trusted?'

'Trust no one.' Sylvester repeated his constant advice to her. 'Especially now. We have had messages,' he continued, 'from the churches in Bythinia.' He paused. 'As you know, the Emperor

Licinius, ruler in the East, also flirts with Christianity. Licinius,' Sylvester added drily, 'drinks too much. At a banquet recently, he let slip that something dramatic was going to happen in Rome that would shift the sway of empire. Now, if you apply logic, what could shift Constantine's empire in the West? The army love him. The people regard him as their saviour. The patricians and merchants are falling over themselves to give him money. Even the Christian Church is prepared to bestow its blessing.'

'Assassination?' Claudia intervened. She told Sylvester about the threats Helena had received.

'It's possible,' Sylvester agreed. 'The Sicarius has declared his own private war against the Empress and, perhaps, against her son. Now what would happen, Claudia, if an attack was made on the Emperor or his mother? If Helena died, Constantine would be devastated. If Constantine died, Helena would have no reason to live. The Empire would go to someone else. But what if,' he held up a warning finger, 'this assassination, successful or not, was laid at the door of the Christian Church? We would lose everything we had gained. Fresh persecution, the return of the night, back down in the catacombs, meeting by candlelight or oil lamp: droves of us being herded into the Colosseum.'

Claudia leaned her head back against the shabby wall. Sylvester had the right of it, she thought. More Emperors died of assassination than old age, disease or battle wounds.

'If they were to be assassinated,' she replied, 'it must be someone near them, someone they trust. Though, there again . . .'

'What?' Sylvester asked.

'I was thinking of the courtesan Sabina,' Claudia replied, 'who was killed in Constantine's private quarters. What if

someone like her got close to the Emperor? Someone pretending to be what they are not? That's the way it will happen,'
she continued. 'Poison is too dangerous. Both the Emperor
and his mother have their tasters and cooks. Why don't you
warn them yourself,' she added, 'about this new threat?'

'How can we, Claudia?' Sylvester replied. 'We have no proof.
The Emperor might think we are bluffing or trying to enhance
our reputation; or, even worse, believe the Christian Church
does threaten him.'

'But he will blame Licinius in the East?'

'Again no proof, though I suspect our assassin would be
quick to collect his reward from that quarter.'

'So, what must we do?'

'Trap the Sicarius,' Sylvester replied. 'Trap him and kill him
before he can do further damage.'

'And you expect me to do that?'

Sylvester got to his feet and stood over her.

'We must all do it, Claudia. Soon it will be summer.
Constantine will go on his campaigns again, protected by his
beloved troops. The Empress Helena will travel to Palestine.
Oh yes.' He smiled. 'We've heard of her dreams, her ambitions
to find the true Cross. If the Sicarius strikes, it will be within
days rather than weeks. Come, I'll walk you back to the
tavern.'

They left the temple. A beggar man sitting on the steps raised
his hands beseechingly and whined from the dirt-darkness of
his robes. Sylvester dropped a coin in his hand and, taking
Claudia by the elbow, led her back down the alleyway. The
beggar watched them go, eyes intent. The coin was tossed
aside. The beggar rose quickly: showing no sign of weakness or
deformity, he strode across the wasteland back into the city.

*   *   *

Later that day, Locusta, self-proclaimed witch, brothel-mistress and owner of the Horse of Troy tavern, left her opulent chamber, locking the door behind her, and walked down the stairs to the dining hall. The place was beginning to fill up. The games were over and everyone was thronging in to eat, drink and chatter about what they had witnessed. The girls were busy: even as she watched, two of them took customers out into the alleyway to pleasure them. The servants scampered about with trays of food. The bully-boys Locusta had hired nodded their heads and raised their hands in salute. Locusta felt pleased. Tonight would be a prosperous one. She stood at the foot of the stairs and stared around, searching for any face that was not recognisable: police spies, informers. Locusta smiled. No one would be so stupid! If a stranger appeared, he or she would always be closely questioned.

'Come over here, my lady!' A large, burly boatman staggered to his feet. 'I placed money on Murranus and Crixus and both won. I'm two sesterces richer!'

An immediate discussion took place on the games. The boatman imitated some of the unfortunate malefactors being pursued by the bear. Locusta snapped her fingers and ordered a round of drinks for them all. She had been to the games to make sure that some of the gladiators came here this evening. Yet she felt uneasy. She sat and sipped at her wine, half-listening to the banter around her. The meeting with the Augusta Helena had not brought the profit she had thought. On her journey to the palace she'd wondered if, like her namesake under the tyrant Nero, her services as a poisoner would be required. Instead she had faced harsh questions, from both the Empress and that mouse-faced little maid. Oh, she'd remember the latter! If she was a maid, Locusta was a priest! One of the Empress's many informers, even a member of the

Agentes in Rebus? Locusta was also nervous about what she had learned at the palace. Ever since that fateful day when she had delivered the invitation to meet Helena, there had been no sign of the Sicarius. There had been gossip that Sicarius had been killed, but Locusta never really believed it. Nor, apparently, did the Empress. Of all the men and women in Rome, Locusta feared only the Sicarius, a ruthlessly dedicated killer who would never tolerate being crossed. Once, two years ago, she had been too friendly, too inquisitive, and her favourite lapdog was sliced in half and placed on either side of the tavern doorway. The Sicarius had not said anything, and she had been too frightened to ask, but Locusta could recognise a threat. Whenever she'd received the token she would always go down to their meeting place. The Sicarius paid promptly and generously. Never once had he failed. Locusta sipped from her cup.

'Madam.'

Locusta looked up. One of the girls offered her a token, a silver coin from the reign of Domitian. Locusta spluttered on her wine. The coin was Sicarius' calling card, his demand to meet. The routine was always the same. She would wait a short while, then make her way through the gardens to the outhouse. Locusta drained her wine cup. She had no choice but to go. She left by the kitchens, past the fountain, the fish pond, the bird nets, the small arbours which guests could hire if a lady took their fancy. She opened the door to the outhouse and went in. The large window at the end was shuttered but she made out the form of someone sitting on the stone wall shelf beneath it. As always, Locusta closed the door behind her, bringing down the bar. She cast about nervously for the three-legged stool and sat down like a scholar facing a teacher.

'Good evening, Locusta.'

She smiled into the darkness. This time the voice was deep. Sometimes it was high. On one occasion it was tinged with an accent. She had seen no distinguishing signs except once, when the Sicarius had moved and she had glimpsed a balding pate.

'Charon always sails.' She offered the recognised password.

'Good!' the voice breathed back. 'Charon always sails!'

'What do you want?' she demanded. 'Maxentius is dead. Rome has a new ruler.'

'Aye, so it has, and you've been to see her, haven't you?'

Locusta felt a chill of apprehension.

'I was summoned.'

'Why?'

'They think I know who you are.' Locusta laughed nervously.

'And do you?'

'Of course not!'

'Do you remember, Locusta? It was through you that the invitation was issued for me to meet the Augusta Helena.'

'It is not right for the messenger to be blamed.'

Locusta closed her eyes at the terrible mistake she had made.

'Blame, Locusta? What on earth should you be blamed for?'

'I heard stories,' Locusta stammered, 'gossip in the marketplace. I meant no harm.'

'Of course you didn't, Locusta. Here, give me your hand on it.'

Locusta stretched out her hand; her fingers were seized in an iron grip. Before she could cry out, she was dragged forward and the dagger was driven deep into her heart. Her assailant twisted and turned it. Locusta opened her mouth to scream but choked on the blood bubbling there. She was aware of faint laughter from the tavern, the last sound she heard. Her killer lowered her gently to the floor and arranged her body carefully, as if she was being laid out at a funeral feast. The Sicarius breathed in deeply, and, ever so gently, closed Locusta's eyes. Then he placed a penny over each.

'For the ferryman.'

The Sicarius opened the shutters and slipped out into the gathering night.

Chapter 10

'Now banish your cares with wine.'
Horace, *Odes*, I.7

By the time dusk fell and the oil lamps were lit, the She-Asses was full of people thronging in from the games. Murranus, of course, was the hero of the hour. He sat like a Caesar in the best chair, a laurel wreath around his head, a garland of white flowers about his neck. Januaria had greeted him with squeals and cries of delight. Polybius had broached what he called his best cask of Falernian. Poppaoe was busy serving up fish pies, eel stews and other delicacies from the kitchen. Polybius hailed Murranus as the hero of the games and everyone commented on his skill.

Time and again some young man sprang to his feet to imitate what the gladiators had done. Granius, particularly, his arm round Faustina, led the cheers and paeans of praise. Paris arrived, his hair all oiled and coiffed. He was dressed in a salmon-pink tunic of the costliest silk which brought oohs and aahs from the ladies. His face was painted, even his fingernails, to match the colour of his outrageous tunic. He sidled over to sit beside Claudia.

'Victor eternus,' he whispered. 'Why do all the girls love a gladiator, Claudia?'

There was no malice in his voice and his bright eyes gleamed impishly. Claudia stared across at Murranus. Now and again he would catch her eye and look mournfully back. He had not referred to the incident beneath the amphitheatre, though she could tell from Polybius' face that her uncle knew about it and was deeply worried.

The only cloud over the celebration was the arrival of the Vigiles. They swaggered in, roaring for Polybius, then took him outside. Claudia made her excuses and followed. The police, dressed in leather corselets and kilts, sword belts wrapped round their waists, had pushed her uncle down the alleyway and were grouped around him. The officer in charge, a small, thickset man with thinning hair and the ugly face of a mastiff, held his hand up, fingers splayed.

'Five days, Polybius. You have five days to produce Arrius' silver. We don't give a damn about the murderer!'

'Or else what?' Polybius retorted.

'We'll close your tavern until you pay a very heavy fine.'

Polybius took a step forward.

'So I'm damned whichever way I go? All you want is the money, isn't it? Arrius' and mine. Whatever happens, some of it will stick to your fat, greedy fingers.'

'What's the matter?' Claudia asked.

The policeman turned round, looked at her and laughed.

'Go and wipe your bum!' he growled. 'Or I'll do it for you!'

Polybius lurched forward but the policeman knocked him back.

'Leave my niece alone!'

'Niece, is it? Niece or nice?' The policeman laughed at his own joke. 'You can pay in either cash or kind.'

'And I can go to the palace,' Claudia said softly.

'Can you now?' The police officer broke free and swaggered over to her: his breath smelled of stale onions.

'And what will you do, little one? Bring down a legion?'

'No, I won't,' Claudia replied quietly. 'I'll ask for an audience with the Divine Augusta, or her secretarius, the priest Anastasius.'

The officer's eyes flickered nervously. Who was this tavern wench? How did she know the name of one of the Empress' closest favourites? He became even more nervous when he looked over Claudia's shoulder. She turned: Oceanus and Murranus now stood at the mouth to the alleyway.

'I really think you should go,' Claudia offered.

The police officer stepped back.

'We'll be gone.' He lifted his hand, his eyes never leaving those of Claudia. 'But in five days, we'll be back.' He snapped his fingers. 'Come on, lads!'

The policemen swaggered off. Polybius, arms across his chest, slouched down the wall of the alleyway.

'Are you all right, master?' Oceanus called out.

'Yes, yes,' Polybius shouted testily. 'Go back into the tavern. Watch the customers! Claudia, come here!'

Polybius made himself comfortable on a narrow ledge at the base of the wall. Claudia did likewise.

'What happened today in the Colosseum?'

'A stupid joke,' Claudia replied. 'I thought I saw the man with the purple chalice on his wrist. I was foolish.

161

I went down, a cage had been left unlocked. The rest you know.'

'Thank God for Murranus!' Polybius murmured. 'But what are you up to, Claudia? You go to the palace as a servant, yet you stand here and talk as if you are on intimate terms with the great ones, the wearers of the purple and gold.'

Claudia leaned over and kissed her uncle on the cheek.

'You know full well what I am and you know why I do it. So, why ask questions? Do you also know,' she continued, 'an assassin called the Sicarius?'

'Who doesn't?' Polybius retorted. 'Particularly after the death of Severus. Yet, in the end, I know nothing of him, Claudia, and neither should you. I am more concerned about those stupid policemen and the crime they can't solve.'

'I've been thinking about that.' Claudia caught at her knees and settled herself comfortably. 'Poppaoe and Oceanus can keep an eye on the tavern. Tell me again, Uncle, exactly what happened?'

'Arrius arrived here, left his pony in the stables and took his saddle-bags upstairs.'

'He followed the same routine as always?'

'Yes.'

'But why should he be carrying broadsheets,' Claudia asked, 'about these murders?'

'I don't know. I thought he was a wine merchant.'

'Continue,' Claudia demanded.

'Granius took him up to the room, made him comfortable, asked if he wanted anything. Arrius, of course, being a miserable old bugger, told him to go away. Granius came out into the passageway. Faustina was at the top of the stairs. They both heard the key being turned in the lock and the bolts being drawn. Some time passed. The miserable sod never showed his face. The rest is as you know. We forced the door. Arrius was inside, his throat cut and his silver gone.'

'But you're not telling me the truth, are you, Uncle?'

Polybius chewed on his lip.

'Those broadsheets. Arrius never brought them in, did he? He wouldn't hide them under a mattress. You did that, didn't you?'

Polybius coughed nervously.

'If Arrius had brought them in,' Claudia continued, 'he would have hidden them more carefully, in some secret place. What I suspect, dear Uncle, is that you have been up to mischief again, haven't you? I can just imagine what happened. One dark night you are called out to this alleyway, where you do most of your real business. A man, woman, girl or boy, I don't know which, is standing here in the shadows. He makes the usual offer. Would you see certain broadsheets are posted up around the quarter? You've done it before, haven't you, for this politician or that? So why refuse now? How much were you offered?'

'Two silver pieces,' Polybius grumbled. 'Two silver pieces with no questions asked. The posters were to go up wherever I thought fit. I took them off him – this was two days before Arrius arrived. I didn't think twice until I got to my chamber and read them. I thought they were the usual rubbish. Vote for this person or that! Or why has the price of bread gone up? Or why are our police so bloody corrupt?'

'But you realised these were different?'

'Of course I did! Everyone has heard about the murdered courtesans, the marks left on their faces, whilst the story of the Emperor's vision before the battle at Milvian Bridge is hailed as a great miracle. I didn't know what to do. When Arrius was murdered, I thought what a marvellous opportunity it was. I pushed them under the mattress and thought, "Let that dead bugger take the blame." Politics is one thing, treason and murder another.'

'But the person who brought them?'

'Oh, Claudia, I don't know. Go round Rome, ask any tavern-keeper. We are always being approached.'

'Uncle, tell me the truth. You don't hand over two silver pieces and forget about it.'

'No, no, you don't. Of course, he came back. I don't know who he really was. Back into the alleyway I go. "What happened to my posters, Polybius?" So I told him. A merchant had been murdered. I was frightened when the police came so I burned them. Whoever it was just stood there, deep in the shadows. I remonstrated. I said it wasn't up to me; if the police had found them . . . !'

'And what did this midnight visitor say or do?'

'Nothing. I offered the two silver pieces back. "No, no," the reply came. "Keep them, Polybius, but next time . . ." Then he was gone.'

'You shouldn't do that,' Claudia declared. 'Uncle, one of these days you are going to come wandering into this alleyway and be trapped by some spy from either the police or the palace.'

'Well, if that happens,' Polybius retorted, 'I'll go and see my niece, who hobnobs with this person and that.'

Claudia glanced down the alleyway. From the tavern she could hear Murranus' voice as he mimicked some court lady at the games.

'How heavy was the money Arrius carried?'

'Fairly heavy.'

'So you couldn't actually go round the tavern carrying it?'

Polybius laughed. 'There's one sound, Claudia, as you well

know, which creates immediate silence in the She-Asses, and that's the clink of money. Why, what are you getting at?'

'What if,' Claudia offered, 'the money is still in the tavern?' She turned and grasped Polybius' arm. 'And before we begin, dear Uncle, I want your assurance that you did not kill Arrius.'

'I did not.' The reply was flat and emphatic.

'Fine, then come with me.'

'What are you going to do?'

'We are going to go to the eating hall, stop all the revelry and organise the most thorough search of your tavern.'

Even in the poor light Claudia sensed Polybius' nervousness.

'Everything except your room,' she offered.

His sigh of relief was audible.

'But you won't find anything.'

'No, but when you lodge an appeal to the Emperor against the police, you can say you have done everything humanly possible.'

Polybius needed no further encouragement. They re-entereed the She-Asses, Polybius touching the phallic sign on the doorway for good luck. Inside everyone was grouped round the table on which Murranus stood. He was now mimicking a court fop: his mincing walk, the way he flapped his wrists and looked at the rest from under his eyebrows provoked shouts of laughter. Everybody had drunk deeply. Oceanus' nose had turned a bright red whilst Januaria could hardly sit up straight.

'Get off there!' Polybius shouted.

Murranus jumped down and bowed. Polybius called Oceanus over, a sign for everyone to be quiet.

'I am in a lot of trouble with the police,' Polybius began.

Cat-calls and jeers greeted his words.

'So I am going to show them that I mean business. We are all going to divide into pairs to search this tavern from garret to cellar for Arrius' silver. And the garden as well. The only place you don't go is my chamber.'

'Why?' someone shouted. 'Is that where the money's hidden?'

More laughter and protests, but Polybius was a popular taverner, and when he offered them a reward, everyone, drunk or not, agreed to help. Claudia, standing in the shadows, watched faces carefully. On her return from the meeting with Sylvester, she had sat and thought about her uncle's problem. She smiled quietly in satisfaction. The solution she had come up with must be the correct one.

Under Polybius' direction, the wine bowls and jugs were removed. Many of the customers, even Simon the stoic, saw it as a game to be played out. There was a great deal of pushing and shoving. Januaria cried that she would only go with Murranus. Paris tried to inveigle Claudia to go with him.

'We could have a kiss and a cuddle,' he whispered. 'Down in the cellars.'

Claudia blushed and shook her head. Paris was seized by Poppaoe, eyelids fluttering.

'You can always go into the dark with me.'

Paris went off happily, ignoring Polybius' glowering looks. Claudia sat at a table and listened to the sounds: shrieks of laughter from the garden, pounding on the stairs. Voices echoed in the cellar below. Her mind went back to that murky chamber beneath the Colosseum: the lion bounding towards her, the locked door, the stench, the flames leaping up. What would have happened if she'd died there? She glanced around the eating hall and, for a moment, wondered what it would be

166

like not to work at the palace. She looked at a shelf above the counter where Polybius had placed a wooden soldier, Felix's favourite toy, in a place of honour. She would rest once she had vengeance, had done justice for her dead brother's soul.

The evening drew on. Polybius and Oceanus imposed order. It was obvious that no one would eat or drink until the search was completed. Paris and Poppaoe were out in the garden. A few shouts and exclamations as various items were found, things Poppaoe and Polybius had lost over the years. Even the occasional coin, or goods belonging to some long-forgotten customer. Claudia stayed where she was. She was fearful. For all she knew, any one of Polybius' customers could be a spy or informer working for someone else. And the Sicarius? Could he have slipped in, looking for an opportunity to do mischief? Hours passed. Claudia had to listen to the moans and groans of disappointment. Some of the customers had had enough and left, but then, just before midnight, she heard a cry of triumph from the garden, and Poppaoe screaming: 'Hoc habet! Hoc habet! He has it! He has it!'

Claudia sprang to her feet. Murranus, Paris behind him, came into the eating hall, in each hand a dripping, bulging sack of coins. He beamed triumphantly at Claudia and put them down on the table. Polybius came hurrying down the stairs. Everyone thronged in. Polybius squatted down and looked at the seals on the string tied round the neck of the sacks.

'That's old Arrius!' he exclaimed. 'He used the same seals on his wine jars and amphorae! Where did you find them?'

'In one of the bird bowls,' Poppaoe explained. 'You know, Polybius . . .'

The taverner nodded. Claudia walked over.

'Which one?' she asked.

'At the far end of the garden,' Poppaoe explained in exasperation. 'There are six earthenware jugs, dug into the ground, about a yard deep.'

'But you couldn't stretch that far,' Claudia insisted.

'I didn't stretch,' Paris simpered. 'I'm far too intelligent for that. Murranus took a stick and poked about. I told the rest to stop screaming. I heard the clink of coin and that was it!' He stood dramatically, one hand on his chest, head held back. 'You are not going to accuse me or Murranus, are you?' he simpered. 'We weren't anywhere near smelly old Arrius the day he died. I have been to the tavern before, but,' he winked mischievously at Claudia, 'that was for the wine. Now I am here for the company.'

'I am not opening the sacks,' Polybius declared. 'They are going into my strong box and I'll take them to the Treasury myself.'

'But one problem remains.' Murranus spoke up.

'By the way, aren't I going to be thanked?' Paris exclaimed.

He closed his eyes, puckered his lips and stretched towards Claudia. She kissed him quickly on the lips. The actor opened his eyes and rolled them dramatically.

'Oh, the ingratitude of women!'

'That's all you are getting from her.' Polybius clapped Paris on the shoulder. 'But every time you come here, you and Murranus get one free cup of Falernian, starting now.'

'You said there was another problem?' Claudia asked Murranus, who was standing back, letting the actor take the credit.

'You know there is, my little sweetmeat,' Paris simpered. 'When dear Uncle returns the silver, they are going to say that the person who stole it also murdered Arrius and probably works here.'

'Not necessarily,' Claudia riposted. 'Somehow the assassin got into Arrius' chamber, killed him, smuggled the money out and hid it in the earthenware jars. They planned to come back for it afterwards.'

'If you believe that, you'll believe anything,' Simon the stoic declared. 'But come on, we've found the money. Where's our reward, Polybius?'

Even though the hour was late and they were all tired, both the servants and the customers demanded their reward. Poppaoe went back to the kitchens. Polybius broke out more wine. The doors and windows were shuttered against the police and everyone settled down. Polybius was worried that they would stay there the whole night, but tiredness and the effect of the wine soon made itself felt. One by one, Paris and Murranus included, they made their farewells and slipped out into the night. Claudia went up to her chamber and bathed her hands and face. She took out her best blue tunic, still marked and torn from the chase in the catacombs.

'I only wore it once,' she murmured. 'Perhaps it's unlucky?'

She held it up and wondered if Poppaoe could do anything with it. She heard Polybius calling her. She left the tunic outside Poppaoe's chamber and went downstairs.

'Nobody asked the question!' Polybius exclaimed.

'What question, dearest Uncle?' Claudia blinked her eyes in mock innocence.

'Don't play the coy minx with me. How did you know the money would be here?'

'Why, dearest Uncle, because the murderers are.'

'Murderers?'

'You yourself said, Uncle, that only a fool would go out of this tavern with money bags clinking. So, where else could they hide it?'

'Who?' Polybius demanded angrily.

'Why, dearest Uncle, the people who stole it. They live, work, eat and sleep here. So they can't hide it anywhere else. If they took it to a banker or a silversmith, suspicions would be aroused. So why not hide it out in Poppaoe's bird garden? No one goes out there. Few people would even dream of putting their hands into the deep water jugs.'

'Who?'

'Ask Granius and Faustina to come down,' she insisted.

Her uncle obeyed. Granius came swaggering into the kitchen. Faustina trailed behind him: her face was pale and she was biting her nails.

'Are you disappointed?' Claudia asked as they sat down opposite her.

'Why should we be disappointed?'

Granius tried to put a brave face on it though his voice quavered. He licked his lips and stared through the doorway as if he expected the police to come bursting through.

'You know full well,' Claudia declared. 'And we are not going to tell the police; well, not yet. Arrius was a wine merchant. He went out to the countryside to collect his profits, then came back into the city. He visited the She-Asses at the same time every month, and went through the usual dreary routine. He hired a chamber, washed, filled his belly and demanded a girl. Of course, he would stay in his chamber, the window shuttered, his precious silver stowed away. An objectionable old man, yes? So you precious pair decided to murder him.'

'How could we?' Granius interrupted. 'He locked and bolted the door behind him.'

'Well, I'd like to suggest,' Claudia replied, 'that we go upstairs and examine these locks and bolts but they are

gone, aren't they? You have had plenty of time to cover up
the evidence.'

'What do you mean?' Faustina snapped. 'What's all this
about? The money has been found.'

'And so have the murderers,' Claudia replied. 'I was at the
Colosseum today. I don't agree with what they do; it is a
terrible way for a murderer to die.'

Faustina's petulant mouth trembled.

'I'll tell you what happened,' Claudia continued. 'The bolts
and clasp were weakened so that when the door was pushed
open it would look as if they'd been forced.'

'And the lock?' Polybius asked.

'Uncle, the locks you buy are cheap. The keyhole is large. I
don't think it would be all that difficult to insert a small iron
rod with sharpened sides which could turn the lock back, even
though the key was in it.'

'You've got no proof of that!' Granius' eyes were full of fury.
Not so much at being trapped as at losing the plunder he had
so carefully stolen.

'No, no!' Claudia retorted. 'This is what happened. Arrius
arrives. He goes up to his chamber. You go with him. You
close the door behind him and, when his back is turned,
immediately cut his throat and lay him out on the bed.
You then steal his silver, probably hiding it in something
you carried, a pot, jar or bag. Arrius dies quickly. It's all
over in a matter of minutes. You pull across the bolts but
tear out the clasps in preparation for the door being forced.
The window shutters are kept closed and barred. You leave
the chamber. Your accomplice Faustina is waiting at the top
of the stairs. She is probably carrying a big bowl or jug, of
which there are many in this tavern. You quickly put the
money in there. Faustina turns and goes downstairs. She

171

is now your guard as well as blocking anyone who might come hastening up. Whilst she does, you crouch down, insert a specially prepared metal rod into the lock and turn it. Arrius is now sealed in his chamber. There are no secret entrances, the shutters are barred, and to the honest enquirer, the door is locked and bolted.'

'But it's common knowledge,' Polybius objected, 'that the door was locked and the bolts drawn. People heard.' He paused. 'Of course,' he conceded. 'The only people who heard it were Granius and Faustina.'

'Most perceptive, dear uncle. That's what intrigued me from the beginning. We hear doors close all day and night. I can't accurately remember whether they are locked or bolted but these two could. Of course, no one would think that untoward. First, Arrius always locked and bolted his chamber and kept everyone away . . .'

'Secondly, when we came up to the chamber,' Polybius interrupted, 'that's what we found.' He went over and grasped Granius by the shoulder. 'And you were there, weren't you? You helped me break the door down. I remember you shouting directions. First we tried the top but then you told us to concentrate on the centre.'

'By the time you'd broken the door down,' Claudia explained, 'the lock was smashed and it looked as if the bolts had been forced, though as I have said, they had been carefully prepared beforehand. The real evidence of the murder had been cleverly removed. Am I telling the truth, Faustina?'

The tavern girl was now shivering, rubbing her arms, lips moving wordlessly.

'It was simple logic,' Claudia offered. 'First, no one went into that room apart from you, Granius. I thought it was a remarkable coincidence that Faustina was at the top of the

172

stairs at the very time you came out. Even more remarkable, both of you could remember, so clearly, the locks and bolts being drawn. Granius also played a role in forcing the door. And as for the silver?' She shrugged. 'You told me you were thinking of leaving the She-Asses, so why not hide the silver in some deep, dirty water jar at the far end of the garden? You couldn't very well hide it in your chamber here or take it to a silversmith or banker. You planned to leave it there till the day you went. You'd leave Rome as beggars but arrive in some other town as quite wealthy people.'

'What are you going to do?' Granius asked.

'I'm going to show you mercy,' Claudia declared. 'Or at least my uncle will. If you pack your belongings you can be gone by dawn. Uncle will simply say he's found the silver; the police might learn of your disappearance and become suspicious. But,' Claudia smiled, 'by then you'll be miles away, won't you?'

Chapter 11

'Do not ask, it is forbidden to know what fates the Gods
have in store for us.'

Horace, *Odes*, I.11

Domatilla's villa was a spacious, quite beautiful property just
off the main thoroughfare stretching across the Esquiline:
cool colonnades, shady porticoes, a well-laid-out garden with
small orchards and arbours where lovers, if they wished, could
become lost. Silver pools glistened in the early spring sunshine; fountains splashed in sun-washed squares. Ornamental
ponds, ringed with lush reeds where fat carp lazily swam,
dotted the grounds.

'A veritable paradise,' Domatilla described it as she showed
Claudia around before leading her into the house. This was an
elegant two-storeyed building connected to other apartments
by colonnaded walks, protected from the elements by sloping
red-tiled roofs. The luxurious chambers boasted marble walls

175

and intricately carved mosaics on the floor. The air was perfumed, the calm atmosphere broken now and again by the hum of conversation, the laughter of the ladies or the tinkle of a bell as a servant was summoned to bring refreshments to this chamber or that.

'As opulent as a palace,' Claudia agreed.

Domatilla stopped at the end of a corridor and grasped her arm.

'But never forget, Claudia,' her eyes, puffy from lack of sleep, twinkled in amusement, 'it's nothing more than a common brothel and I'm little more than the Emperor's whore-mistress.' She brushed away the dyed curls from her forehead. 'I'm tired and I look it,' she remarked, 'but you look as if you haven't slept a wink.'

'I was busy at my uncle's tavern,' Claudia replied.

'How busy?' Domatilla asked archly.

'Not that!' Claudia snapped. 'We had a few problems which had to be resolved.'

Domatilla walked on, one arm around Claudia's shoulder.

'I know who you are,' Domatilla whispered conspiratorially. 'If the Empress, the Divine Augusta, sends a servant like you, then it's not to help with the washing-up, is it?'

She opened a door and ushered Claudia into a chamber. A large bed in one corner, furniture of different varieties scattered around: two low tables, a couch, stools, a chest with bronze clasps. Pegs were driven into the wall on which to hang clothing. The high window was closed and shuttered. The air smelt faintly of beeswax candles.

'This room is just like those of the other girls,' Domatilla commented. 'Perhaps not as well furnished, but you've only just arrived: only the Gods and Divine Augusta know how long you will stay. The windows are high because we do have troublemakers who like to break in and have a good look. However, the walls too are high, whilst I have a few bully-boys with dogs patrolling the grounds at night.'

She ushered Claudia to the edge of the bed, kicking the door closed behind her. She took a pole, loosened the bar of the shutters and opened them, then, wheezing and muttering to herself, she pulled up a cushioned chair to sit opposite Claudia.

'This chamber is next to mine,' she explained, her podgy, bejewelled fingers emphasising her words. 'Ostensibly you are my servant.'

'In reality?' Claudia asked.

'Keep your eyes and ears open,' Domatilla retorted. 'We have had four girls murdered. The last, as you may know, was killed in the Imperial Palace itself, but the other three were enticed out.'

'Enticed out?' Claudia asked.

'Well, we only take the best here.' Domatilla sniffed. 'Girls from good families, not your common whores or strumpets. They are not slaves but freed women with kinfolk in the Imperial service and army. You met them all yesterday at the games. By the way, where did you go?'

Claudia studied this fat, cheerful whore-mistress. Domatilla had explained that she had spent the night following the games carousing or, as she put it, acting as hostess to leading members of the senate. She was a friendly, chatty woman with few pretensions about herself and even fewer about the rest of humankind. She smiled a lot, making her fat cheeks quiver. She reeked of perfume and would break into squeals of high-pitched laughter, but her eyes, tense and watchful, never changed. Her face reminded Claudia of that of an actor covered by a mask. Was she the killer? Claudia wondered.

Had she enticed her own girls to their deaths? After all, she had sat at the games yesterday and watched men being killed by gladiators and wild animals. Was she the Sicarius, or did she know who he was? Domatilla leaned forward, waving her hand before Claudia's eyes.

'Have you fallen asleep, girl?'

'No, no, I am sorry.' Claudia shook herself and apologised. 'Yesterday I had urgent business at my uncle's tavern.'

'Rufinus said you were strange.' Domatilla laughed, lifting her fingers to her mouth. 'He said the Divine Augusta called you her little mouse. And if that's the case, I'm her little plump rabbit, aren't I? Anyway, what was I talking about?'

'Your ladies,' Claudia replied. 'You said that they were free women of good quality.'

'Yes, yes, I school them myself. I provide clothing, perfume, food and boarding. They lack for nothing: hairdressers, manicurists, doctors, leeches. Their health is the best in Rome. Now, grateful customers pay me direct. I give the girl an agreed share: what she does with that is up to her.' Domatilla grasped the front of her white silk gown and flapped it as if she was hot. 'However, the little minxes aren't above earning a bit on the sly. They all have great hopes of contracting a favourable marriage or becoming the personal mistress of some senator or general. After all, they are skilled in the arts of love. One of their first assignments when they arrive here is to learn couplets,' she grinned at the slight pun, 'from Ovid's *Art of Loving*.'

'So, in other words,' Claudia broke in, 'if they get a message to go and meet so and so . . . ?'

'Oh, they hasten away like a bee for honey; it's difficult to stop them. If they climb into a litter and tell the slaves to take them here or there, how can I object? They are allowed to visit friends in the city.'

'So, how do you make a profit?' Claudia asked.

'Men always get tired.' Domatilla gave a look of mock grief. 'They always want something different, so they come trotting back to Domatilla and share their secrets.'

'So, the first three who were murdered,' Claudia asked, 'had gone out on some secret assignation?'

'Yes.' Domatilla sighed. 'And I don't know who delivered the message or where they were going. The first I knew about it was when their corpses were brought back here.'

'And each of them had been with the Emperor?'

'Yes, each of them had lain with the Emperor.'

'How had they been killed?'

'Strangled; those Christian symbols carved on the forehead and cheeks, with a scrap of paper tossed near the corpse with the words, scrawled in blood, "In hoc signo vinces."'

'Was a coin found?' Claudia asked.

'A coin?'

'Yes, the sort you put on the eyes of a corpse to pay Charon the ferryman.'

Domatilla pressed her fingers into her cheeks.

'On one of them, yes, but the others.' She shrugged. 'I understand a curse was laid next to the corpse of Sabina. The Emperor would not like that. He's a soldier: for superstition they are worse than sailors.'

'And why do you think,' Claudia asked, 'your ladies were chosen? Because they have lain with the Emperor?'

Domatilla rose and went across to a table. She removed the linen cloth from a tray, filled two cups and brought them back.

'See,' she pressed a cup into Claudia's hand, 'you are not

179

my servant. Drink this. It's from vineyards in the north. It's cool and light and doesn't require water.'

Claudia sipped obligingly.

'I don't think my girls were killed just because they had slept with the Emperor,' Domatilla explained. 'Constantine is a stallion. I would wager my litter to a purse of silver that he mounts quite a few of the ladies of Rome. You know men, Claudia, there's nothing like victory and the cry of the crowd to make them feel like they are the only cock in the barnyard.'

'But none of these other women have been murdered?'

'Of course not.'

'So why?' Claudia insisted.

'The assassin undoubtedly hates both the Emperor and his mother,' Domatilla replied slowly. 'And,' she blinked quickly, 'he undoubtedly hates me. I'm losing good custom, Claudia. No more girls come to see me. I'm like a butcher: my customers are always crying out for fresh meat. Four of my girls have died, been killed in a savage, gruesome way. The killer is teaching me and the Divine Ones a lesson.' She breathed in. 'I can speak honestly, Claudia?'

Her companion nodded.

'I blame the Divine Augusta. The Sicarius was a professional assassin. He worked for, and was paid by, the dead Maxentius. Everyone in Rome could see that Maxentius' star was starting to dip. He lost control of the city, and if it hadn't been for his own praetorian guard, someone would have murdered him sooner or later. He left Rome to his minister, Severus. Everybody else was on the run. I fled to a villa in the countryside: Severus took over my house. He used to be a customer and always liked the place.' She sipped from the wine. 'You know the story. The Divine Augusta sent a message and managed to buy the service of the Sicarius. Apparently an agreement was reached and Severus' life wasn't worth a candle flame. Now, during the last days of Maxentius' rule, Severus used this villa for his own purposes, carousing and drinking late into the night. The details are few, but on the day after Maxentius was killed at the Milvian Bridge, a mysterious woman, dressed as elegantly as any courtesan, visited Severus. They met in the banqueting hall; Severus took her to his private chamber.' Domatilla raised her cup in a mock toast. 'When the door was forced, Severus was found dead, his throat slashed from ear to ear; his corpse had been laid gently on the bed, two coins placed over his staring eyes. He received a pauper's funeral.'

She paused, blowing her cheeks out. 'I came back here and cleaned the mess up. The place had been looted but nothing that couldn't be put right. The Divine Augusta, of course, came to thank me for my support. She mentioned that she wished to meet someone here. I don't know who it was, but she took over one of the wings of the house. There were a few guards and she was accompanied by that huge beast Burrus. I know nothing about what happened, except that a corpse was taken out, discreetly of course. The Divine Augusta thanked me and left. I searched the chamber from ceiling to floor. She had been a good guest,' Domatilla added drily. 'Even the blood-stains had been wiped up.'

'So, you know the Sicarius was supposed to have been the Divine Augusta's victim?'

'Yes, yes, I learned all about that later. I believed, even then, she had made a dreadful mistake.'

'Do you know anything about this Sicarius?' Claudia asked.

'Claudia, Claudia,' the whore-mistress replied. 'Do you want poison? I know poisoners. An abortion, a loan, safe passage out of the city? These are people I can do business with. I can even hire thugs and footpads. The Sicarius is different. He was the dead Emperor's man. His reputation has grown over the last three or four years. If someone is a traitor, you send the guards round to his villa and ask the culprit to open his veins or take a dish of poison. But what do you do with men who are guilty of no crime, or at least, one that can't be proved? Or someone who acts the friend but is really an enemy? Maxentius curried favour with the Senate, with the bankers and the merchants. But,' she lifted a warning finger, 'if he wanted someone removed or took a dislike to them, it was always the same: an accident, a fall downstairs, a seizure in the bath, attack by a footpad. That's how the Sicarius came to be known.'

'Too many well-planned deaths?'

'That's how one of my customers put it.' Domatilla smiled. 'And always the same. No trace, no clue, so the legend of the Sicarius began. At first people thought it was some story to frighten Maxentius' opposition. After a while the Sicarius became flesh and blood; he was a real person.'

'And the connection with Locusta? How did that emerge?'

'Oh, that evil bitch! One night at a supper party, Maxentius had been drinking deeply, and someone mentioned an enemy. Maxentius replied, "Oh, yes, him! He should go for a drink with Locusta at the Horse of Troy!"' Domatilla sucked on her lips. 'A few days later, the man in question suffered an unfortunate accident. He was travelling by the Basilica Nova and a piece of masonry toppled on to his head.'

'So, that's how people connected Locusta and the Sicarius?'

'Clever girl!' Domatilla replied sardonically. 'What concerns me, however,' she added, 'is that with Maxentius, the Sicarius could go where he wished. Undoubtedly he had an Imperial seal, some sort of pass. But,' she continued, 'Maxentius is dead now, his head rotting on the end of a pole. Yet once again, the Sicarius can go tripping through the Imperial palaces committing murder and disappearing like smoke on a spring morning. Ah well!' Domatilla drained her wine cup and put it on the floor. 'I must make ready for tonight.' She raised one eyebrow. 'Of course, you wouldn't know, the Divine Ones are coming here: Constantine, his mother, Anastasius, Rufinus, even that strange Christian priest Sylvester.'

Claudia recalled the carts she had glimpsed lining up outside the kitchens.

'It's a banquet,' Domatilla explained, 'to celebrate the end of the games, and for Constantine to show his patronage of my house. I have hired that poltroon Paris and his troupe of actors to entertain them.'

'Do you know Paris well?' Claudia asked curiously.

'Well? He sheltered with me when he fled Rome, hid in a cellar. At one time he even fled further into the countryside. He can be very funny, our Paris. He didn't return to Rome until after Severus was dead and Helena and her son had firmly ensconced themselves.'

She paused at a knock on the door. A serving-girl entered and handed her a small scroll. Domatilla snatched it out of her hand. The parchment was of fine quality, the ribbon red silk. Claudia half-suspected what it might be: the look on Domatilla's face told her everything. The courtesan's cheeks sagged, her lower lip jutted out and quivered.

'What is it?' Claudia demanded.

Domatilla handed it over. The writing was like that of a child, though the letters were carefully printed. At the top a Christian symbol, and beneath it what a slave used to whisper to a victorious general as he conducted his triumph through Rome: 'Sic transit gloria mundi': 'Thus passes the glory of the world.' Beside the words was a smudge of dust, and beneath them 'In hoc signo vinces.' Quotations from the poet Horace were written below. The first was from his odes:

'We have all been gathered for the same end. The lot of every one of us is turning about in the funeral urn. Sooner or later, we are pushed into Charon's boat, out into eternal exile.'

The second was more pointed:

'Believe every day that has dawned to be your last.'

'It's a warning.' Domatilla swallowed hard, then got up, hastened to the door and brought the servant girl back.

'When did this come?'

'An officer brought it.'

Domatilla stared in stupefaction.

'What do you mean, an officer?' Claudia demanded.

'He was an officer. He wore a cloak, breastplate and a red leather kilt, greaves on his legs. He came to one of the postern doors and the porter let him in.'

'What did he look like?' Claudia asked.

'He had a red face, blond moustache and beard. He said he came from the Emperor, that's why he was let through. My lady, is anything wrong?'

Domatilla dismissed the girl. She refilled the wine cup, her hands shaking as she raised it.

'Will I be next?' she whispered, not even bothering to turn round. 'Will my corpse be found in the dark beneath some olive tree?'

'You have nothing to fear,' Claudia reassured her. 'This assassin will soon be caught.' She tried to sound more confident than she really was. 'You are well guarded. Do not leave the villa and you'll be safe.'

'That's right.' Domatilla finished the wine in one gulp. 'I'll hire more guards, bully-boys. At the banquet tonight the Divine Augusta has already insisted that all food and wine be tasted.' She seemed lost in her own world, fat jowls quivering, the kohl running in rivulets down her painted cheeks. 'I must do what I can! I must do what I can!' And, mumbling to herself, Domatilla left the chamber.

Claudia locked and bolted the door behind her. She put her ash cane next to the door, undid her bundle and took out two daggers. One she placed on a stool near the door, the other under the pillows. She closed the shutters and went and sat, as she had done as a child, in a corner, bringing her knees up, wrapping her arms around them. The elation, the feeling of triumph she had experienced in trapping Granius and Faustina had long disappeared. Both had confessed, collected their belongings and fled into the night. They had apologised to Polybius, explaining how Arrius had once tried to rape Faustina. His death was an act of revenge as well as the means to become rich.

'It was easily done,' Granius conceded. 'I killed him immediately. The bolts I had already broken on the inside. I had fiddled with the lock so I could turn the key from the outside.' He glanced guiltily at Claudia. 'It wasn't a piece of metal but a pair of pincers. I chipped away at the keyhole. I practised and found it could be done. At the top of the stairs I gave the money to Faustina, who was waiting on guard. We thought the garden was the best place, those earthenware pots sunk deep into the soil to collect water for Poppaoe's birds.'

Polybius and Claudia had heard them out. Uncle had even given them a little money, a change of tunics and sandals, some food and wine, and told them to be well away from the She-Asses by morning.

'Will you tell the police?' Claudia asked after the guilty pair had gone.

'I'll tell those greedy buggers nothing!' Polybius growled. 'I'm going to take the money straight to the Treasury.' He drew his dagger and cut the twine round the necks of the money sacks, which he'd brought down from his strong box. 'Mind you, I have to take my expenses. If you don't tell anyone, Claudia, I certainly won't!'

Claudia had left him to it. Dragging herself wearily upstairs, she had packed her possessions and come here. But for what? The Sicarius was alive and kicking, conducting his own private war against the court. The assassin could move around the city at ease, like some wild animal probing a stockade, eager to get in. He was playing a game. The murder of the courtesans was a clear warning to both Domatilla and the Empress. Now he was edging closer. Both Helena and Domatilla had received warnings. It was only a matter of time before he struck. But who? And how? Claudia got to her feet and sat on the edge of the bed. The other murders had been easy to explain. The whores had been attracted to their deaths by greed, except for Sabina: that was puzzling. The killer was undoubtedly someone with power. Claudia still wasn't convinced of Domatilla's total innocence. What if she had arranged to send the letter herself? And when would the Sicarius strike? Tonight, during the banquet? But that would be difficult: the villa would be swarming with guards and spies. Claudia heard a rapping on the door.

'Who is it?' she called out.

'Claudia, it's me, Domatilla!'

She rose and let her in. The whore-mistress now looked more composed and serene.

'I've just heard news from the city about that evil bitch Locusta. Last night she was found stabbed in one of her outhouses.' She closed the door and leaned against it. 'What does it mean, Claudia?'

'I've been thinking.' She studied Domatilla closely.

'Why are you staring at me like that?'

'I always do when I'm thinking.' Claudia half-smiled. 'I suspect the Sicarius is preparing to leave. He's going to do something very dangerous and wishes to leave no trace behind.'

Domatilla's gaze fell away.

'I sometimes wonder . . .' she stammered.

'What?' Claudia demanded.

'Whether you are the killer.'

Domatilla made no attempt to conceal her blushes. Claudia just stared in puzzlement.

'Why not?' Domatilla continued. 'I've watched you: you can act the part, running hither and thither.'

'I could say the same for you,' Claudia countered. 'And that's the beauty of it.' She took a step closer. 'If the Sicarius had his way, he'd have all of us at each other's throats.' She emphasised the points on her fingers. 'A courtesan would come out to meet me if she thought I was bearing messages. I could have killed Fortunata. I could have arranged for that message to be delivered by an army officer.'

Domatilla sighed and held out her hand.

'I didn't really mean it,' she stammered. 'I am very worried.'

She made to go but Claudia caught her by the arm.

'Tell me, Domatilla, if I said I was looking for a man with

a purple chalice tattooed on his wrist, would you know the reason why?'

Domatilla looked over her shoulder and grinned.

'I'd like to lie but those cat eyes of yours would know the truth.' She walked away from the door to face Claudia squarely. 'Yes, I know the story. It's more common than you think. I mean, you have no boyfriend. No one at all. You've found out about me, I've found out about you.' She smiled thinly. 'We pride ourselves on being spies, informers to the Divine Ones. In reality,' her face became ugly, 'we are all animals, Claudia, and the powerful feed on the weak.' She noticed the dagger lying on the stool and smiled. 'I have met girls like you who've been abused and raped. I am no different: that's how I became what I am. In my case a kinsman, someone who pretended to be my friend. You are not alone: half the girls in this villa hate the men they meet and harbour deeper feelings for each other.'

'Do you know of such a man?' Claudia demanded.

'No. Such men don't come here, Claudia. They are fright-ened of an adult woman, and . . .' She was going to finish the sentence, but shrugged.

'You know something?' Claudia's curiosity was now aroused.

'When did this happen?' Domatilla asked.

'Over a year ago.'

'You should see the police.'

'My uncle did.'

'And?'

'They were no help.'

'No, go higher. Some day, when you have time from your snooping and your listening, ask our patroness to search amongst the police records.'

Claudia's heart skipped a beat. She had never thought of

that. Her uncle had done what he could but the police had just shrugged it off as some drunken nobleman or priest out for an evening's pleasure.

'You know what fat-heads the police are,' Domatilla continued. 'They couldn't care for the likes of you. They are more interested in their paperwork, taking bribes or watching what the great ones do.' She picked up Claudia's dagger and sat down on the stool. She noticed how Claudia walked away. 'I'm no danger, little mouse,' Domatilla declared. 'The Divine Augusta told me your story. She said that you had been raped and gave me a few details.' She pulled a face. 'Yes, that's it. I asked her if you would be a rival for any of my girls or be interested in a little business yourself. The Divine Augusta told me and a memory has stirred.' She balanced the dagger between her fingers. 'More than a year ago . . . Yes, it must have been about then. Don't forget, Claudia, the police are interested in politics: who's rising, who's falling. Rome has not been the quietest of places. Anyway, I heard tittle-tattle and gossip about young women being attacked in various parts of the city. That's one of the good things about being a whore. You collect more information than the police ever do. The attacks took place over a considerable period of time. The police didn't give a damn. They've got better things to do than bother about an assault on some poor slum wench. I also heard a tale, albeit secondhand, about another victim; she too survived, to describe a man with a purple chalice on his wrist. I thought he'd be easy to trace. I mean, every time he stretches his hand out to buy something, or drink a cup, or eat, someone would notice.'

'I thought he was a priest.'

'You should have come to Domatilla beforehand. I've seen that tattoo.'

189

'Where?'

'On many a man's wrist. It's not just the mark of a priest but a soldier, some sect which worships Mithras.' She clicked her tongue, enjoying Claudia's puzzlement. 'Yet, little one, it can also be hard to trace.'

Claudia drew her brows together.

'Soldiers wear wrist bands,' Domatilla insisted, getting up, 'which show their rank but can also hide any tattoo. Now look, I must be going. Oh, by the way, the gladiator Murranus wishes to see you.'

Chapter 12

'Fortune favours the brave.'
Terence, *Phormio*, l. 203

Murranus was waiting in the porter's lodge. The guards who manned the gate had been only too willing to take him into the small tiled room, offer him a cup of wine and discuss the finer points of the previous day's games. Murranus sat politely answering, though he was ill at ease. He had his hair newly cropped, face shaved, and wore a simple green tunic which hung down beneath his knees. His arms and the side of his neck still bore bruises from his victorious fight, whilst his eyes were shadowed and showed the effects of poor sleep and a hard night's drinking. He extricated himself from the incessant questions and took Claudia out on to the gravel path.

'You can use the bushes!' one of the guards shouted. 'But you don't go far! We are under strict instructions!'

Murranus and Claudia sat on the grass in the shade of a laurel tree.

'Januaria wouldn't like this,' Claudia began. She plucked at a wild flower and handed it to him. 'They'll start gossiping about you.'

Murranus wasn't in the mood for jokes.

'Why did you go so quickly?' he asked testily. 'One minute you are in the tavern directing us to search for this and that. The money is found. The next morning I find Granius and Faustina have vanished whilst you have stolen away like a thief in the night.'

'Why, did you miss me?' Claudia asked quickly.

Murranus glowered at her.

'You did miss me,' Claudia insisted. 'Oh, stop scowling, Murranus. It doesn't suit you. You are quite handsome, but smile. Look at the flowers, you'll distract the guards. Come on,' she teased. 'I saw you act the mimic last night. You have a sense of humour, you can relax. Januaria knows that.'

Murranus sat twiddling the stem of a flower.

'I like Januaria,' he said, 'but . . .'

'That's what I'll call you,' Claudia teased, 'Senator But, but . . .'

Claudia felt a twinge of compassion at Murranus' discomfort but she did like teasing him.

'Are you soft on me, Murranus?'

'I'd like to know you better.'

'And I'd like to know you, Murranus.'

His head came up, eyes watchful.

'What do you mean?'

'Whom do you work for?'

'I'm a gladiator. You know that. I kill people in the arena. If

I continue to kill people I'll become rich, but one day I might make a mistake and that will be the end of me.'

'Do you work for the Emperor?'

Murranus laughed. 'You mean as a spy?'

'Where do you live?'

'In the barracks with the rest of them.'

'Now you are lying.'

'I am,' Murranus conceded. 'I have a small garret in the Street of Perfumes. I pay a rent. It's a place I go to when I want to be alone.'

'Or to be with Fortunata?' Claudia queried.

'I told you, my sister was strange, that's why I am here. I don't know what business she was involved in, but she asked me to take her down to the Horse of Troy. Oh, by the way, have you heard the news? Locusta's dead.'

'Yes, half the city must know it by now. You were talking about Fortunata?'

'Yes, we went down to the Horse of Troy. As I've told you, we sat there drinking and eating. Fortunata was all eyes, peering this way and that. If she had been by herself, Locusta's bullies would certainly have questioned her, but they recognised me so they left her alone. Nothing happened. We left the tavern and went up a side street. When we reached the crossroads, two muleteers were having a fight. You know how it is? They were slashing at each other with their whips. One of those movable stoves had overturned and the cook was about to join in.' Murranus looked down at the flower. 'There were people shouting and screaming. The police came along and were busy helping themselves. A runaway slave had also been caught. They were fastening an iron ring round his neck and then it happened. I am sure that was the only thing that went wrong.'

'What did, Murranus?'

'Well, it was dusk, the young bloods were out looking for fun: gentlemen and their ladies going to parties. We managed to get through the confusion and were halfway across the square when we passed a lady's litter. The curtain had fallen back.' Murranus waved his hand. 'Perfume was billowing out. I saw a painted face, a silver tiara. Fortunata had a better glance. She wanted to go back but the press of the crowd was too strong and the litter disappeared. When we reached the far side of the square, Fortunata just shook her head. "I can't believe it!" she whispered. "I just can't believe that!"'

'Did she say what?'

Murranus shook his head. 'I had drunk deeply but Fortunata was distracted, I am not too sure what it was about.' He glanced up at Claudia. 'It could have been the person in the litter or one of those carrying it. At the time,' Murranus slipped the flower into his leather wrist-guard, 'I didn't think anything of it except that my sister may have seen the source of some juicy tidbit or scandal: a high-born lady being taken to her lover, or something along those lines.' He pulled a face. 'Last night I remembered. So, I thought I'd come and tell you.'

'Why should you tell me?' she asked quietly.

'You know full well,' Murranus retorted. 'Do you think we are all fools, Claudia? Polybius knows what you are up to. Searching for that man with the purple chalice on his wrist, pretending to be a palace domestic. Those police came last night to rough up Polybius. They soon disappeared when you went out. I've also got friends amongst the guards. You've been seen in parts of the palace a poor servant girl would not be allowed.'

Claudia leaned forward and pressed a finger against his lips.

'We are what we are, Murranus, or what life makes us.'

'Will you come back to the She-Asses?' he asked.

'When I'm finished.'

'Do you want any help? I mean . . .'

Claudia shook her head. Murranus was staring at her beseechingly.

'And where will all this end, Claudia?'

She got to her feet and brushed the grass off her tunic.

'It will end, Murranus, when I trap the man with the purple chalice on his wrist and when Murranus the gladiator no longer strides into the arena.'

Claudia kissed him on the forehead and, before he could stop her, ran back across the grass and into the villa.

She was touched by Murranus' concern. She felt slightly uncomfortable. Her face was hot with embarrassment. She wanted to go back and talk to him some more but she was wary. Murranus was more than he claimed to be. Back in her chamber, Claudia splashed water over her face, drying herself slowly with a towel. She half-listened to the sounds of the villa: the patter of feet and the shouts of servants as the preparations began for the evening's festivities. There was a knock on the door and Paris poked his head round. He had a pair of satyr horns on his head and he had painted his face black. Claudia burst out laughing.

'What are you doing here?'

He came in, closing the door behind him.

'Tonight's the night, Claudia.' He rubbed his hands, then struck a dramatic pose. 'I am,' he declared in a pompous voice, 'obliged to perform before the Emperor.' He clasped his hands together and rolled his eyes heavenwards. 'Who knows where this will lead?' he declared in a falsetto voice. He pointed to the bed. 'Are you tired? Would you like to lie down?'

'Don't be impudent!' Claudia snapped, but she found it hard to be angry with this gaudy peacock of a man.

'Paris! Paris! Where are you?'

'Domatilla calls.' Paris gave a mocking bow. He had his hand on the latch when he turned. 'If I get tired, can I come back and lie down with you?'

He saw the dagger on the stool and pulled a face.

'You were expecting me, Claudia?'

'Paris!' Domatilla's voice was now raised to a screech.

'I'll be back.'

The actor blew a kiss and disappeared through the door. Claudia went and locked it behind him. She was about to undress and wash when there was a further knock and she opened the door to one of Domatilla's servants, a red-faced, orange-haired harridan.

'Domatilla says you'll serve the Emperor tonight. You are not to splash his wine.'

'Yes, yes, I appreciate that,' Claudia broke in testily.

'And you are to wear this.'

The woman laid out on the bed a long tunic in the Greek style, sea-green in colour, with gold edging, and held at the shoulder by a silver clasp: a pair of sparkling sandals were put down beside it.

'You can use the baths!' the woman shouted, so loud, Claudia half-suspected she was slightly deaf. Then, without waiting for an answer, she flounced out of the door.

'Now I'm going to have peace and quiet,' Claudia vowed.

She re-locked the door. She lay down on the bed, rolling to one side, bringing her knees up. Murranus was still distracting her. She diverted herself by thinking about what he had said. The gladiator and his sister had left the Horse of Troy and were going across that square. Fortunata had seen someone in a litter, a noblewoman whom she recognised. She must have been intrigued, which meant that she saw someone who shouldn't have been there. So who was it? The Empress Helena? Domatilla? Or one of her ladies?

Claudia drifted into sleep, and when she woke, she realised she must have slept for at least two hours. The heat of the day was past and the water clock in the corridor outside showed that the period of festivities was drawing near. Claudia washed and changed, slipping on the gown Domatilla had given her. The sandals, too, were a perfect fit, though the leather was new so she tied the thongs lightly. A small jar of rosewater distilled with other fragrances had been left on the table and she rubbed some of this into her hands and face. She then sat, eyes closed, and composed herself. She must remember who she was: nothing more than a high-ranking servant in the house of Domatilla. She must remember Anastasius' rules. She must betray no sign of a relationship with him or any of the Imperial household. She must not assume airs and graces but act as she was supposed to: a maidservant responsible for pouring the Emperor's wine, nothing else.

Claudia left her room and hurried down to the atrium. The great marble dining hall was long and opulently furnished. On the floor were extensive mosaics depicting the legend of Hercules, particularly his amorous pursuits. Similar frescoes and paintings covered the walls. The couches in the banqueting chamber had been arranged in a horseshoe shape. The small tables carefully laid together in front of them were already burdened with precious cups, plates, spoons and knives from Domatilla's treasure house. The couch in the centre, where the Emperor and his mother would sit, was draped with purple silk trimmed with gold. Alabaster jars full of precious oils had been lit. Musicians in the far corner were busy preparing flute, lute and lyre. Servants, under the watchful eye of Domatilla, hurried backwards and forwards, and the air was fragrant with savoury smells from the kitchens.

Domatilla's main concern was the makeshift stage which had been set up. Behind a large dais made out of wooden blocks pushed together rose an enormous and ornately decorated stage wall, the backdrop against which the actors would perform. These latter were the real source of the confusion. Clothed in gold and scarlet, their hair covered by high wigs, their faces hidden by crude masks, they were all thronging about, putting the final touches to their performance. Some machinery had been brought in to simulate thunder. Lamps were being arranged to create flickering shadows. Everyone was screaming and shouting at each other, Paris leading the pack, issuing directions, moving from angry tantrum to sugar-sweet pleading. Domatilla glimpsed Claudia and waved her over. The Emperor's hostess had been transformed, her face beautifully painted, her black hair coiffed in oils. She was dressed in perfume-drenched ivory silk. Jewellery flashed and winked on her fingers, wrists, arms and neck. She fluttered her false eyelashes and gave a quick smile.

'I am trying not to lose my temper, shout or laugh,' she whispered. 'The paint on my face is not yet dry. I don't want it to crack. Now look, Claudia, all you have got to do is make sure the Emperor's wine cup is kept full. You don't do it all yourself. His steward or wine-taster will pick up the cup, then you fill it. On no account must you fill a cup and give it to any of my guests without it being tasted. The same goes for food. Now, it should be a pleasant evening . . .'

She paused mid-sentence at the distant braying of trumpets.

'Oh, the Gods be praised! The Gods be praised! The Emperor

has arrived!' she screeched. Hands waggling in the air, Domatilla waddled off.

Her chamberlain swept into the banqueting hall. Paris and his actors were bluntly told to 'piss off and wait for your call'. The final touches were made: baskets of sweet, fragrant flowers laid out, more oil lamps lit, couches pulled back. Servants arranged jugs and jars. In the kitchen the chef was laying about him with a ladle in preparation for his triumphant procession of food. Shouts and orders came from the corridor. Claudia felt it was like a theatre just before the play began. All clamour and noise followed by a swift and sudden silence. There was the sound of marching feet in the corridor. Members of the Imperial guard, under the command of a young tribune, trooped in and took up their positions round the room. Constantine and his mother entered, followed by the high priestess of the Vestal Virgins and others whom Claudia recognised: Bessus, Chrysis, Anastasius and, looking rather sheepish and out of place, the priest Sylvester. Rufinus headed a small coterie of favourite courtiers. Chamberlains ushered them to their seats. Domatilla placed a laurel wreath, embossed with silver, on Constantine's head, a similar one on the Empress Helena. Constantine cracked a joke, the tension relaxed. There were toasts to the Emperor, to his mother, the victory at Milvian Bridge, and, of course, the games. Constantine turned to Helena and began to converse quietly, a sign that the banquet had begun.

Claudia noticed how every cup of wine was tasted and the same for the dishes brought in. Chamberlains would probe the food with a small knife, cut off a portion, taste it, then nod the dish forward. Claudia, when she was ordered, filled the Emperor's cup with wine. His mother nudged him and he indicated to his taster to add water.

'The Divine Augustus,' a chamberlain whispered, 'knows he has to be on his best behaviour.'

Claudia looked along the line of guests to where Sylvester sat eating his food. Only once had he caught her eye and made a slight movement of his lips in recognition. Helena, too, had winked as she moved behind her son's shoulder; the rest ignored her.

The dinner party was decorous, not one of the Emperor's drunken debauches with his fellow soldiers. Domatilla sat further down the line next to Anastasius, her shrill laugh ringing through the room. Her face was pink, damp with sweat, eager to please and very flattered at this sign of Imperial favour. Most of the conversation revolved round the games or what the Emperor would do once summer came.

Claudia watched the guests carefully. She could detect nothing suspicious and conceded that only a fool would make an attempt here. The banquet was convivial but the soldiers stood in the shadows and other officials milled about. Nothing had been left to chance. Domatilla's chefs had surpassed themselves: dishes of wild boar, turbot, plump chickens, sows' udders, followed by apples and other fruits, shellfish, oysters and snails. The banquet progressed. The laughter and conversation grew. Syrian girls appeared and performed a sinuous dance. Constantine encouraged them warmly, getting to his feet and clapping loudly. He glimpsed Sylvester watching him so coughed and immediately sat down, to the muted laughter of the rest of his guests.

Jugglers and fire-eaters appeared. The wine was changed, this time white, cool and fresh from Domatilla's cellars. The stage was prepared, Paris and his actors appeared in their garish robes with their masks over their faces. Paris, wearing that of Heracles, gave a flourishing bow and the performance began. It was not a proper play but rather different scenes from mythology or Rome's history: Thyestenes eating his children for dinner; Oedipus killing his father; Hercules slaying some mythical beast; the quarrel between Romulus and Remus. The performance lacked real skill but, led by Paris, the actors sang about their pain and fury in resounding emotional arias. Scene swiftly followed scene, and then there was a change of mood to a knockabout farce with clowns acting out the stock characters of pantomimes.

Claudia recognised some of the characters she and others had played when travelling around Italy with her acting troupe. There was Pathos, the ridiculous old dodderer, always keen on the girls; Maccus, the nincompoop who could so easily be fooled. After these disappeared, the performance continued: tales of new-born babies kidnapped by pirates; maidens abducted by slave-dealers; pimps and bankers, soldiers and parasites, misers and spendthrifts. Their antics provoked Constantine to bellows of laughter. The Emperor was thoroughly enjoying such theatre. Now and again he'd stop to clap or, snatching his purse from a chamberlain, interrupt the performance by throwing silver coins at the stage.

Paris surpassed himself, particularly with his satirical imitation of a fop parading in the Forum. The clowns joined in the fun. Towards the end, as a pièce de résistance, the troupe enacted the last days of Maxentius in Rome: the worry of the old Emperor, the agitations of his advisers. Constantine clapped and clapped, summoning the actors nearer and nearer so he wouldn't miss any words. The chamberlains became visibly anxious. At one point, when Paris was lying on the stage, a huge mask over his face, the actors mingled with the guests. They pinched food from their plates, sipped from their goblets in the time-honoured tradition in which actors were allowed to mock the audience, play the jester and suffer no reproof. Girls sat on Constantine's couch: one even threw her arms round his neck and kissed him roundly on the lips. Two young men, masked and cloaked, sat beside Domatilla. Time and again the actors flowed backwards and forwards. The guests also rose and milled about until Paris jumped on a chair and clapped his hands. The whole troupe gathered around him and bowed towards the Emperor as a sign that the performance was over.

Constantine was very pleased. More largesse was distributed. The actors made one last flourish and disappeared behind the screen. The banquet progressed. Constantine, now in the best of humours, clambered to his feet and toasted Domatilla. The little fat whore-mistress staggered up. She began to thank the Emperor in grandiose, flowery terms. Abruptly she stopped. The goblet fell from her hands and she leaned over as if she had been struck in the stomach. Claudia watched in horror. Domatilla's face came up with a look of absolute agony, her mouth opening and closing. She slumped to her knees, retching and vomiting. The Emperor jumped up, hastening towards her. Domatilla was now in a paroxysm of agony. She knocked a small table over, legs and arms thrashing out.

The Emperor's physician was called. Claudia pushed her way through. Many of the guests stood back, unable to accept what was happening. A light froth had appeared at the corner of Domatilla's mouth. Face now rigid, body jerking, she gave a choking sound. The physician, his finger down her throat, was trying to see if something was stuck. He took his hand away. Domatilla's head fell to one side. The Tribune was now rapping out orders: soldiers hastened off to seal doors and gates. Domatilla's sweat-soaked corpse was laid out on a couch. Now all beauty had gone. Her face had a pale greenish tinge, her lips seemed more red, her hair was awry. The physician was feeling her neck.

'A seizure?' Helena asked.

The doctor prised open Domatilla's mouth.

'I noticed this before,' he murmured. 'Her tongue is blackened. Divine Augusta, I believe this lady has been poisoned.'

Domatilla had knocked over one of the tables when she fell but not her own. Under the direction of Bessus the chamberlain, her silver dish and goblet were taken away by the physician to a far corner of the room and carefully examined. A slave was brought in, and with the Tribune's sword pricking the nape of his neck, the man, trembling with terror, was forced to drink the wine and eat the food. Claudia noticed how Sylvester had kept to his place, his only movement being the sign of the cross. He made to object at what the slave was forced to do. Claudia walked towards him, warning him with her eyes not to intervene. In the end such intervention was not necessary. The physician brought both dish and goblet back.

'Well?' Constantine had slumped back on his couch.

'If the lady was poisoned,' the doctor declared, 'then it was nothing she ate and drank here. No food is tainted. There's no potion in the wine.'

'That stands to reason,' Helena intervened. 'Everything was tasted, food and drink.'

'Did she take from any other plate?' Rufinus spoke up.

Anastasius, who had been sitting to Domatilla's right, shook his head, making a sign with his hands for the Empress. Bessus also confirmed this, whilst the Tribune, a cool-nerved young man, pointed out that he had watched the tables from the moment Domatilla had collapsed.

'Why?' someone asked.

'To make sure nothing was removed,' came the calm reply. 'And nothing was.'

'What about the acting troupe?' Bessus asked.

'But they had no food,' the Empress replied.

'Some poisons take hours,' the physician declared. 'Others a few seconds. The Lady Domatilla could have eaten or drunk something before the banquet ever began.'

'What kind of poison?' Helena asked.

'Augusta, how many feathers are there in a swan's wing? Rome is full of poisons and poisoners.'

Helena, who had drunk and eaten very little, now asserted herself.

'Have the body removed and taken to her own chamber!'

'And the acting troupe?'

'What can be proved?' the Empress retorted. 'All we do by questioning them is publicise Domatilla's death to the rest of Rome.' She sat down next to her son. 'Tribune, have the room cleared! Ladies and gentlemen, as you can see, the banquet is over!'

She gestured at Rufinus, Chrysis and Bessus to stay. Turning on her couch, she glared at Claudia.

'You too, girl! My son and I will need wine.'

Claudia expected Anastasius to be invited but the Empress rose, summoned him across and whispered quietly. The priest quickly left. The banqueting chamber was cleared, the doors locked.

'What have we here? What have we here?' the Empress asked in a half-whisper, as if talking to herself.

Rufinus was about to reply when there was a pounding on the door. Bessus went to answer and came back agitated.

'Divine Augusta, I think you'd all best come with us.'

They left the banqueting hall and, guarded by a military

escort, made their way along the corridors to Domatilla's room. Her corpse now lay hidden under a gauze sheet on the bed. Claudia, whom Helena had summoned to walk behind her, gazed round in horror. The bed and the walls had all been daubed with blood.

'Someone has taken a wine-skin full of blood and squirted it around,' Rufinus whispered.

His face was pale. Claudia noticed a bead of sweat running down from his forehead.

'This is too much,' he added in a shocked half-whisper.

'Divine Augusta, look!' Bessus pointed to the walls just inside the doorway, to letters crudely drawn in blood: 'IN HOC SIGNO VINCES'.

'I want them all arrested!' Constantine rasped. 'I want everyone who was here tonight, actors, servants, taken to the prisons beneath the palace!'

'Don't be stupid!' Helena hissed. 'That's what the killer would love: a mass arrest.'

Constantine nodded.

'Have the guard called,' he murmured. 'Let's leave this benighted place.'

The Emperor and his mother, their courtiers clustered about them, abruptly left the villa. They were hardly in the grounds before the looting began. Servants, the courtesans themselves, now knowing their mistress was dead, began to help themselves. Claudia stood in the passageway listening to the sound of breaking glass, shouts and cries. She went to enquire if the actors were still there but was informed that they had been given a military escort to the gate. She returned to her own chamber, locking and barring the door. Only when she lit the oil lamps did she realise that someone had been here too. On the wall next to her bed had been scrawled the words: 'IN

HOC SIGNO VINCES'. The killer was sending her a warning. Tonight it was Domatilla; tomorrow it might be her, or the Empress, or her son.

'I can't stay here,' Claudia murmured.

She took the rough military cloak she always used, piled her belongings into it, grabbed her ash cane, climbed out of the window and lowered herself carefully to the ground. She ran at a half-crouch across the garden and paused under a tree, fearful of the guards and their dogs. However, all order had broken down. The porters, the burly oafs Domatilla had hired, had all flocked into the villa to help themselves.

Claudia remained hiding for a while, collecting her thoughts. She doubted if Domatilla had been poisoned before the banquet. She'd been hale and hearty enough, so how? Her food and drink had not been tainted. A piece of food offered by a guest? Had she sipped from a cup belonging to someone else? Or been pricked by a needle? Had she left the chamber to relieve herself? Or, as was the custom, to vomit? Claudia breathed in and shook her head. She had watched both actors and guests carefully and noticed nothing suspicious. She grabbed her bundle and cane and walked quickly towards the gate. She was going through, towards the narrow lane which would take her on to the main thoroughfare, when she heard a sound behind her. Paris stepped out of the darkness.

'What's the matter, Claudia? What's going on?'

'Domatilla's dead. Someone even blamed you and your troupe of actors.'

Paris stepped closer. The paint was still on his face.

'Well, it wasn't us! I never left the stage, and why should the other boys and girls poison that poor bitch?' He put his hand on Claudia's shoulder. 'Anyway, you've got nothing to fear.' He gestured with his head.

Claudia spun round. Murranus, who had been standing beneath a line of laurels, came swaggering towards her.

'What are you doing here?' she asked.

'I don't know,' he stammered. 'I just came . . .'

'Oh, never mind!' Paris snapped petulantly. 'It's the She-Asses for the three of us. Polybius owes us a cup of wine!'

Chapter 13

'He himself teaches what I should do: it is right to learn even from an enemy.'

Ovid, *Metamorphoses*, IV.428

Claudia rose late the next morning. The sounds and bustle of the tavern drew her from a deep sleep but one plagued by nightmares. She washed and made her way down to the garden. She sat and watched Poppaoe prepare a bird nest, all the time chattering away about this or that. Claudia did not know what to do. Polybius, now Granius and Faustina had disappeared, was short-handed and was bustling about, cursing softly beneath his breath. Nevertheless, he was more than happy with the turn of events. Claudia nibbled at the dry chicken Poppaoe had placed in front of her. The beer tasted musty and curdled her stomach so she quietly poured it away. Should she go to the palace or wait for fresh orders? And what could she do? Domatilla was dead. Locusta killed. Of course, she could go down to the Horse of Troy, but she doubted if there would be much to find. By now the tavern, like Domatilla's house, would have been plundered by servants, not to mention the police, who would cluster in thick as flies upon a dung heap.

Claudia sat back on the wooden bench and stared at a golden songbird in its silver cage. The morning air was fresh. She felt she could sit here all day and just relax, let the terrors and the fears slip by her. She was intrigued by Murranus meeting her last night. He and Paris had walked her back to the She-Asses, where there had been more feasting and celebration. Polybius, of course, couldn't keep a still tongue in his head. He said he had found the silver, but everyone knew, or at least suspected, that Granius and Faustina had been responsible. Claudia chewed on her lip. What had Murranus been doing lurking in the shadows? Had he really been concerned? Or was he responsible for Domatilla's slaying and had visited the villa to watch the effects of his handiwork? Of course, Paris was sharp-eyed. Once he'd spotted Murranus it would be very difficult for the gladiator to walk away.

'Are you going to sit there all day?' Polybius broke into her reverie.

'Why, what can I do?' she asked.

'You can go down to the pottery. I need some more cups, a few jugs. Oceanus will go with you, he can carry them back.'

Claudia got up, slipped her sandals on. Oceanus was at the front door, his great ham-like hands hanging down by his sides. They walked into the busy streets, a sharp contrast to the quiet of the garden. The weather had turned fine, and the crowds were spilling out, to shop or simply take the air: tinkers with their pack mules; soothsayers and fortune-tellers setting up their small, shabby stalls. A group of mercenaries from the city garrison, resplendent in their barbaric armour, swaggered around, eyeing up the girls and looking for a fight.

They crossed a small square, Claudia half-listening to Oceanus mumbling on about the games. They reached the pottery shop and Claudia made her purchases, signing the wax tablet on her uncle's behalf. The sharp-eyed, close-faced potter would be down before the day was out to claim his money and seal the bargain with a free cup of wine. They were walking back, Oceanus holding the wooden tray, when a litter drew alongside them and a hand came snaking out. Claudia stopped so quickly Oceanus bumped into her. She was about to struggle when she recognised the amethyst ring on the right hand as Anastasius'. She turned to her companion. He was staring at her, bushy eyebrows joined together.

'Go on home, Oceanus. Tell Polybius I have business.'

Her hand was released. The litter moved on, carried by six slaves wearing the Imperial colours, white tunics with a purple stripe down the middle of their backs. Two soldiers from the palace strode behind it. Claudia knew the routine. She would follow the litter until it stopped and then Anastasius would meet her. It seemed to take for ever. They crossed the market-places, into which the whole world seemed to be packed. Along shady colonnades, dealers shouted and touted for business: boot-makers and linen merchants, sellers of bronze vessels and minor implements, vendors of hot spiced sausages, boys offering bread and dates, women hawking fruit and vegetables, scribes offering their services to country folk or writing letters to someone's son in the army. A deafening hubbub of voices, the hoarse cries of beggars, cheap-jacks, snake-charmers and bird-sellers rattling out their own patter. Old men hobbled by, resting on staffs. A young woman, with cabbages piled high in her barrow, stared so lecherously at the men, Claudia wondered whether she was selling herself or the vegetables beside her.

At last Anastasius' litter went down an alleyway into the garden of a tavern. He got out and Claudia followed him in. It was a more spacious and elegant place than the She-Asses. The paintings on the walls and floors suggested a world of sensual gaiety: Bacchus fighting Mercury; Venus going fishing; two young satyrs dancing with a puppy, huge bunches of grapes hanging from their plump fingers. The tavern-keeper shuffled forward. He recognised Anastasius, who simply clicked his fingers and the man led him down a stone-paved passageway into a small private chamber.

Claudia followed him in. Anastasius, looking heavy-eyed, just stared at her. He waited until the taverner had brought two cups of watered wine and earthenware bowls full of fruit. The Emperor's secretary closed the door behind him and, making signs, told Claudia to sit on the stool opposite. For a while he sat staring sadly at her. Claudia grew uneasy. The look was searching, as if Anastasius was seeing her for the first time. Claudia wondered what had gone wrong. She suppressed a slight shiver. She understood that look! Helena and her council must have been up most of the night discussing possibilities. Did they now suspect her? She recalled Domatilla's words, as well as the first rule every spy learns: 'Do not trust anyone.' In the early days, before Constantine had seized the purple, she had worked with spies who had a finger in every pot: men and women who tried to serve more than one master. She kept her face composed under Anastasius' critical scrutiny. After all, how could she blame him? She had been in that chamber when Domatilla had died. She had served the wine.

Claudia decided to break the silence.

'Do you trust me?' Her fingers sketched the air.

No reply.

'If you don't trust me,' Claudia repeated, 'then you should dismiss me.'

'You are never dismissed,' came the signed reply. 'Usque ad mortem: To the death!'

'You must trust me,' Claudia affirmed. 'You must not do what the assassin wants.'

'What is that?' Anastasius queried.

'To set us at each other's throats, to create such distrust we do nothing: like what's happening now,' she declared hotly.

Anastasius sighed. This time he mouthed his reply, emphasising his words with signs.

'We trust you. But the Empress is at a loss. We took advice from the priest Sylvester.' Anastasius paused and smiled slightly.

Claudia again wondered if he knew about her relationship with that powerful emissary.

'The Empress,' he continued, now using both hands to communicate with Claudia, 'has told him everything. This is what Sylvester thinks.' He paused, rounding his eyes. 'Sylvester believes the Sicarius is a soul sick with fury and anger. He wages his own private war against the Empress.'

Claudia nodded. She agreed with that.

'He is also very skilled,' Anastasius continued. 'All these murders, well . . .' He shrugged his shoulders. 'He may well get rewarded by the Emperor's enemies, but he is doing it because he loves it.'

'Why do you say "he"?' Claudia asked. 'It may well be a woman.'

Anastasius shook his head. 'The priest Sylvester pointed out that last night no woman was seen near Domatilla, of that we are certain.'

'But the poison may have been given earlier in the day.'

Anastasius shook his head.

'That is why I wanted to meet you. Domatilla's corpse has been carefully examined. The Empress herself has graciously agreed to see to its burial. The poison was distilled from a plant, a very rare potion imported from Syria. It would have killed in a very short while.'

'So it must have been administered during the feast?'

Anastasius nodded in agreement.

'And there's something else.' He moved on the stool. 'Sylvester has learned from bishops in the East that Licinius is massing troops along his borders. It's as if our Emperor in the East knows something might happen.'

Anastasius drained his cup and got to his feet. He gripped Claudia's shoulder with one hand, the other making signs in the air.

'The Sicarius must be trapped and caught: that, Claudia, is the Emperor's wish.'

He left the chamber. Claudia waited until he was gone and then followed. She kept to the main thoroughfares, now and again stopping to look over her shoulder until she was satisfied no one was following her. She reached the alleyway leading down to the She-Asses and jumped as a figure came out of a shop. Paris raised his finger to his lips and beckoned her over. He looked hot-faced, eyes gleaming.

'Claudia, the man with the purple chalice!'

'What about him?' Claudia demanded.

'I think I can help. Tonight we are putting on a performance of an Aeschylus play. There are rumours that we may even be summoned to the palace. You will be there, won't you?'

'Why?' Claudia demanded. 'What has that got to do with the man I am searching for?'

'He might be there as well. Claudia,' Paris stretched out a hand, 'be my guest tonight. Why not even take a small part yourself? You will be able to watch the audience.'

'How do you know all this?' Claudia asked curiously.

'I don't. One of my troupe recognised a soldier last night.'

'One of the Imperial guard?'

'An officer. He had a wrist band on but it slipped.' He grinned. 'You know how sharp-eyed actors are. He thought it was strange: it's a sign used by members of the Mithras cult, yet the Empress usually surrounds herself with Christians.'

Claudia felt her stomach clench with excitement.

'I can't stay now, Claudia. Meet me about an hour after the theatre's first performance, near Quintilian's tomb on the Appian Way. You know where that is?'

Claudia recalled the great marble sarcophagus with grotesque heads at each corner. A quiet, secluded place in the cemetery where lovers were accustomed to meet.

'We'll have a picnic,' Paris offered. He glimpsed the uncertainty in Claudia's eyes. 'Look, if you want, bring Oceanus or Murranus, I don't care, or some girlfriend.' Paris fingered the key round his neck. 'I'll bring Maccus.'

'Who?'

'The actor who saw it. He's frightened.'

'Why?'

'When our actors went amongst the audience, this officer drew close to Domatilla. Look!' Paris spread his hands. 'Maccus is at the theatre. Like me, he's frightened. He'll only speak well away from the rest.'

He turned and went back into the shop and brought out a small tub of a man.

'This is Callistus, he's a good cook with sharp ears. I was here with Maccus?'

The shopkeeper nodded.

'Well, tell the lady!'

'He left frightened, shouting at Paris that he'd only talk well away from the city.'

Claudia nodded. 'I'll be there.'

'Good!' Paris smiled and dismissed Callistus. 'I'll bring the food, you supply the wine.' The actor was about to turn away when his hand went to his lips. 'Oh, and we'll go straight from there to the theatre.' He smiled. 'So wear that beautiful blue tunic, it becomes you.'

And then he was away.

'I'll be there!' Claudia called after him. 'But give me a little longer!'

Paris lifted his hand in agreement. Claudia returned to the She-Asses. Oceanus had dropped the tray of cups and jugs so he was sulking in a corner. Polybius, hands raised, was raging at the ceiling. Claudia slipped by him up to her chamber. She was determined to meet Paris and hastily made herself ready. She washed and applied some paint to her face, took the new sandals and tunic Domatilla had given her and laid them out on the bed. The tunic was slightly stained and she remembered what Paris had said to her. She opened the chest and took out her blue tunic. Poppaoe had washed and repaired it. Claudia was about to slip it on when she went cold, a sick feeling in her stomach. She crossed to the door, locked herself in, then lay on the bed, her cloak wrapped about her.

She must have lain for at least two hours, ignoring the sounds from the tavern, as a myriad of thoughts and images teemed through her mind. Her fear was replaced by anger, by cold determination. She was a spy, she was an informer, she would do what was necessary. She hastily finished dressing, took a small leather bag and put a dagger in. Then she grasped her ash cane and went down the stairs to the eating hall. Polybius was about to berate her but one look at his niece's close-set face and he changed his mind.

'Uncle, I need two small flasks of wine, the best you have. Please don't ask why. I do need them. I'll be gone for a while but do me one favour.' She pointed to the water clock in the far corner. 'Wait for half an hour, then would you come out to meet me at Quintilian's tomb on the Appian Way.' She grasped her uncle's hand. 'Please! As a reward for finding Arrius' silver? Oh, and bring Oceanus with you.'

Her uncle went to the cellar and brought back two flasks. He was about to question her but Claudia seized them and almost ran out of the doorway. She was late but she stopped at an apothecary's and bought what she needed. Then, scampering like the little mouse Helena called her, she raced through the alleyways, out of the city and down the Appian Way. This was not so busy: most of the traders were now in the city and it would be some hours before their business was done. She left the broad thoroughfare, making her way across the City of the Dead. She must have walked half a mile until she reached the cypresses which shaded Quintilian's tomb. She stopped, made her preparations, then crept forward.

Paris was waiting. He had already laid a cloth out for the linen and parcels of food. He got up as Claudia approached, seized her by the hand and kissed her on both cheeks. He acted self-consciously, rather embarrassed.

'You brought the wine?'

Claudia nodded and handed over the small amphora of white wine.

'And I've brought the cups,' he said. 'They are only tin but they'll do.'

He filled one and handed it over. Claudia raised it to her lips and pretended to sip.

'Where's Maccus?'

'Oh, he's coming, he'll be here soon.'

She smiled. 'So will Oceanus!'

'Good, then we'll wait. Did you have trouble getting away?' Paris asked. 'I am sorry it was such short notice.'

Claudia studied his girlish face: the soft olive skin, high cheekbones, lustrous eyes and black curly hair falling into ringlets round his neck.

'Why don't you eat?' he offered.

'I . . . I am not hungry,' she replied.

His eyes took on a guarded look.

'Is there anything wrong?'

'No, no, why should there be?'

Claudia looked across the cemetery at the gravestones, some marble-white, others grey and cracked. The day was cloudy, the sun kept slipping in and out. What a quiet place Paris had chosen: the ideal location for murder.

'Where are you from?' she asked.

'Well, from Capua originally, but I've travelled around.'

'And your parents?'

Only then did she notice the change: a slip of the eye, a tightening of the lips.

'Oh, they died whilst I was young.'

'How did they die?'

His eyes became even more guarded.

'They owned a small farm, nothing much, poor soil and a few vines. It was a time of trouble. I had gone out into the fields to play. I was by myself. It was the breeze which brought it first:

that terrible smell of burning. It was a beautiful day, Claudia. The sky was a deep blue and I saw the black smoke rising like a dirty thumbprint against it. I was very young, no more than four years old, but I sensed something was wrong. I ran back through the fields. The farm was a lonely one. The soldiers, mutineers, had already killed my father. The farmhouse was burning and they raped my mother before they slit her throat. I watched it all from behind an outhouse.'

Paris extended his cup and Claudia refilled it.

'I stayed hidden. The rest is simple enough. I scrounged for food, a travelling troupe of actors came by. They took me in and,' he shrugged, 'since then I am what I am.'

'Did you kill the men?' Claudia asked.

'What do you mean?'

'The soldiers who murdered your father and raped your mother? Did you find out which unit they belonged to? Or the officer commanding? Did you track them down and kill them?'

Paris sat back on his heels, a look of puzzlement on his face.

'How did you know that?'

'I just thought you might have.'

Claudia opened the flask of red wine and filled his cup. Paris picked up a leg of chicken and gnawed at it. Claudia noticed how he drank the wine quickly. She had time enough, there was no real hurry.

'And you like the colour blue?' she added. She pulled at her tunic. 'You asked me to wear this.'

'Yes, yes, I did.'

'And when have you seen me in it before?'

Paris lowered the cup. 'Oh, Claudia, don't be such a minx. When we searched the She-Asses,' he grinned, 'naturally, I chose your chamber. I looked in the chest where you keep your clothes.'

'No, it wasn't there,' Claudia replied. 'I had given it to Poppaoe to wash. She had taken it down to the bath house to bleach out the stains.' She leaned over and filled his cup.

'Claudia, what are you saying?'

'I've worn this tunic twice, Paris. Today and, strangely enough, when I came here to meet the priest Sylvester in the catacombs. You remember that well, don't you?'

Paris acted nervously. He drank again and Claudia knew the danger was past. He'd drunk enough. It would take about another half an hour for the poison to work, though already his eyes had a heavy look.

He shook his head. 'I don't know what you are talking about.'

'You are Paris the actor, but you are also the Sicarius, the professional assassin. You mix both roles together. You can mimic male or female, young or old, a beggar or a fop, a dilettante or a serious scholar. You have so many souls inside you I doubt if you know which is the real one. You have a taste for killing, for sudden death. You enjoy it,' Claudia continued, 'and the power it gives you. You see, it was your job, a task to be carried out. Only the Gods know how Maxentius met you.' Claudia moved on the grass: the ground was hard and littered with pebbles. 'You see yourself as some avenging angel. You won't kill for anyone. You like the protection of the law, or at least those who exercise it.'

Paris was cradling the cup in his hands, staring fixedly at her.

'Did you kill one of Maxentius' opponents and then take the credit? Tell the Emperor how you had done it and, if there was other business, how you could be contacted through that harridan Locusta?'

'Locusta!' Paris exclaimed.

'Yes, the tavern-owner, the wicked witch who ran the Horse of Troy. You'd go down there to receive your commission and your payment. You probably terrified her out of her wits. A fine life you led. You must be a very wealthy man, Paris: all that gold and silver hidden away. But, of course, everything has an ending. Your fame grew as Maxentius' fortunes declined. Constantine and Helena came marching from Milan. They got to know about you, or at least, the Empress did. One of her spies slipped into the city with a fresh commission: Maxentius is going to die in battle, and when he does, the Empress Helena wants no opposition to her beloved son in Rome.'

'But Severus was killed by a woman! Everyone knows that!'

'Oh come, Paris, with a bit of silk, a wig, some make-up and lady's shoes, you could pass for a comely courtesan. Severus died and you must have felt like a cock on a dung hill. One employer goes and another takes his place.'

Paris was now rubbing his stomach.

'But Helena has used you and Helena wanted to dispense with you. She invited you to a meeting at Domatilla's villa, but our Paris has the cunning of a fox. Somehow, I don't know your method, you persuaded another to take your place, bribing him with gold and silver, telling him he had nothing to fear. Who was it, Paris? Someone you seduced, who'd do anything to win your favours? You're a skilled hand at pretence: did you tell Iolus and Callistus, even Maccus, what to say? They'd do anything for Paris! As would those thugs who followed us that evening, all little dramas arranged by Paris.'

'You were talking about Helena?'

'Ah yes, your suspicions were proved right. The pretend Sicarius was killed by Burrus, his bloody carcass tossed in the Tiber.'

Claudia leaned forward. There was a slight sheen of sweat on Paris' forehead.

'You will let me finish my story?'

She fished in a leather bag and took out a short stabbing dirk.

'I can run and I can defend myself, Paris.'

'Then finish your story, Claudia. It's an amusing piece of theatre.'

'No, no, Paris, it wasn't amusing to you, full of arrogance and fury. How dare anyone threaten the great Paris, thc Sicarius? The man who decides who lives or dies? Some upstart Empress? A tavern-keeper's daughter? You'd teach Helena and Domatilla a lesson. Helena because of what she plotted, and Domatilla because she was Helena's accomplice.'

'But I loved that silly fat bitch!'

'You have the face of Adonis, Paris, and a heart of cold iron. Our noble Emperor has a liking for soft, perfumed flesh and so the murders begin. Domatilla's ladies are easy prey. You can masquerade as a rich man, as a lover, male or female, draw them to some secret assignation, then kill them.'

Paris stifled a yawn.

'The one that intrigues me,' Claudia continued, 'was Sabina, killed in the Imperial quarters. We know a woman entered: that was you. But how did you get by the guards?'

Paris smiled languidly.

'I wager you had the impudence to leave by the way you entered, only this time unnoticed?'

Again the smile.

'Sabina, of course, would let you in. She'd think you were

someone sent by the Emperor, or Domatilla; her murder would have been quick. Then, of course, there was poor Fortunata. You recognised her, as you did me, as a spy from the start. You wined and dined her. She was reckless enough to go to the Horse of Troy. Of course, she found nothing. On her way home, however, she glimpsed something incredible. I doubt if you went to meet Locusta dressed as you are: you'd be an old man. Another time a beggar or a servant, sometimes even a woman perfumed in silk. On that particular night Fortunata glimpsed you in a litter. She saw through your disguise.'

'There's no law, my dear,' Paris intervened, 'which says I can't dress up like a woman and be taken round the city in a litter.'

'Oh, I am sure Fortunata thought the same, but it started her thinking. After all, she did see you in a quarter where, perhaps, such ladies are seldom glimpsed. I wager she wondered whether you were going to the Horse of Troy or coming away from it. Of course, there may have been other little items of gossip Fortunata picked up, perhaps an instinctive feeling that something was wrong. So, poor Fortunata had to die. You, arrogant as ever, wanted to teach the Empress a lesson, to demonstrate that no one ever came after you. You slit that poor woman's throat and, pretending to be a butcher or a carter, smuggled her corpse into the slaughterhouse behind the palace. You left her body hanging as a warning, like the farmer does rats, then it was back to your killing. Like an animal slowly eating its way towards the heart, you drew closer and closer to the palace.'

Paris shook his head and put his hands down on the grass to steady himself.

'I could kill you now,' he stammered.

'My dear Paris,' Claudia mimicked, 'you won't be killing

anyone. I have given you two potions: the one in the white wine makes you a little sleepy.'

'And the red?'

'Oh, you are safe enough so long as you don't move violently or suddenly.'

'You're a clever little bitch!'

'No, Paris, I'm a frightened little bitch. You told me to bring someone out here with me but you knew I wouldn't.' Claudia shrugged. 'Even if I had, he or she would have died as well.'

'You were taking a gamble. I could have killed you on sight.'

'No, no, Paris, I don't think you would. Killing to you is like a good meal to someone else. You like to savour it, plot it. I suspect it would have been a lovely afternoon, eating and drinking. You'd have cursed Maccus but promised we'd go looking for him. Meantime, you would have entertained me with a song or a poem, and then, just as I thought it was time to go . . .' Claudia threw down her cup. 'You would have enjoyed it, allowed me a little time to realise what a superior person you were, to accept that I had been tricked, to know that you were better, faster, more cunning. You are a hunter, Paris. You hunt human beings. You would have killed me and done the same as you did with Fortunata: strung me up on some branch, perhaps with a curse attached to my tunic or a warning that you were getting closer to the Empress. Days would pass before it was noticed I was missing. And when would you have struck at Helena? Tonight? You are a cunning, cruel, cold-hearted bastard. The Empress or her son, possibly both, would have been your last victims.'

'Why do you say that?'

'That's why you killed Locusta. Time for farewells. Success or not, Rome was beginning to pall. Locusta had to be silenced before you went on your travels. Where to? Nicodemea? To collect your reward from Licinius?'

'And Domatilla?' Paris was determined to keep his poise, show he was not frightened.

Claudia secretly wondered if he really believed he had been poisoned. The consummate actor, so detached from the real world, perhaps he thought all this was a dream.

'Domatilla was an easy victim. You probably got yourself invited, and after the feasting had begun and the actors were supposed to be preparing, you slipped down the corridor to Domatilla's room with a wine-skin full of blood. Locked doors are no problem to you, are they, Paris? You probably carry all sorts of implements to gain access to this door or that. That's why you were so good with our crime at the She-Asses. I suppose,' she jibed, 'if you have the mind of a criminal, it is easy to hunt others.'

'Are you a criminal, Claudia?'

'There's a touch of you in me.'

'If I had my way,' he sneered, 'there'd be more than a touch!'

'Why not?' she retorted. 'Robbery, murder, rape. Your own private war against the world, eh, Paris? Playing out that dreadful drama you witnessed as a child.'

For the first time since she had met him, Paris lost his nerve. His mouth parted in a snarl and he would have lunged forward, but Claudia held her dagger up.

'I promise you,' she whispered, 'my story won't take long.'

'We were talking about Domatilla, yes?'

Paris sat back on the grass, crossing his legs. You are dying, Claudia thought, I've killed you and you don't even suspect me.

'I should also talk about Polybius, my uncle: you brought

those treasonous broadsheets to the She-Asses, as you did to other taverners, in order to fan the blaze of gossip in Rome.'

'Oh, forget that!' Paris winced. 'Domatilla!'

'Very well, Domatilla. Your actors and their masks.'

Chapter 14

'Who will guard the guards themselves?'
Juvenal, *Satires*, VI

Claudia paused. She turned and looked over her shoulder. She thought she'd heard a sound and wondered if Paris had come by himself. But of course he would. She looked at her victim. She must hurry, because the potions were having their effect: his olive skin had turned slightly grey, a sheen of sweat glistened on his high cheekbones.

'Domatilla was easy to kill. All those actors in their masks. Did you persuade one of your troupe to exchange his for yours? And when the actors were circulating amongst the guests, you sat next to plump Domatilla. She was full of wine and gaiety, no thought of any danger. You offered a specially prepared sweetmeat or a grape or some fruit. She ate it and back you ran. You, and your fellow actors, were on and off the stage or behind the scenery. Masks were exchanged. No one could really tell who was who or who had gone where. At the end of it all, Domatilla was dying as you are now.'

'What?' Paris gripped his stomach and leaned forward.

'The potions I have given you, they will start working soon. Something very similar to what Domatilla swallowed. It's better this way, Paris. Constantine would have crucified you in the arena. It's also justice for Domatilla, Fortunata, Sabina and the rest, as well as for me!'

Paris winced at the pain in his belly.

'You followed me here, didn't you?' Claudia continued. 'When I came to meet the priest Sylvester? I escaped and put that ash cane across the doorway. When I first met you, you lifted your ankles as if to show there was no bruise, so clearing yourself of any suspicion. However, that particular morning, you were disguised as a soldier, as you were when you delivered that warning to Domatilla. You later followed me back to the city and had the impudence to return my ash cane.'

Paris drew a deep breath as the pain receded.

'I never thought it would end like this,' he said.

'You were wearing boots that morning, weren't you?' Claudia continued. 'Stout leather marching boots which protect the ankles. I must have been easy to follow wearing that tunic. It was your one mistake which forced me to think. As for the attack beneath the Colosseum, that was cruel. You knew all about me. You paid some urchin to lure me down at a time when the wild beasts were unattended.' Claudia paused.

Paris was now drawing deep breaths as if to control his giddiness. She herself felt cold in the presence of this great killer. Three times he had tried to take her life, and if it hadn't been for her tunic, perhaps she would now have been drinking the poison or being led away to be knifed or garrotted.

'I could have bargained for my life.' Paris had now sat back, clutching his belly. 'You and I, Claudia, we could have helped each other. The man with the purple chalice tattoo. I would have found him for you.'

'I don't think so, Paris. You share with no one. You would have killed me, struck at the Empress and left Rome. Milan, some other city would have become acquainted with the Sicarius. A lifetime of murder and good profit.'

Claudia got to her feet. She picked up the wine jars, emptied them over the cloth and walked away.

Paris called her name, but she ignored him. She sat on a tomb and read the inscription: a dedication to some cavalry-man. She concentrated on the etchings, the skilful drawing of a mounted soldier thrusting a lance at some grimacing barbarian. Only once did she turn. Paris was sprawled across the cloth as if he had tried to crawl after her. The sun was growing warm. Claudia stared up at the sky. When this was finished, she would remind the Empress, oh yes, of many things. She wondered idly if she would ever trap the man who had slain her brother and cruelly ravished her. She heard a sound like the cry of a wounded animal but steeled herself. There was nothing she could do.

After a while she got up and went back. Paris was lying in the centre of the cloth, eyes staring sightlessly up at the sky, mouth gaping. The skin of his face had turned a mottled hue; a streak of vomit trailed from the corner of his mouth. She knelt down and pressed her hand against his neck, then picked up his leather bag. She spilt the contents out on to the grass: small jars of paint, two or three wigs, a false bald pate, two cloaks, a dagger and a length of rope, possibly disguises but nothing incriminating. She sat back on her heels. Something was missing. Paris would never have told her, but how had he managed to penetrate the Imperial quarters? And why was it his acting troupe that had been hired by Domatilla?

Claudia picked up the wig and sniffed at the perfume. Paris had been a consummate actor, almost a shape-shifter, able to go where he wanted. He had loudly proclaimed that he couldn't stand the sight of blood, but he had been in the Colosseum all the time. He had deliberately incurred Maxentius' wrath when he sensed that Emperor was about to fall. She glanced over at the sprawled corpse.

'You only pretended to flee Rome,' she murmured softly, 'acting your favourite role of a frightened rabbit. In reality you could slip back whenever you wished.'

She clicked her tongue. Paris must have had a protector. Someone who helped him. She went and examined the corpse. She found a purse full of coins and slipped it into her own bag. She felt the clothing and smiled. The key Paris always wore round his neck! He'd either plucked it off in his death throes or tried to hide it. The chain had snapped; Claudia put her hand down Paris' tunic and drew the key out. It was of delicate bronze, small and squat.

'Not to a door,' Claudia murmured. 'It's too small for that: Paris would always keep an eye on what he wished to hide.'

She slipped the key into her own purse, picked up the wine flasks and smashed them on some rocks. The tin cups she put down a crevice of a derelict tomb. She threw the food away and, wrapping the corpse in a blanket, pulled it under the shade of the trees. She grasped her own belongings and went back along the track leading to the Appian Way. She had scarcely reached it when she heard her name called: Polybius, followed by Murranus, was striding towards her.

'Claudia, what is it?' Her uncle grasped her by her shoulders.

'You look pale. Whom have you been meeting? I brought Murranus; Oceanus is in disgrace.'

'Do you know Quintilian's tomb?' Claudia replied. She tried not to catch Murranus' eye. She felt guilty about her earlier suspicions.

'Yes, yes, I do. It's near a copse of trees.'

'Go over there!' Claudia urged. She grasped her uncle's hand and stared up at him. 'Paris is dead!' she burst out. 'He lured me there but I killed him!'

'What is this?' Murranus jostled her uncle aside. He crouched down. 'You killed Paris?'

'He tried to murder me. He's the Sicarius.'

'But Claudia, he's a popular actor!'

'Not any longer.' Claudia half-smiled. 'Do not touch any food or wine, it is poisoned.' She took from her bag what she had bought at the apothecary's and thrust it into Murranus' hand. 'Get rid of that,' she pleaded, 'but be careful. I must get into the city.'

'I'll come with you,' Murranus offered.

'No, you won't,' Claudia warned. 'This matter is not yet over. It's best if you know as little as possible.'

Both men would have objected but Claudia stepped round them. Uncle Polybius called her name; she just raised her hand and hastened on up towards the city gates. When she reached Zosinas' theatre, a porter tried to stop her at the door.

'I am Paris' friend,' she lied. 'He sent me back.' She held up the key. 'He wants me to get something for him.'

'He sent you with that?' the porter exclaimed. 'Then you *must* be Paris' friend. He always wears it round his neck and never gives it to anyone.'

She was allowed into the theatre. A servant took her to Paris' chamber, a small, cell-like room behind the main stage. It held nothing much: a cot bed, table and stools.

'Shall I stay with you?' the servant asked.

'No,' Claudia replied. 'You know what Paris is like.'

'Oh, don't we all,' he replied. 'You must be very special. He allows no one in here.'

Once he'd closed the door, Claudia began her search. The shelves bore some pottery and greasy rolls of parchment, lists of items the actor had bought. She found the wicker baskets full of interesting costumes: ladies' clothes and sandals; military helmets, greaves, boots, the leather marching kilt of a legionary; wigs of different varieties. Pots of paint, eye-patches, women's perfume and make-up. Although the room was small, Paris had carefully stowed a variety of items away. In one corner a legionary shield and a lance; a sword in a scabbard hanging from a peg. More interesting, various passes sealed by this official or that officer in the police.

'You had the run of the city,' Claudia murmured.

Paris would have flirted with both male and female to get his own way. Nevertheless, she didn't find what she was looking for. She felt beneath the bed: more costumes, bric-a-brac, but nothing extraordinary. She sat on a stool and stared up at the ceiling. It looked solid enough. She tapped all the walls, climbed on a stool and pressed her hand against the cold lime-washed plaster. She jumped down and smiled at the hollow sound her feet made. The floor had been of polished wood but this had faded. She crawled round on her hands and knees; the planks were held fast by wooden pegs. She pulled the bed aside and continued her exploration.

It was then that she noticed that a piece of hard-boiled leather had been fitted in one corner. It looked as if it was nailed down but it came away smoothly enough, revealing a small trap door. She opened this and felt inside. More items. Her fingers touched a small metal-bound coffer. She pulled this up on to the floor beside her, and fitted the small key into its lock. The key turned, and she opened the coffer, spilling the contents on to the floor. The first scroll was what she expected, a piece of parchment displaying the Imperial seal, allowing Paris to go where he wished. Other pieces of parchment, dry and yellowing, bore the seal of Maxentius or some of his officials. Claudia then undid a small roll bound by a scarlet ribbon. It contained three documents in all, two signed by Severus and dated a few weeks before the battle at the Milvian Bridge. The third document was more interesting. Claudia went cold at the list of names: Fortunata's, Domatilla's, her own and others, including the gladiator Murranus. Each entry was, according to the memorandum, a spy employed by either Helena or her son.

'No wonder you knew so much,' Claudia whispered.

She took the manuscripts and pushed them into her bag, placed the chest back and made the room presentable. Then she threaded her way through the streets to the She-Asses. She ignored the stream of enquiries and went straight to her chamber. She was standing staring out over the garden when Murranus knocked on the door and came in.

'You shouldn't have killed Paris,' he said. 'The Divine Augusta would have racked him for days.'

She glanced over her shoulder.

'What for, Murranus? So other people could be arrested and crucified?' She sat down on the stool. 'Why didn't you tell me?' She spread her hands. 'I make no secret of it. I am an Imperial spy. I work for the Agentes in Rebus.'

'You shouldn't say that,' Murranus retorted.

'Why not? If necessary, I'll say it again. What a strange world we live in, eh, Murranus? Everyone watches everybody else and nobody trusts anyone. Oh, sit down on the bed. I can't keep staring up at you, it hurts my neck.'

Murranus obeyed.

'So, Fortunata wasn't your sister, was she?'

Murranus shook his head.

'You probably worked as a pair. Yes?'

'We were given tasks together.'

'And did you suspect Paris?'

'No.' He sighed. 'Fortunata was arrogant. She very rarely shared information. She wanted to win the Empress's favour. Afterwards, yes, I wondered if Paris was involved.'

'But, of course, he had been exiled by Maxentius, and when Severus died, he was supposed to be in Capua.'

Murranus shrugged. 'He was such a, well, a butterfly.'

'Not like you, eh, Murranus?' she joked. 'I watch people, you watch me. Poor Januaria thinks you come here for her, but it's to guard me, isn't it? Was your opponent in the Colosseum specially chosen to give you the victory? Afterwards you came looking for me.' Claudia laughed. 'I am glad you did. That's what you were doing outside Domatilla's villa last night, wasn't it?' She got up and kissed him gently on the brow. 'No, that's not an invitation, it's a thank you. Paris was also waiting for me but to kill not to kiss. He realised you were there so acted the jovial friend. In his cold mind what did it matter? There was always the prospect of the picnic the following day.' She turned to the door and opened it. 'Oh, by the way, give my love to Anastasius. I am sure it was his idea for you to be my guardian!'

Later that day a special consistory was held deep in the Imperial quarters. Constantine, dressed in the armour of a general, sat on a camp stool, his mother beside him, holding his hand. Bessus, Chrysis and Rufinus were present, as were Anastasius and Sylvester. Claudia gave a succinct description of what had happened, omitting certain details. Constantine, slightly bulbous-eyed, studied her closely. Now and again his harsh face would break into a half-smile. Helena, however, was furious. She betrayed this by constantly tapping one sandalled foot against the floor. Sylvester was amused, Chrysis and Bessus slightly jealous. Anastasius smiled, as if taking credit for Claudia's achievements.

'Well, he's dead!' Helena snapped when Claudia had finished. 'If I had my way the bastard would be crucified for everyone to see!'

'No, it's best not,' Constantine soothed. 'Paris was a favourite actor. Actors come and go, they disappear. Paris has disappeared and he will stay that way. What concerns me is whether he had an accomplice.'

Claudia shook her head.

'If there's an accomplice, Your Excellency, then he resides in Nicodemea.'

'Ah, Licinius!' Constantine wagged a finger. 'One of these days I must return the favour. If one assassin can be bought, so can two.' He detached himself from his mother and leaned forward. 'You did very well, little mouse. Much better than I thought you would. Bessus?' He half-turned. 'Make sure my favour is shown at, of course, the appropriate time.' The Emperor got to his feet. 'Well,' he sighed, 'the danger's past. I am sorry Domatilla is dead.' He laughed. 'Her poor ladies will need consoling!'

Followed by Chrysis and Bessus, he bowed to his mother and swaggered out of the chamber.

'Typical son!' Helena snapped. 'The danger's past and for a

while he won't give it a second thought. But he'll come back, Claudia, he'll start asking me questions about the gaps and holes in your story.'

'Such as, Your Excellency?'

Anastasius was no longer smiling but gazed warningly at her.

'Why, little mouse, you know full well. True, true, we have Paris in disguise doing this and doing that. He must have felt like the God Jupiter assuming whatever guise he liked, but he wasn't a God! I'd like to know how he was able to get so deep into the Imperial apartments to murder Sabina.'

Claudia shook her head. 'Your Excellency, I don't know. Perhaps he bribed a guard or palace servant?'

Helena sucked on her lips, her eyes glinting with annoyance.

'That may be so, that may be so. But a bribe?' She shook her head. 'I doubt it. He carried a pass. I'd like to know who issued it. Nevertheless, you did very well, little mouse. Didn't she, Rufinus?'

The banker smiled. He had been lounging in a chair, staring at Claudia curiously, as if unable to assess her true worth.

'And Murranus?' Claudia asked.

'Yes, my dear, he's one of us.' Helena leaned over and caressed Claudia's cheek. 'I must look after my little mouse. So many cats around, eh?' The Empress got to her feet. 'You know how dear you are to me, Claudia. Anastasius, let's rejoice in the news. A walk in the Imperial gardens will freshen the mind! Dominus Sylvester, will you join us? And you, Rufinus?'

The banker got slowly to his feet.

'I am dismissed?' Claudia asked impishly.

'You are dismissed, little mouse, for the while. Go back to

the She-Asses. Tell your beloved uncle he has nothing to fear from those oafs who masquerade as policemen. The Emperor will not forget, and neither will I.'

Helena ruffled Claudia's hair and made her way to the doorway.

'Rufinus, are you coming? Or are you staying to seduce my maid?'

Rufinus laughed. 'Your Excellency, I wish to reward this remarkable young woman myself.'

The Empress shrugged and left. Sylvester threw a warning look at Claudia and followed. Claudia sat self-consciously. Rufinus opened his mouth to speak.

'Not here, sir,' Claudia whispered. 'Perhaps in another part of the gardens?'

The banker agreed. They walked along the corridors. They heard Helena's voice shouting for servants so they left by another door. They crossed a pebble-dashed path to a broad marble seat overlooking the gardens. In the hollow below, surrounded by flower beds, stood a huge fountain: two maidens holding a vase from which coloured water spouted. The sun was beginning to dip, and the evening breeze felt quite cool.

'When you began to speak,' Rufinus murmured, 'I wondered what I should do. Throw myself upon the sword? Take poison? Or run home to open my veins in a warm bath? Do you have them? How much will it cost? What do you want?'

Claudia opened her bag and handed across the documents she'd taken from Paris' coffer.

'These are the originals, and I don't want anything.'

Rufinus looked startled. He narrowed his eyes and chewed the corner of his lip.

'Well, when I said you were remarkable, it was flattery. Now I mean it. Everybody wants something.'

Rufinus drew a small dagger from beneath his toga and cut at the parchment, carefully slicing the documents into small pieces. He scooped these together and walked over to a small brazier wheeled out not for warmth, but to provide billows of perfume from the spice blocks deeply embedded amongst the coals. Using his toga, Rufinus lifted the top off and shoved the scraps in. He replaced the lid and watched the flames turn the scraps to feathery ash, then he walked slowly back, carefully scrutinising the ground lest he had dropped some. He sat down beside Claudia.

'I could walk away,' he murmured, 'and say it never happened, but you deserve more than that. I am a frightened man, Claudia. I am a banker who supported Constantine. I'm also a man with a wife, children, kinsmen. You weren't in Rome in the last days of Maxentius? A constant nightmare. I can't remember the sun ever shining; it seemed like eternal night.' He sighed. 'Spies and informers swarming everywhere, Maxentius lashing out, Severus trying to raise money for troops. My heart was, and is, with Constantine, yet I didn't dare leave Rome. If I had fled, others would have died. My treasure would have been seized and dissipated. No, that's not totally true. A small part of me plays the banker. You invest in one venture but you close no door. Severus came to see me. Maxentius' chief minister was a treacherous fox. He wanted a letter from me, a bond, promising money to fight against what he called the usurper Constantine. I had no choice. My wife sat white-faced, my children clustered about her. I drew the letter up and sealed it. I guaranteed to supply Maxentius with silver.'

'And did you?'

'No, of course I didn't! But you see . . .'

'I don't understand,' Claudia broke in. 'Constantine would

have understood such a forced letter. You certainly wouldn't be the first to be compelled to sign such a sham.'

Rufinus looked back at the brazier as if to ensure everything was destroyed.

'That's what I thought. When Constantine marched into Rome I could explain everything. He'd bellow with laughter, slap me on the back and order a cup of wine. Of course, I took matters into my own hands. When Maxentius marched out to fight and Severus fled to Domatilla's villa, I organised a gang to ransack the Imperial records. I got my letter back and burned both it and the bond. I thought that was the end of the matter.' He blew his cheeks out. 'I heard Severus was killed by a woman. I didn't think anything of it until one night a scrap of parchment was pushed into my hand. Nothing much, except it made a reference to the bond I had signed. I was told to go out into the gardens of my villa, to a small orchard near the far wall. I was to come alone, unarmed, carrying nothing but a lantern.'

'The Sicarius?' Claudia asked.

'Yes, the Sicarius. He was masked and hooded, waiting for me beneath the trees. He claimed to have a copy of my letter and a bond. I laughed at him. I was about to call my guards when he showed me, in the light of the lantern, the seal. It was Severus'. Maxentius' chief minister had an evil soul. I had not really co-operated with him but he had drafted a letter to me, signed and sealed on behalf of Maxentius, thanking me for my support and for the hundreds, indeed thousands, of gold and silver coins I had poured into their treasury. Don't you see, Claudia, what it meant?'

'But you hadn't given it?' Claudia asked sharply. 'Couldn't you open the ledgers?'

Rufinus threw his head back and laughed.

'Claudia, Claudia, I could write ledgers which look accurate but are no more true than the legends about the Gods. In the days before the battle of Milvian Bridge, I was drawing silver and gold, moving it about like pieces on a chess board.'

'So, it was Severus' revenge?'

'Yes. He was writing to me as if I was an accomplice. True, it might not be conclusive proof of my treason.' He snorted with laughter. 'When does an Emperor need that? The least I could expect was confiscation of my goods and exile. Oh, Constantine would reassure me at first, but the doubt would nag at his soul like a maggot in a piece of meat.'

'And the Sicarius had acquired this letter?'

'Apparently. When he killed Severus, the assassin ransacked the few records the minister had brought with him. He found the letter and thought he would use it. He gave me very careful instructions. I was to persuade the Emperor to take his pleasure with Domatilla's ladies. I was also to provide him with a pass from the Imperial chancery.'

'And what else?'

'A list of the Emperor's spies. It was either that or Severus' letter would go to Constantine. I had no choice but to agree. We met again, I gave him what he asked. I demanded that be an end of it but the Sicarius just laughed. He said he would have his revenge and then be gone. I asked him what he meant, but he just mocked me. When the murders began, I suspected what had happened.'

'And Paris' involvement?' Claudia asked.

'The Sicarius made one demand: when the Emperor attended Domatilla's reception, I was to ensure that Zosinas' troupe was hired. Of course, I suspected Zosinas. I never guessed it was Paris.' He wiped the sweat from his brow. 'It was easy to arrange. I made sure I never showed my hand. A word with Bessus, a hint, a nod, and of course, the chamberlain would accept. After all, Zosinas' principal actor, Paris, had been proscribed by the dead Maxentius, so the troupe was high in Constantine's favour.' He turned to face Claudia squarely. 'I had no choice,' he murmured. 'There was nothing I could do. Once I had been shown that letter, once I had agreed to co-operate . . .' He paused. 'So, what do you want, Claudia?'

'A man with a purple chalice tattooed on his wrist.'

Claudia glanced back at the palace. Sylvester was standing in the doorway.

'I want a man with a purple chalice tattooed on his wrist,' she repeated, 'to die like he watched my brother die. You have tremendous wealth, banker?'

Rufinus nodded. 'But you've already been paid.'

'What!' Claudia exclaimed.

Rufinus smiled sourly. 'The Empress hasn't told you? The man's undoubtedly a soldier, an officer. There were others of his ilk responsible for attacks on girls from the slums, serving wenches.'

Claudia bit back her anger.

'Don't worry,' Rufinus assured her. 'The Empress will probably tell you in her own time and in her own place.'

'But there's more?'

'Oh yes, Claudia, there's more. The men belong to one cohort of the Sixth Illyrian stationed in Dalmatia. We've had reports of similar deaths and rapes amongst native girls there.'

'I must go there!' Claudia declared.

Rufinus stretched out his hand.

'Are we in agreement, Claudia? Are we friends and allies?'

She clasped his hand. 'Friends and allies.'

'I will move heaven and earth,' Rufinus declared, getting to his feet, 'to bring that cohort back to Rome. I have my life; you will have that man's head.' He looked over his shoulder and glimpsed Sylvester in the doorway. 'Oh,' he turned back, 'be wary of him!'

Claudia just stared.

'Always remember,' Rufinus declared, 'in the great scheme of things, what is most important? A little mouse, albeit a clever one, or the souls of the Empress and her son?'